Noble
Death

PATRICK RAIN

Noble

Death

TempesT
LORE

Noble Death

Published by Tempest Lore Press

Cover design by Tempest Lore Press

ISBN 978-0-9979789-0-2

First Edition: August 2016

Prologue

I OPENED MY eyes, and I found myself staring at the wall in front of me. I was nearly snoozing in a black, plastic chair. The hallway was sterile white, almost to the point of being blinding. When I looked around, I noticed that the hall stretched to no end, and there were absolutely no doors. No exits. The whole place had a feel, look, and smell of a prison. It was a location where once you entered, you might be unable to leave. You start to feel like a thousand little arms are grabbing you, holding you tighter and tighter, and not letting go no matter how hard you struggle.

Oblivious to why I was here, I felt like I knew this location. This obscure, characterless, distant place felt like a familiar one where nothing can happen to you, but on the other hand, you feel this horrible uneasiness. To my right, the corridor seemed to draw closer, magnet-ized by my consciousness. Losing momentum, it stopped completely, forming a dead end. Soon, an outline of a door emerged as if someone traced the wallpaper with a razorblade. The doorknob appeared next. My feet sunk into the floor as if I was walking on quicksand. My vision became soaked in a deeply saturat-ed blue. Without thinking, without hesitation, I stood up, walked to the nearby door and entered.

The room on the other side was almost completely empty except a desk was located in the far back. It closely resembled a teacher desk, although most teacher desks I've seen were metal and this one was wooden. The very light brown color wood had many scratches and multiple words engraved on the top and the front of it.

As I walked closer to read the markings, someone interrupted me, speaking in a calm voice. "I can't decide if I should reprimand you or praise you."

There was a man leaning against the back wall, awaiting my arrival to the point of boredom. The man appeared to be in his 30's at most, but gave of a childish aura. He had a rather long haircut. Its color was a combination of silver and gray. He wore a tailor-made black suit and a pitch black cotton shirt under-neath, but what really stood out was his tie which was completely black covered in smiling, crimson skulls. They seemed to be staring and following me wherever I went.

"I realize you're lost every time you arrive here, but we've met countless times before, and you still keep me waiting." The man said. "Even when you make it here, you're still half-asleep and lack attention."

"I don't think that I feel lost. Sleepy would be a better way to describe it." My attire came to my attention as it was my favorite and most-worn outfit. I was wearing a white shirt and a black two piece suit: a pair of trousers and a jacket.

"Nonetheless, I have to commend you for the last story that you told me. It was very engaging, and it somewhat reminded me of my origin."

"Yea," I said, "I remember."

The top of the desk was occupied by a lone, vermilion hardcover book with torn edges. It was most likely his note-taking tool of choice. The men walked closer, snatched it up, and opened it on what seems to be the exact page he was looking for. "Yes, that's the one." The man said. "A man limps through the forest chased by a hooded figure. The man's leg appears to have multiple stab wounds. As the hooded figure catches up, he grabs the man be the shoulder. Taking a hold of the man by the garments, the hooded figure drags him to a dark, deep pit and shoves him off the edge."

"Thank you for the elaborate explanation. Can we move on to something else?" I gave in to my impatience.

"Oh, come on," The man replied. "This is where it gets interesting. The man reaches the bottom of the pit with countless injuries, and he is slowly hugged by the cold arms of death. After a second, the hooded figure begins to scream. The figure kneels and tightly holds his right leg with both hands as blood pours out. The blood begins to drip down the side of his head. He loses his consciousness and falls into the dark pit as well. The man wakes up seconds later with no wounds. He notices injuries similar to his own on the hooded figure. It was as if …"

"As if the injuries were transferred from the men who was running away to the hooded figure." I cut in.

"Quite a story! Memory? Imagination?"

"Unfortunately, I can't give you a definite answer because I'm sure you already know it." By now, I was fully aware of what was going on. I realized that I have been here and spoken with this man countless times, despite not knowing anything about him. He was the master of dodging the question. He almost never had any emotions, except his mischievous smirk which showed up from time to time. It wasn't long before the smirk became a synonym for his mockery." This was the one thing that I was completely sure about.

"I know the answer?" The man chuckled, staring into his notebook. "Let me ask you this, what if it's here?" He pointed to his head. "But I don't have access to it? Is the info still classified as something I know?" He then stared back at me outfitted with the irritating, impish smirk.

"Looks like it's no use trying to inquire about your understanding of this story."

"That's correct. I believe that the only natural way to gain knowledge is through an experience, a fight, a crafting of story, a solving of a problem, a struggle," he whispered, "and struggle you will. It wouldn't be right for me to spoil all the secrets and give them to you on a plate."

I was reassured he knew something about this story. "Remind me again, when was it we first met and why are you here?"

"I think we met around three months ago. As for my purpose here, that's a secret."

"I do remember you were kind enough to introduce yourself as Mankind's Most Persevering Teacher. Now that I spend more time with you, that one statement sure is a goldmine of info compared to what you reveal on a daily basis."

Having been haunted by the presence of this man every time I fall asleep, I had enough time to rid myself of all complaints. It was the only way to mentally survive our ambiguous discussions. At first, I detested these visits, which not only freaked me out but questioned my sanity. However, I quickly grew uncaring and indifferent, having lost all hope of getting rid of him.

"You can't even comprehend how much I am lamenting because of that." The man uttered.

"Our acquaintanceship, if you can even call it that, would have just ended right then and there. I'm lamenting because of a missed chance."

"Sure." The man smiled. "But believe it or not some people listen and answer, and they do it obediently without questioning."

"So there are others?" The man seemed a bit agitated by the question.

"You sure are persistent today, picking at my every word."

"You're the one who complained about my lack of attention."

"Would you like to know when you'll meet your end?"

The question caught me off guard, and just before I could proceed, I was interrupted by a girl's voice calling for me. "Hey, what do you think about the killings, Sebastian?"

"Time to wake up!" The man's last words echoed in my mind as the whole room melted into darkness.

◆

The hall was brimming with extremely loud idle chatter. The classroom was almost empty, except for the teacher stuffing his case with his entire book collection, and a couple classmates texting on their phones.

The bold-headed teacher shared my enthusiasm with his hideous smile, celebrating the end of the class. He arranged for an early exam last week, so today was more like a closing ceremony. One down, two to go, I thought.

Fully awake, I noticed a girl leaning toward my desk from her seat in front of me. The girls name was Heather. She was quite a cheery one, but because of that sometimes she leaned into the territory of being annoying. She frequently forced herself to help and protect others. It was a yearning she couldn't fight against. On the outside, she seemed like a vivid optimist, yet you can never be certain what one thinks on the inside. Her tiny posture only amplified her friendliness. Her long blond hair was pulled back into a ponytail behind her head. She wore light blue jeans that were torn around her knees, and a plain blue T-shirt. She always had an azure wristband around her petite hands, resembling one that is used by tennis players. "Hey, spacing out again?" she waved her hand.

"As far as I know, they're considered suicides for now?" I said. That's right, it started 23 days ago and each day one person has taken their life. Once a day as if someone was counting down, marking of each twenty-four hours with an evil celebration.

"But don't you think it's weird? I mean most of those people were not depressed or something?"

"You never know. It's not like everybody goes around talking about their problems. Plus there are so many incidents a day other than the suicide and we only have one policeman. I doubt he has the time to investigate everything."

"Your point being?"

"There is truth yet to be uncovered." With more info this case could turn out to be anything. Either it's just an epidemic of suicides and everybody who is mentally stable is fine, or there is something more to it and people might be in danger. I kept the long explanation to myself.

"I wonder if the policeman knows something we don't. What if he doesn't? This whole thing might never end."

"Well, there is no use contemplating about all this. I mean, you can't do anything about it, right?"

"Hey, I'm the one who is supposed to say that." She put on her happy mask before continuing. "Let's change this dreadful topic. Once you finish here, are you going to leave this town?"

"Maybe, how about you?" I kept my plans to myself like there ever were any. At the moment, all I considered was the end of two more meaningless classes that stop me from my art major.

"I can't. Sure, I live alone, but it's my home here. I will probably run the small local restaurant that was left by my parents."

"So you could say that restaurant is waiting for you? I guess the residence will be thrilled about the opening."

"Yea, it's been closed for around 5 years. Soon, I'll be

forced to open it." She had the look of someone who isn't ecstatic with the idea. The girl fell silent as if lost in thought. Heather was honestly bothered be something.

"Hey, Heather, do you play tennis?"

"What's that?"

I didn't really enjoy this idle chatter, yet on many occasions I had to continue the dialogue. "You wear a wristband, so I was wondering if you play tennis."

"No, my sister use to play. That's why I have this accessory." Heather said, pointing at the wristband. "But that question sure did surprise me." Her smile was pale.

Someone has been prying on our little dialogue and decided to finally join in. "I heard you talking about the suicides. I don't know why you're so worried. I am on the other end of the spectrum; I believe that this town finally became interesting. Detectives, interesting cases and other things just like in a real city" The eavesdropper's name was Kasper. He had a buzz cut and a baseball cap. He wore jeans and a t-shirt with a logo of his favorite baseball team. He was a talkative person, and a gossip lover, who would lie to you straight in the face unaware of his obvious tendencies.

"Anyway, I have an exam really soon, so I have to get going." The girl avoided eye contact with Kasper like she deemed him unworthy of her attention. I was unsure if they had some history together, but to be honest I didn't really care.

"Do your best!" Kasper tried to be kind.

"Good luck!" I said.

She didn't reply to my comment. When she was right at the door, she turned around, gave a soft smile and said, "Thanks."

"She must like you." Alex commented as if he was trying to mock me in some weird, twisted way.

"What makes you think that?" I pretended I didn't know.

"She left as soon as I joined the conversation, and she didn't look at me even once, yet you had her full attention. I wander what it is she likes about you?" The whole time speaking, Alex was looking away.

"Who knows? Maybe it's that I mind my own business" I commented, attempting to leave class.

"She's so selfless, yet she associates with you every day, you selfish bastard. You can't take what's yours." He roared all of the sudden. "But I promise you that I will take what rightfully belongs to me."

Did he really encourage me to take what's mine? Taking what is rightfully his? Was he talking about …? The questions were gone before I decided to give an answer to any of them. I left.

◆

My aim was returning home which was located just around 20 minutes of walking distance from the university. Walking outside, it was only lightly pouring so the streets were barely wet, but the rain seemed to increase in strength with each minute. With no umbrella, I was forced to advance with some paper held over my head. Upon leaving, I remembered that I also had to do some groceries, or else I won't have anything to eat today. I live alone after all.

Before the suicide incidents started this town was a really tranquil place where one could remain undisturbed and relax. The town has an official name, but most resident just call it the nucleus of the forest. It has a population of about 2000 people, and it's is located in the United States. The whole location is surrounded by a dense forest. Sometimes when you look at the town from a high viewpoint, it seems like the forest is slowly eating it up, and sooner or later, the town will be swallowed.

The place is very much isolated from the rest of the world. If you leave, you might not see another human being for days. In a remote place like this, you start to philosophize about life to the point where you finally begin to feel alive and at peace. Tranquility is the whole reason I came here, and that sole reason has kept me here for almost four years. On the other hand, all good things must come to an end. By now, the town degraded, and the same dangers and nuisances of a big city surfaced.

The Main Street runs through the entire town from north to south at a slope. It is populated by various stores, bars, a theater, a police station, a church, and a university. The university is located at the very north edge of town, and it's at the highest elevation. Right next to it is the rain-soaked cathedral that's in the state of renovation since the roof collapsed last year. As you continue south down the incline, you encounter more and more entertainment related places. The whole street is sporadically decorated with tall buildings that uncomfortably loom over the tiny village-style contraptions. Various streets and roads branch off where all the citizens reside. I live in a small apartment on the second floor of a building that's a quarter of a way down the descent.

Upon reaching the halfway point, I noticed a commotion at the side of the street right in front of the police station. There was a man on an antique wooden pedestal claiming, "We have to unite and fight against this inhuman evil. Sometimes, men have to stand up and unite, and this is exactly the time!" He argued. There was a crowd of around 20 people bunched up, listening patiently to the man. He wore a brand new black suit, and a light brown overcoat on top, pockets filled with paperwork. His unfathomable gestures were amplified by an aura of enthusiasm. His hunger for power hidden somewhere in the pit of his huge stomach.

The man was a spokesman of a growing sect that's called The Unity. The sect was here when I first arrived in town, but it consisted of only around ten people. However, around two weeks ago it started to gain momentum. Its slogan changed, and it seems like its priorities evolved as well. The head of the sect claims its goal is to gather people, and to fight the suicide incidents. To fight? I guess so far, he didn't specify how. Sure, the number of people more than doubled, yet the sect is still a small faction. However, who knows what will happen if the suicides don't stop. Slowly but surely, it seems like day by day people are losing motivation, energy, and fall into the depths of depression, weakness, helplessness, and pessimism. A sect feasts on those ideals, and it looks as though this one might be in for a feast of a lifetime.

As I was about to leave, a lady to my side uttered. "How about everyone tries to think for themselves for once?" She stared at me. I instinctively ignored the comment and tried to make my way past the crowd, but the woman insisted, "I'm not a fan of gatherings like those as well." The women had a pixie cut, her hair pure black. She wore a dark blue skirt suit and a white shirt under a jacket. This was an apparel just like those that are worn by women office workers. Although hidden under her jacket, I could see that she had something tucked onto her belt, possibly a gun. The woman had a keen eye since she took notice of me staring at her belt. Before I could say a word, she introduced herself as Detective Judith Page, showing me her badge and putting my worries of the gun at rest.

"Nice to meet you. So you're a detective, I'm sure you'll be able to help this town, considering we only have one policeman. Are you here because of the suicides?" I made an attempt at being casually friendly.

"Yea, so I'll be here for only a short time." She spoke in a firm voice.

"True if the case is an easy one, and so far it seems like it's not." I challenged her resolve.

"That's precisely why I took the case, plus I'm not alone. Greg Dench is here as well. You know, his father, the famed detective, passed away recently."

"Yea, I heard. Dench has been working all his life to surpass him so he should be of great help." The statement I spoke was false. The word on the street is that he will never be able to surpass his father. All his accomplishments were compared to his father's and in the end criticized. This probably let him on the wrong path, and that's why he turned into a drunkard whose high abuse of liquor overshadowed his sense of justice. All his recent cases were failures or small fry that had almost no meaning to his overall career. Is this why he came here? Is he hoping to solve this whole thing and gain prestige? Of course, I didn't voice any of this, but it was mostly common knowledge.

"You must be thinking about the rumors surrounding Dench, right?" She bowed forward.

"Try finding one who doesn't when that name comes up, Miss Detective." The detective froze as if I angered her in some unimaginable way. I answered too casually as if talking to a close friend. I let my guard down as if I was home in a safe place, but this was no safe place. Needless to say, a second later I was sorely regretting taking that stance as her personality took a 360 spin. The detective change from a kind woman to an anger-fueled madman ready to attack anyone in the way. Her hand twitched at the sole sound of my reply. She was aiming to grab her gun, but the only thing that was stopping her was the very thing she was defending, the law.

"I'm sorry if I offended you in any way." None of what I could say seemed to matter as the woman was completely spacing out, staring me down in the process.

As she was about to grab her gun, Detective Dench called out behind her. "Let's go, Page. The doors are open!"

She finally stepped back, ready to make her way "You should really show some respect to your superiors. You might not get a second chance next time."

Was she for real? She was going to turn to physical violence just because I said something she didn't want to hear. Her dichotomy of behaviors left me stranded. Kind and insane, her two polar opposites dropped an enigma into my mind which sent me searching for a logical way to comprehend the recent events. Bound by the chains of surprise and astonishment, I realized something that was true.

At that one instance, Judith Page had the eyes of insanity.

◆

After dismissing the feeling from that situation, I made my way to the store to get all the necessary things for dinner. The grocery store was quite small. In size, it related a gas station store. Walking in, a lady over 70 years old running the register, greeted me in her solemn voice. The place was filled with rush decisions: a housewife judging vegetables based on what would be best for her child's healthy diet, a lost husband searching for his favorite spice, and a teenage girl consumed by her boyfriend's message, played on her phone.

I have to admit, I was no cook. The only dished I could prepare were cold meals such as various sandwiches. Can you even call that a dish? To be honesty, I disliked cooking, so I was frequently forced to run on canned food and pay tribute to the pizza delivery business in town. Although I didn't enjoy it, I was hard pressed to eat or else I would starve. Once I finished picking out my least hated, future meals, someone screamed in panic "Thief! Someone stop him! He has my purse!"

A man wearing mirrored sunglasses, a baseball hat, and a hood dashed between the sets of shelves, tripping and falling to his knees where I stood picking out my food. As he fell, his glasses dropped to the floor allowing me a second of eye contact with him. It was then that I discerned that he had a scar running through his right eye. Clearly the man dressed so that no one would recognize him, but in reality he stood out like a basketball player in a crowd of dwarfs. Anyone in the store would label the man as suspicious since he looked just like he jumped out of a crime drama TV series. He was the cliché robber. The thief stood up, gained momentum, and zoomed close to me. The purse in hand, he was ready to attack me to make his escape. I stood back letting him pass. Once he escaped outdoors, I observed the evocative scene where this town's only policeman began a sudden chase.

I heard chatter behind me.

"Why didn't the man stop the thief?"

"He never helps anyone."

"Yea, I heard the rumors. Someone once died in a brutal fight, and he was sleeping on a bench, oblivious to the cries for help."

"I heard all about it. Vile. I wonder how terrible the sister must have felt when her brother died in that incident."

Returning to my shopping, a girl in mid-twenties stood staggered and staring at me. Her fingers were twitching for her missing purse. The girl had really appealing long auburn hair that went to about her waist-line. She was wearing a blue t-shirt with the slogan, "It's the time to stand up and unite!" and a skirt that fitted her beautiful curves perfectly. The girl was really elegant and alluring.

A homeless man was stationed at the counter, trying to pay for a cold meal, but apparently he didn't have enough to compensate for the food. I could see the lady behind counter slightly shaking her head horizontally. Helpless, the man asked aloud, "Please someone, I haven't eaten in more than 24 hour."

A Good Samaritan responded, "That's fine. I'll cover the cost." It was a gesture of pure kindness, one that's very rare these days. It was an act devoid of any outside motives and ultimately lacking in selfishness, a selfless act.

By the time it was over, 8:00 PM ticked on my wrist watch. It was the norm for me to arrive home quite late since most of my classes took place mid to late afternoon. Closing in on my home, my cell phone started to ring thunderously. The caller was Heather, the girl from my classroom. Standing outside, I had second thoughts before I decided to answer.

"Hi, Heather."

"So you remembered my name?" She asked as I detected a nonexistent sense of joy pulse from her.

"I don't think I could ever forget." Her comment made me recall how unmindful she was to my take on those little conversations in the classroom. The girl just didn't want to give up and was always chatting with me. Almost as if she was a stalker, one that is obsessed for reason unknown.

"Sorry to disturb you, but I think I need your help."

"What is it this time?" I run my hand through my hair.

"You see …" A prolonged pause commenced. "I'll get to the point. I live alone, unable to cover all my costs; I was given some money from someone. Now they …"

"Want it back obviously." I said empty of sympathy.

She fell silent.

"So what do you expect me to do?" I asked without any intention of getting involved, yet propelled by moral customs.

"They're right in front of my place, waiting. I'm here too. They told me I must repay now." She shuddered into tears.

She screamed, and before I knew it, a third voice joined in. The man spoke in a stern voice, filled with harshness and determination. "So you're the one she decided to call? Ain't much of a support? Couldn't even cheer the girl up a bit in what could be her last moments."

"How much does she owe?"

"Well, that sum is quite hefty, around $9000. That's of course because she made us wait far too long."

"Oh, well." I chuckled, ready to hang up, but didn't. "I bet you'll manage to fill the whole she busted in your pocket."

"Look, I don't know what you pulling, but you have ten seconds to give me an answer."

The countdown started.

"Three … two … one."

I flipped the phone, ending the call. I had no intention of paying for her, and I had an intuition that they're just bluffing. They were not of a high caliber. This is probably one of the first times they did something like this, so they're just practically starting out. Either way, I doubt they'll have the guts to make a life or death decision. Walking up the steps to my apartment, I heard a fight upstairs. My landlord was up and about her usual business of drinking. Although a beautiful and kind woman, once alcohol reached the pit of her stomach, she turned into her loud, fight-yearning alter ego. She was making a huge ruckus. Dismissing the idea of going home as fruitless, I turned to kill some time.

Before long, my phone began to ring again. There was no one else on the other side but the weeping Heather. "So they let you go." I exclaimed.

"Yea," she was still crying, "What did you tell them?"

"They didn't hurt you, right?"

"No, only a couple bruises."

"They left, so for now all should be well."

"How did you know they were going to let me go?" She insisted.

"I didn't."

There was a profound silence before she replied. "Is my life worth so little to you? How can you just gamble with it on the line?" Her voice was trembling.

"Nothing I can say could justify my actions in your eyes." I answered earnestly. As I recalled all my words and actions, I heard her weeping in panic. She hung up, disappointed. I felt a little feeling of relief because nothing happened to her.

◆

The bar was only a few minutes from my home. It is a place occupied mostly by full-time workers sick of their jobs, trying to forget. It was a place where there were no fights, and most people there just wanted some peace and quiet. I opened the door, and a bell rang softly as if it was there to alarm all the bar's patrons of a new presence. One the right was a counter that stretched almost to the end of the room. Behind it, needless to say, was a barman who served drinks. The wall behind him was inhabited by bottles of whiskey, vodka, and other alcoholic beverages. At the time, all tables were busy, peaceful debates ensuing. In one of the back corner, a single spring door squealed piercingly as someone fought to get into the deserted, filthy bathroom. The spring door wasn't used often, for it was really difficult to open. Eyeing the only empty stool at the counter, I took a seat and called out "A shot of whiskey!"

"Having a bad day?" the barman inquired.

"No, not really. Although, if we consider the norm, this one is a bit more annoying." I poked fun at his question.

"Whenever you come here, it must be a bad day. You don't even like to drink. What is it this time?" He poured some whiskey. "Work?"

"No, nothing like that. The closest word that comes to mind is life."

"Are you still working as the librarian?"

"No, I quit two days ago." My work as a librarian was there to pay for my expenses only. I will be done with my major after this semester ends in only a couple of days. I have enough to get me to that day, and after that I am planning on traveling somewhere else. That's why I made the conscious decision of quitting that some consider careless.

"And what now?"

"I guess life continues." I resisted disclosing my plans.

"Always willing to talk, never telling any info."

"That's true." I continued to drink.

As the barman served other customers, someone next to me left, leaving their seat open.

"One more." I called out again.

A man with a crew cut chose to sit on the empty stool.

"It must be my lucky day. I stumble upon my most hated person in just a couple hours of searching." The man wore a pair of gray sports shoes resembling those worn during running. His gray trousers had cuffs very tight around his ankles. As for his dark green jacket, it was one of those field jackets that are supposed to be worn in harsh weather conditions.

His hoarse and brooding voice sounded in my ear to the point of being painful. The voice was upsetting as if someone violated my sanctuary of peace. The words he spoke were once that could ruin anyone day. They were words dipped in poison, one that had no antidote.

"You're not the first one today." I commented. I put my temporary stress attack at peace, and dissolved all my emotions right inside my body. I was proficient at not showing emotions, as well as dealing with any emotion I had ever felt. It was almost second nature for me to never wear any emotion other than those I rationally deem fit. By the time he could respond, I was not only at peace, but I didn't care about his offensive stance. At least, I tried to not care.

"That's alright, you can finish your drink, and then we'll have a little talk outside. We have to act civilized here, but outside it'll be a little different." He padded me on the back as if mocking me. He was truly struggling to put me into a state of unrest. Nonetheless, upon finishing my drink I had no intention of going outside.

Before I knew it two other thugs soaked in water joined in, standing right behind me. The water followed them from the doors up to their current position. The two looked like exact copies of each other. Their apparel was composed of completely black hoods, jackets, and trousers. One of them also wore a pair of black shades that didn't completely cover a scar on his face. The other wore a smile whenever the boss acted menacingly. I looked behind into the window, where I realized that it was pouring.

"You're finished. Let's go" The man said.

I was forced outside into an alleyway a couple feet from the bar.

"So let me guess, you're the one I spoke with over the phone about Heather?"

"Yea, so I honestly hope that you have had enough time to reconsider your previous decision. Are you going to cooperate, or not?"

"If you're talking about the debt, than I thought my answer was clear."

The man laughed, staring at his backup which begun laughing as well, mimicking the leader's behavior. The leader cleared his throat, and his voice became less hoarse. "Alright, I guess you leave me no choice."

The leader had his back to me when his body swiveled around 180 degrees, and he planted his fist into my abdomen. Pain crept up my spine; my composure crumbled just a little before I fell to the ground onto my knees. The attack even though expected was quite painful. As I swiftly stood up again, I leaned a little against the wall staggered by his attack. "Are we done yet?" I commented. The drinks worked their magic because the awful stress wasn't getting to me. The scene felt like a joke.

The leader was flustered as if he was the clown here being played with. His face grimaced. Anger ferociously consumed his entire face. His hand jerked as he tried to reach into the pocket of his trousers. His hand was now firmly gripping the handle of his hunting knife. He directed the point close to my face, forcing me to retreat backwards a little bit. Still frustrated, the man asked "Ain't you scared of death?"

"Not one bit, you know why? Because no matter

what, it's not my time yet." I tried to keep my cool and play with his mind a little bit. I should have known better.

The man snickered. "You're something else. You're truly not scared, or you are the perfect liar." He paused. "On second thought, would you like to join us?"

"I'm not interested."

"Well, the whole incident with your girl is just the beginning. Let's just say, we want to spread out our wings. Evolve. Expand" The man declared.

"So you're not just going to steal purses from defenseless women that do groceries." Words escaped my mouth.

The man's enthusiasm evaporated in an instant as his voice sounded with almost no emotion, "Excuse me."

"You heard me right. Or is it just a coincidence that one of your thugs has a scar similar to the one a thief had today morning?" I exclaimed, attempting to anger him just a little bit more. If I was sober, I would probably notice it wasn't such a good idea.

The man turned to face me. His menacing eyes were empty of emotions. He was a totally different person He had completely lost his not-so-fine grip on his sanity. His eyes were the eyes of an individual devoid of emotions. The man twisted his upper body just a little so he could reach his companions with his ominous stare. The thugs froze. The one with the scar wiped his sweating hand. Was it from extreme stress? Was he afraid that he screwed up? He then suggested, "Boss, please let it go."

The next thing I knew, the boss lanced his knife into my chest piercing my lung in the process. The edge of the blade tore through my flesh, sending my entire body into turmoil. It was a fatal strike that could never be undone.

As I felt myself barely being able to fill my lungs with the needed oxygen, I lost all the power that I had in my feet. It felt like my body was in the state of crisis, and all resources were pumped back in my upper body. Leaning against the wall, losing strength, I fell to the ground. I sat, my back against the wall. I was in a half-sitting, half-resting position, staring as the attacker waved his knife, blood dripping from it. As small bits of blood reached the asphalt of the alleyway, the smiley thug erupted into panic, "Shit! What did you do? I am getting out of here!"

"No, you ain't, we're brothers now. We are sharing the darkness that flowed into us the moment we saw this."

"But …"The thug was speechless.

"What was I supposed to do anyway?" The leader said. "I mean, the whole thing with the debt, we could probably work it out. He had no proof but … he saw you in the store. That could have ruined out whole initiative. Besides, I cannot lose another member of my family now. We are just starting out."

"Alright, boss, I have trust in you. I'll wait at the mouth of the alleyway." The smiley thug exclaimed, slowly backing up.

"That's fine, but know this, I'll shoot you as soon as you walk into the light." The boss took out a small gun that was holstered at his ankle.

To tell the truth, this day has really something. I almost felt like I was driving a car so worn out that the tires might explode, thrusting me into a collision. I was suffocating even though my throat was free. No matter how hard I struggled today, I have fallen into a pit that was then filled with mud, and I won't be able to dig myself out. It was the feeling of being angry, yet tied down with chains, the feeling of not being in control. This strong sensation cursed through my body, and all actions taken on the inside were in vain.

As life slowly evaporated from me, I could almost sense it. Little specs came into existence during my final moments. Those little specs of illuminating light flowed through the alleyway. I don't think any of the thugs could see it, but to me, it seemed like they were extinguishing the darkness. They were so vivid that one could wonder how something so beautiful could exist here in the dumps of an old backstreet. As the light diminished sending the entire passage into darkness, I finally closed my eyes.

Here in the darkness, I was lured into recalling my past. For I don't know how long, people called me many things: heartless, cold, selfish, unsympathetic, cruel, and some even went as far as labeling me as inhuman. This is because, ever since I could remember, I led the life of an observer and avoided taking action. I hated obligations, and firmly believed that taking action most of the time had lifelong consequences. The reason why I chose to live in this formerly peaceful town was in order to enjoy the life of a hermit. I didn't want anyone to get in my way, nor did I get in the way of the people around me. Yet, everyone had these false expectations. They think you are obligated to jump in when something is happening, but usually those same people, when surrounded by others, don't takes action. They wait for someone else to do something.

That's not to say that I wouldn't help someone in need because I would, but only if it was a life and death matter. Right before death, to some it might seem like I broke this rule. Yes, I didn't rush in and put my life on the line, but I observed the situation and made a choice that would hopefully result in someone's life not ending. Making any decision has repercussions. I made a decision to not get involved, a choice which has a lifelong aftermath.

"At least it won't be a long aftermath" I joked inside.

Most of the time, I shied away from confrontations unless I had a really bad today. I subdued my nature to provoke others. I tamed my nature to play with the minds of others, particularly those that got on my nerves. Today was a day unlike those that came before it. I continued confronting the man and pushed him a little too far. Overall, I didn't expect everything to end up just like this. Did I consciously provoke him? Did I provoke him because I was drunk? Did I misjudge the situation? Falling asleep, my mind was blurry. I couldn't answer any of the questions I had.

"Cold, selfish, heartless, unsympathetic, inconsiderate, inhuman, those observing me called me many things."

A Lesson of Life and Death

———————

AWAKENED, I FOUND myself in the ominous white hallway. It was filled with a heavy mist empty of oxygen as if deliberately aiming to keep me half-asleep. With all the questions that showed up at the time of death, I had no intention of waiting even a second. I sprinted to the door, and into the cold white, adjacent room. I was yearning to know what is going to commence next. I wanted to know more.

Mankind's Most Persevering Teacher was as always dressed in a pure black suit, the blood red skulls on his tie much more vivid. He was writing in his notebook, taking notes. I could barely hold off with questioning, but I wanted to see what he has to say.

"Look at you! You're always dressed in a black suit and a white shirt. I've always thought that it's very impractical, but today I think it fits the occasion." The man exclaimed, walking to the front of his desk. His lighthearted mood was free of any emotional pestering that humans face.

"Is that all you have to say to me?" I asked.

"Of course not! I actually prepared a lesson for to-night, but before we proceed, I would like to know something."

"I'm in need of some answers as well." I said mildly agitated by his carefree attitude.

"How about this, you'll provide me with an honest answer, and I will give you an answer as well." He pirouetted with his notebook in hand. "Agree?"

"Fine, but how will I know if your response is true?" I asked.

"If there is a lie I am guilty of, it's only the lie of omission. Of course, you can try arguing, but I don't think you are in a position to." He smiled as he danced slowly around the room while taking notes in his beloved notebook.

"Ask the question."

"If I could return life to you, would you do anything differently? Do you have any regrets?" He asked with his eyes opened wide, looking straight at me.

"No, not really, I have no regrets. I have done every-thing according to my views." I hesitated. "But if I knew what would happen, I would have tried to take a little bit more risks. Just maybe, I would have tried to take life into my palm and hold it even for just a second."

"That's the answer I wanted to hear." He clapped his hands twice.

"So, my question is—"

"Didn't I already answer one of your questions?" He said. "Of course, I did."

"What?"

"Your question was an inquiry about the truthfulness of my response, wasn't it?" He exclaimed as his attitude rose to new levels of enthusiasm. His vulpine smile showed up.

"Taking advantage of my situation? I'm sick of your trickery."

"Well, I couldn't help myself. Besides, tricks are fair game since you're not one to reveal your sincere beliefs."

"I'm only using what I have learned from you." I grimaced.

"Such a diligent student you are. Would you promise that you'll stick to this mentality in the near future?"

"I'll promise you one thing. If I live and an opportunity presents itself, allowing me to gain more knowledge about this, about you, I won't think twice about taking that chance."

"I count on it." His smile grew brighter. "Anyway, I decided that all we ever do is converse, so maybe I should do a lecture. What do you say?"

"I don't think I have a say in the matter."

"I bet you'll enjoy it." He leaped across the room.

The man opened his notebook and inscribed some remarks in it. As he finished, he took a seat and turned to the window behind him. I noticed that he sat on a simple laboratory chair, one that is often used during examinations.

"So today we will go over a person called Michael Bailey. Bailey was once a loving father and a dedicated husband. He had a wife, Deborah, and a nine years old daughter, Sophia. He worked as an accountant in a small firm, where he tried to do his best, but he was barely able to meet his family's needs. Life was tough for him, but he never gave up. You could say that he was quite an optimist." The man explained. "We'll learn something very important about life from Mr. Bailey." He then pointed to the window and said, "Do take a look! It's quite a pleasant scene, if I say so myself. It's taken directly from his life. At least at first, it's a pleasant scene anyway."

I walked closer, pulled apart the blinds, and twisted the oval knob to open the window. I was greeted by a scene outside. It was almost as if I was looking into the building across the street from me, but I was able to see everything inside because the walls were fully transparent. The building was quite far away, yet I could see every little thing in the room like it was right in front of my face.

The scene took place in a dining room. A really small rectangular dining table with only three chairs was located in the center. A blue tablecloth occupied the space directly on the table, and there was a single bowl and a trio of plates on it. The tablecloth was a very deep azure blue color with a pattern of flowers on it. The flowers were lucid yellow with very light green dots for hearts. It was a rather awkward color combination that looked like the colors didn't want to coexist near each other. Over the table was a small silver metal chandelier that used candles as light source. All but one candle were lit at the time. Apparently, it was a family dinner. The rest of the room was utterly empty.

I could see Bailey with a crew cut, wearing a light pink dress shirt, sitting at the dining table. I couldn't catch even a glimpse of his face because he had his back to me, but I noticed that he was constantly looking back at the cheap watch on his hand. He was acting very restlessly as if he was present at home, but at the same time, his mind was somewhere else. He looked like he might run out any second.

Across from him was, presumably, his wife Deborah. Her long hair looked very messy and unwashed. She was dressed in a distressed smile, her white robe very dirty, almost gray. She was a very plain woman who was overcome by something extraordinary. Just looking at her, I could immediately come to the conclusion that she was struggling with depression. Despite having a loving husband, the woman couldn't smile. She wanted to live happily, but no one ever thought her how to. Despite the distressed smile, she seemed to be enjoying the quiet dinner.

To Bailey's left was seated a child, Sophia, that was an almost identical replica of Bailey's wife, but younger and much more lively. At first glance, Sophia seemed oblivious to the sad atmosphere, but at closer inspection, even she detected that something is wrong. She was seated closer to Bailey, so it almost seemed like the room was divided into two, an optimistic and a pessimistic half.

The whole room had a feel of a really good family, but at the same time, something was very wrong. It was a machine running well, but one gear was broken, and sooner or later, that gear might corrupt the whole thing. It was a machine where the other gears worked twice as hard to prevent anything from going wrong. They were forced to bear the responsibilities of the broken gear. Here the broken gear was Deborah.

A dialogue finally broke out. I could hear everything.

"I will have to go to work soon." Bailey said.

"I am sorry if I'm always sad, but I'm just not as optimistic as you are." Deborah replied.

"It's alright." He forced an uncomfortable grin. "I'll be the one who will fill our family with positive energy."

"Sophia, when you're finished, please go to your room. Mom wants to have a talk with dad." In a moment, the girl was finished and left the room, closing the door behind her. "Today we'll receive the results of the medical examination that was done on Sophia."

"I know. So call me right away, and I'll come back from work." He hesitated. "If I can." Bailey had a gloomy face. He knew that even if the situation was dire, he would never be allowed to leave work early. His only ticket for a fast departure was to fire himself.

The woman nodded.

A phone filled the room with noise. "Michael speaking." Bailey announced after grabbing the phone.

"Hey, Michael!" A voice sounded on the other end.

"Hi, boss. I'll be right at work. I'm leaving right now."

"Michael, you know, you should take a break. Stay with your wife and child. Enjoy the afternoon." The mechanical voice spoke without any particular emotions.

Michael was quiet. He knew what would come next. After a long pause, he decided that he needs to know right away. Just before his boss hung up, he asked. "Wait! Boss, you don't need me anymore?"

"I'm sincerely sorry, Michael."

"But I need this job. It's the only thing that is keeping my family afloat!"

"I didn't make the decision. Michael, you're a good

accountant, and you care for your family, everything will work out."

Bailey ruptured in anger. "What do you know about my life? You have no idea what this means to me. All you do is bullshit me about how you know how I feel and that you're sorry. These empty words mean nothing. You can't even admit that you called not out of kindness, but out of obligation to the firm." Michael shouted before realizing that his family was listening. He tried to calm down. He tried to think positively, but he was a broken container. No matter how much positive energy he could collect, it would all disappear through a hole of doubt in his mind. Lost in thought, he hung up the phone before his boss could reply.

"You lost your job?" Deborah inquired troubled. The moment she saw her husband nod, she took a step back, turning around to escape into her mental confines. She ran for her room. Michael gave chase, but his psyche wasn't equipped for a confrontation, and he was too late. Deborah locked the door.

"Deborah, everything will work out. We have been in many difficult situations, and it always worked out." He heard no response, so he made one last comment which he would regret all his life. "I'll go out and talk with some friends. Maybe they'll help me find some new work."

Bailey wasn't an impregnable individual. Each troublesome situation left a mark on his psyche. Each complication has worn him out. Being an optimist became harder each day. What was once second nature to him, now became nothing more than a farce, a mask that he wears each time he steps home. His original intension, when he left home, was to run away until he would outrun all the nuances. He was sick of all this. He didn't know how much more strength he could gather, and the upcoming fray seemed to be something that he has never faced before. All he could concentrate on was the sad idea of his wife on the verge of collapse and his sick daughter. The gifts of love that they gave him and their problems that he had to bear were two sides of the same coin—a coin called life.

He still looked back, debating on his intension of running away, but he was ashamed of even thinking about it. Family was too important to him. It was all he had. Bailey would be able to kill for the sake of preserving his family.

He spent hours going from one friend to the next, trying to find a rope he could grab, so that he wouldn't fall from the edge. With each disappointment, his step grew heavier until he returned. From the outside, he could see the lights were off, so he thought that his wife and daughter were asleep.

He opened the door to his home and walked into the living room where he faced a nightmare that would break him completely.

The Cause of Death

DEBORAH WAS SUSPENDED over the ground by a rope. A small stool was tipped over near her feet. Her entire face was covered by her oily hair. The rope must have chafed against her neck because it was soaked in blood a little at the noose. Bailey stared at her chin where water, tears, were dripping from. He fell to his knees, broken mentally. As he hurried to get her down, he touched her feat only to realize how cold they wore. At that moment, he knew there was nothing more he could do for her. He cringed, defeated by the mental trauma, but he couldn't cry. No matter what happened, he was unable to cry. He screamed in anger. With a final look at his beloved wife, a piece of paper on the floor was brought to his attention.

"I received a message about our daughter." He whispered, reading. "As always, I was too weak to bear any of life's problems. As always, I was a coward and run, but this time, I was finally able to make it out of this nightmare. I pray that you will forgive me someday. I will be waiting for you and soon Sophia will be too."

He felt profound pain in his chest.

"You're truly selfish, you always chose the easy way out. You never understood how much family meant to me. You have separated yourself from me, and soon you will take Sophia too. I sometimes wish I could be like you." Bailey muttered in grief, realizing that in the long run his struggle to be the pillar that supported his family failed. He turned the note over to see another message. "Sophia is with our neighbors."

The lights went out.

◆

I was once again in the company of the teacher. He rose from his stool and shut the window.

"Before we discuss this any further, I bet you want to see the end of the story, right?" The man asked. Something was telling me he knew the ending already. He was accustomed to death.

I fell silent, waiting for him to continue.

"After all this, Bailey initiated many criminal acts from robberies to blackmail. He became a criminal and much more. With no work, it was the only way to provide for his daughter. Although not too long after his wife passed away, his daughter left him as well. He became completely twisted and uncaring in the face of danger. Lacking concern for his own life, he started to live a life free of sympathy for others. He found another family composed of people united in crime. Bailey was 30 years old at the time of his death. He died today in a dismal alleyway stabbed to death."

Why show this to me? I contemplated, keeping all questions to myself after grasping that none will be honored with an answer.

"What did you think of the story?"

"Discouraging." I said, realizing that to me the story symbolized pure despair and sadness.

"What do you think is the moral of the story?"

"Some things are unavoidable. No matter how strong something is, it can't withstand everything."

"Want to know my take on it?" The teacher wrote in his notebook.

"We went this far, so why not continue a little more." I noticed that my impatience has vanished.

"In summary, mankind can be divided into three classes: pessimists, realists and optimists. All these are basically different levels of mental vitality. Even the strongest can't withstand everything. No matter how strong someone is, there comes a time when he faces a force so massive that it breaks him."

"Care to enlighten me and explain how this relates to me?"

"Maybe it doesn't at this very moment, but at one point it will."

"So, what now?"

"Well, I think that it's about time for you to go back."

"Wait. Hold on. What are you talking about? My life is ..."

"No, it's not, at least not yet. You're going to have to endure it a little bit longer." He smiled.

"Don't tell me it's related to the story I told you."

"I don't want to spoil anything, so you'll see once you get back. Anyway, aren't you happy?"

I avoided answering his question for the answer was obvious. I was tremendously content that I could go back. Anybody would be.

I was a little shocked by the last turn of events. Despite having so many questions, I kept them to myself. At one point, it seemed that by now there are so many unknowns that I don't even know where to start. At the same time, for the first time in my life, I was yearning to take action. I felt a slight tingling in my heart, a sign of anticipation and worry for the things that might come in the very near future. This foreign feeling quickly faded without me even noticing. I was on the verge of waking up.

"What about the time we spend here? I mean, we have been here for what seems like over an hour."

"In this dream world, time flows much slower. In here, hours are equivalent to only seconds in the real world. When you're back, your life will be resumed only a second or two after you lost unconsciousness."

"Fine."

"I'll be awaiting our next meeting with anticipation."

"Anything else you're willing to shed some light on?"

"The story we discussed, the morale of it, keep it in mind. Also, I'll be keeping my eyes on you."

"Don't you do that on a daily basis?"

"Sure, but from now on it'll be a closer observation."

My eyes finally opened up to the real world. The man who attacked me was bleeding from his chest, his clothes dipped in blood. He was barely able to stand. A second later he fell to the ground and onto his back, laying in the pool of blood, which only increased in size. He could not utter an audible word, and the only thing that came out of his mouth was some senseless mumbling. His eyes expressed pure shock.

Apparently, the wound on my body from the knife has closed already. I noticed that there was a lot of blood on my skin and shirt which was slowly peeling off into little fragments. These fragments would than decompose in the air, leaving no trace. By the time the process was completed, there was no evidence that I was harmed in any way. I was back at full strength which cannot be said about the attacker. I finally stood up, fully awake, completely healed. I put my astonishment to the side to deal with the ordeal at hand.

Witnessing something supernatural shook the smiley thug to the core. He seemed to consider it worse than being an eyewitness to a murderer. The instant he saw me rise, the smiley thugs gave in to his discomfort and fear and run away, screaming his heart out and leaving the other one behind.

By now his hood was down and his shades were on the pavement, so I could finally see his face. His brown hair was cut short, and he had multiple piercings in his ear some of which drooped down, chiming against each other. He was standing, looking at the body of his leader petrified and unaware that I stood up. Slowly tears gather in his eyes, and he began to cry, but he ceased immediately as he finally became aware of me. He tripped falling to the ground. "My name is Aidan. Don't kill me! Don't kill me!"

"Shut up for a second." I turned my attention to the body and stared at the knife which was left right in the pool of blood. I was curious to check if my blood has evaporated from it too, but it was impossible to verify, so I hesitantly assumed that's what happened. I considered multiple other scenarios which could lead to me, and upon deciding that I haven't left any clues, I turned my attention to Aidan who was still on the floor dispirited.

"Why didn't you run?" I asked.

"I-I'm, just, just, really scared." It seemed like he had trouble talking when under high stress. "Let's, let's be diplomatic."

"Now you want to be diplomatic?" I leaned against the wall. "I've got an idea. If it works out, it should benefit both of us." I checked my pockets and noticed they took my wallet and my cell phone, so I demanded them back.

Aidan jumped in search of my wallet through his pockets. "Here." He said. "The other guy must have taken the cell phone."

"I hope you understand that you'll need to find him and get it back." I responded after checking and confirming that the contents of my wallet were all intact.

"I-I'll search for him and if I-I find him, you'll l-let me go, right?" He asked.

"Once you have the phone, you'll reach me. By the way, I realize that even if you told someone about this incident, no one would believe you, but you can't go around spreading rumors like there is no tomorrow, and this goes for the other thug too."

"Y-You're not going to kill me? I saw t-this whole t-thing." He pointed to the body. "What about the corpse?" He threw numerous questions at me. By now his staggering was decreasing slightly.

"If I had to pick, I would probably use fear as a

weapon of choice. So my advice is don't do anything foolish, and you'll live. Regarding the body, I think that's mainly your problem."

The man clenched his fist, angered.

"Don't you have any will to fight back? I mean, he must have been someone important in your life; you wouldn't stay behind otherwise. You feel no anger?"

"You know, my boss," he said and took a deep breath. "He was always looking for trouble. I think he wanted to find an opponent who would fight back and end his life. I think this is for the best. Michael is with his family now after all."

"I understand now." I thought about the time in the dream world and the lesson. "What was the whole ordeal with shouting out your name?"

"I heard it's much more difficult to kill someone once you label him with a name. The person than becomes a living being, and not just a bag of meat." Aidan responded.

I didn't respond because I realize how terrified he must have been. If I saw something like what transpired here, I probably wouldn't be able to fight back, but ultimately, I would try to regain my will. It seemed this man lacked that trait.

Prior to my leave, a hazy blue image flashed before my eyes for just a second. It was an image of a man sitting loosely on a stool. His head rested on the counter. The sound of water dripping echoed in my ears. I considered the whole thing as a simple hallucination from a lack of sleep.

At the mouth of the alley was a flower, a light red carnation. Something told me to grab it, but I chose otherwise.

"What was that?" Aidan asked.

"Nothing of importance. One more question, this whole time was one of you watching the street for any witnesses?"

"I'm pretty sure that no one saw this incident. Plus the rain erased our tracks in the back of the alley." He reminded me of the drizzle.

"Looks like it's time to get going." I looked at my watch. The night was growing old.

"They'll find him tomorrow, but it'll be a while before this whole situation dies down." He rehearsed his breathing routine. "Looks like I won't find tranquility any time soon."

"They'll probably think of this as another suicide case." I said unmindful of the importance of those words. A second later, I asked myself the question, "Could this ability allow someone to stage a suicide?"

"You're right. There are no signs of struggle. No footprints. No witnesses. The weapon is right in his hand. Sure it all fits, and I bet our only policeman will think so too, but I am not so sure about the two outsiders." He commented with worry on his face. He looked back at his boss with sadness. He felt disgrace for leaving someone important to him like that, but out of fear, he didn't say anything.

We left the scene in opposite directions.

I still couldn't believe the events that transpired. All of the sudden, I felt a little dizzy and lightheaded. The stress kicked in, and I felt overwhelmed. My calm bearing was gone, and I wished that the situation had no place in my life.

The Weight of Pain

I WALKED INTO the classroom and observed that the lecture has already begun. I found my way to my seat in the back of the classroom, where I could observe the worn-out teacher writing enthusiastically on the black board and acting like what he is teaching is the truth. With all the windows closed, the air that lingered about was heavy, humid. Every classmate had the same exhausted face. Some girl moved to catch a glimpse of the breeze from the fan. Everyone was present except Heather. Her seat, that's two seats away from me, was completely deserted. Kasper was seated to my left. He had a stamp with the logo of a bar called Scarlet Snake that he frequented.

When he noticed that I arrived, he whispered. "Shocked that she's not here?"

"Do you know where she might be?" It was pretty standard practice to abandon class midway through, or even to never show up, but Heather was very punctual and responsible. She had never missed class unless she was terribly sick. This time, she was probably sick from yesterday's events.

"How should I know? Not like she considers me a friend or something." he said.

"Guess that's true, but you know her longer than I do."

"She might be home, I haven't seen her since yesterday."

"Yesterday right after class?"

"Yep, that time when you and I exchanged those comments." Kasper stretched in his seat without hiding his boredom. "We're supposed to do that project for this class, right? Heather is in our group too. Presentation is next class."

"It's not like you to worry about school."

"Just because I'm usually easygoing, it doesn't mean that I completely ignore what is going on here. I want to get through this with good grades too." He chuckled silently. The words sounded awkwardly because he really didn't know what responsibility was.

"Well, we can probably just meet once everyone has completed their portion of the project to compile everything."

"I haven't even started."

"Is that why you're so concerned?"

"You know what I meant." Kasper yawned. "Is it just me, or are you a tiny bit more talkative today?"

"It's just you."

Sitting in the classroom, I was fully consumed in my contemplation. I looked at the professor, but none of his words reached me. All the noise and sounds in class ceased, and I was completely lost in thought. I remembered the incident, the gift, the ability.

To Aidan, it probably seemed like I was in control. He might even blame me for the death of his boss, but I was lost. I couldn't sleep all night, thinking about this power. Yet at the same time, I was in no position to research anything. Perhaps, I didn't know where to start, or maybe, I was instinctively struggling to forget about it. However, yesterday keeps reminding me that I am not going to be able to run away that easily. The events keep saying, "The only way to run away is to dig deeper into this." At first, the power seemed handy, and it sure is in dangerous situations, but it might be troublesome since I hardly know anything about it. It's so unpredictable.

The only thing I know for sure about it is that it's obviously only activated when another person hurts me in some way. My best guess is that it's only set in motion when I am badly hurt, but there is no reason why it wouldn't work from a simple scratch. Normally, this wouldn't be a problem, but what if someone notices, starts yelling and pointing at me, labeling me as evil? It could turn out to be an inconvenience to say the least. To be safe, I'll assume that any wound will trigger it.

I keep coming back to the question if this power could allow someone to fake a suicide. I mean, it wouldn't be so easy, but what if it's true. An attacker could provoke a fight. The victim could be defending against the attacker thus hurting him, and in the end, the victim would be wounded. Sure the theory sounds ridiculous, but so does this power. If I was able to come up with a story like that, I should really be careful with getting hurt. Someone could mark me as the culprit with the use of some imagination. What if the theory is true? That would mean that the culprit has a good understanding of this ability. If I could find him, I would most definitely get some answers. I could get rid of this power. I'm probably getting ahead of myself.

The professor started to pass out sheets of paper, homework. As he reached my seat, I thought that this could be a chance for an experiment. I stretched out my hand and grabbed the handout. I pressed my finger firmly against the edge before the teacher could let go. Blood dripped from my finger, staining the very tip of the paper. As the professor continued with distributing the handouts, he noticed the papercut on his finger. My wound was healed, and the paper spotless. At that moment, I learned that this power indeed gets triggered even by minor wounds, and the other person doesn't even need to have the intention of hurting me. This made me even more determined to find the culprit.

Guess I have my work cut out for today; I will start by trying to find some info about the ability first. Next, I will look closer at the case. Maybe there will be some clues. If only I could find a trend, a pattern. I rehearsed my plan. I though back to that feeling I had the other day, the feeling of excitement at the things to come. This feeling has vanished by now.

Once class was finished, I started packing up. The professor zoomed past me and approached Kasper. "Hey, Kasper, you know Heather, right?"

"Yea."

"Could you give this to her? This is the assignment for next class. We're almost finished with the semester, so she shouldn't fall behind." The teacher said in an emotionless voice.

Kasper glared at me. His face looked like he was asking me to intervene with an excuse for him. It looked like he was surprised with the sudden request and couldn't create a plausible excuse for himself. For some reason, he didn't want to help or even meet Heather, despite his usual tendencies to pester and talk to her in class. I briefly listened to the conversation and decided to let the teacher do his thing. Kasper was hopeless and reluctantly accepted the task. "Professor, I completely forgot I have work today, so I won't be able to stop by Heather's place."

"At the start of the semester, didn't you say that you don't work? You claimed that you don't need to work because you're parents pay for everything."

I chuckled. Kasper had neither diligence nor a feeling of responsibility which made it tough for him to find work even if he tried. Of course, he never had a care in the world, and so it seemed like the idea of working was very much erased from his mental dictionary at birth. I was curious how he would escape the situation.

He tried thinking of something. His eyes kept wandering the classroom, avoiding eye contact with the teacher which made it obvious he was lying. "Yea, that was true until this week. I finally got a job. But you know what? It's no problem. I'll get the assignment to Heather."

"Thank you" The teacher walked off, complaining.

"Where are you going?" Kasper asked.

I left the classroom.

The brick building was a three floor structure. It was

used for classes ranging from art, to design, to sawing, and all the other so-called arts. The building was newly renovated. The white walls were painted a new, the hallways were clean as if never used, and all the exits now had a pair of brand new doors. However, the smell of paint lingered in the air, reminding everyone of how much work was done in the building.

I took the almost-broken elevator down. The sound of metal jerking resounded. Most people avoided taking the elevator because of the heart tearing sounds, so I regularly took advantage of that. It allowed me an exit that was free of the crowd bunching up at the door.

The elevator stopped. I made my way to the exit of the building where I was stopped by a kid, who was hanging out flyers, with a small puppy. The kid forced me to take one, or else he would follow me around for all eternity. The flier was a tactic used by The Unity. They tried to spread the word and persuade people into joining their ranks. The flier was in the form of a little booklet, and it had a simple design. There were multiple pictures posted on a dark green background. I didn't care to read it until I saw a new proposal they were trying to pass. They suggested that if the town united, they could search every home and interview everyone until they found the culprit of the suicides. It was an outrages idea, but there was a chance that if people are desperate enough, it might pass. The thought was unsettling.

"Hey, wait!" Kasper screamed, trying to catch up to me. He was smoking something.

"If you want to talk, cease with the smoking." I hated the smell of smoke. I avoided any contact with it because it would gradually irritate my throat and lungs to the point where it felt like someone poured something into them, preventing me from breathing in oxygen. Ultimately, it would feel like the inside of my lungs was coated by some dried out substance. To my amazement, he obeyed. It was a bad sign. Kasper was a person who wouldn't comply with anyone's advice or request unless he had ulterior motives.

"So, I was hoping that you would take this to Heather." He was lugging the paperwork under his arm.

"What makes you think that?"

"Well, you're friends, right?"

"Didn't you say that you're interested in Heather? This whole thing should be like a gift from the heavens. The paperwork should be enough to justify seeing her."

"I'm not sure if she would like to see me after what happened yesterday." Kasper commented.

"So what happened?" Guess I wasn't the only one to get into conflict with her.

"It's a private matter!" he said. "So what's it going to be?"

"I'll pass."

"Oh, well." Kasper took out and lit a smoke. He left the handouts by the trash can before running off.

Unwillingly, I decided that if Heather is to get the assignments, I should take them. Moved by the recent events, I pressed on with the good deed in mind. I sighed.

Heather lived not too far from the school. It was only about a ten minute walk. Today, I had only one lecture, so I made it there a little past noon. When I first reached the parking lot of the apartment complex, I realized it was very similar to the one I lived in. It was a two-story building with outdoor stairs that led to the second floor walkway. I claimed the wooden stairs. They were soggy from last night's rain. I make my way to the cherry colored door with the number 12 on it, and I knocked. There was no answer. The parking lot was empty, but I couldn't tell if that meant Heather wasn't home because I didn't know if she had a car. I argued against knocking again and started to walk away. A sound came from deep within the apartment. She probably decided to check who tried to disturb her peace.

I came back to the door. "It's me. I have no intention of giving excuses, nor am I here to try to win you over with meaningless words and apologies. The professor wanted you to get the notes and homework that was given out today."

Without saying anything, the door unlocked and opened inviting me inside, but to me, this was no invitation. Walking into these doors would most likely result in nothing good. The apartment itself consisted of a very small living room, an even smaller bedroom, and an almost nonexistent kitchen and bathroom. The inside was quite messy. There were dirty and unwashed clothes scattered on the floor, an uncountable number of dishes in the sink, and so much garbage that some of it spilled from the trash can.

I found Heather in the living room. She had a gauze covering the right corner of her lips and her bruised cheek. Her hair was the messiest I've ever seen. She also had a pair of black shades, and a robe over her shoulders. She held it tightly around her body, hiding both of her hands. "What do you want?" She exclaimed in a voice very different from her usual cheery one.

"This is the stuff from class." I gestured, trying to give her the paperwork.

"The professor never asked you to do anything, why now?" She grabbed it.

"In truth, it was Kasper who was commissioned to do this." At the sound of those words, she turned her back to me, struggling to hide her despair in the face of some horrible thought that she was unable to bear. She tightened her fists until her nails drew blood.

"So now you're his delivery boy?"

"Quite on the contrary, I chose to get it to you because it landed in the garbage can, courtesy of Kasper's feeling of responsibility."

"So you don't feel obligated to give me an explanation?"

"As far as I'm concerned, my gamble must have upset you, but everything worked out."

"Worked out? You don't even know what I have been through that night!" In fury, she took of the shades to reveal a black eye. At the same time, her robe fell of her shoulders, revealing numerous bruises and a broken hand.

I was pretty sure that I wasn't at fault for this. After all, when I spoke to her that night, she was way too tranquil for someone with so many injuries. She said it herself that she only sustained a couple bruises. While the thugs could have come back to ask about me, I see no reason to hurt her this much. A simple inquiry combined with her anger would yield the info they desired. She would have disclosed any info they wanted without much of a fight. I tried to avoid angering her anymore, but I failed. "Likewise."

"I can only imagine! They asked for your info, and

you know what? I gave it to them! I truly hope they'll find you one day!" She shouted, but to me, it seemed like she wasn't screaming directly at me. Heather was just hopelessly venting of her rage, a rage that possibly drifted through her veins for many years. It was a feeling of desperation that would otherwise dwell within her dormant, but yesterday someone lit the fuse. "Why are you so cold? Why are you so heartless?" She cried out.

I kept silent. I couldn't find the right words.

A prolonged period of stillness commenced. Unable to continue the empty dialogue, she took a seat on the floor in the corner and curled up. She held her legs to her chest with both hands. Although I felt like an unwelcomed guest, I was under the impression that if I left her, she might do something foolish, so I chose to take a seat on the floor and stay.

In the silence, it was very easy to lose track of time. Seconds, minutes, and maybe even hours passed as we sat there on the floor. I was counting on a quick visit, but my plans fell apart. If someone asked me the reason for staying with Heather, I honestly don't know if I would be able to answer that question.

"I'm not as ignorant of what other people think as it might seem." Heather muttered "I know that I annoy you, that you don't enjoy my company. I know that look when you look at me in class. It's the look that tells you 'Just leave me alone. I'm tired of this nonsense chatter.' I'm sure every day you wanted to ask me why I insist on talking with you."

"Does all that really matter?"

"A little over four years ago, I still had a family that I could depend on. One day, they were taken away from me by an accident. On that day, I lost my name. I wasn't called Heather anymore. When people looked at me, they said, 'It's the girl whose family died in the accident.' One summer day, you arrived and thanks to serendipity we met. You didn't look at me with pity. I prefer your look of dislike over the look of pity."

"You know." I looked at the sun outside, "We are all bound by intangible and invisible chains. Those chains can take up many forms, but in the end, all they do is prevent us from evolving and changing favorably. Some people are guided by chains and others struggle against them, until they break them completely." I exclaimed.

"Which one are you?" She calmed down a bit.

"I am still the former. And you?"

"I think there is one more category. Some people pretend that they don't have any chains. They act positively, but that's all they are doing, acting. I act kind and always do my best. I play the part of a happy-go-lucky." She wept. "It's the only thing I can do. It's a mask I wear all the time. I'm deeply hoping it will protect me against anything out there. That it'll help me forget about everything, but I'm still bound by sadness, by despair."

"Well, everyone is running away from something."

"What are you running away from?" She pointed at me, making me remember that she wasn't the only one who disliked her past.

"Realities of life in the suburbs."

"There it goes again, your tendency to hide in the shadows. Now that I think about it, I don't know anything about you. When I look at you, all I can say is that I see a 26 year old man with a slightly messy, rather out-of-control, dark brown hair, who always wears a white shirt and a black suit." She looked at me through her watery eyes.

"There really isn't much of a story to me. I came here four years ago after an overdose of traveling around."

"What about your bystander tendencies?"

"I'm still looking for the cause. Anyway, I should get going."

"I have a favor."

"One more? I though you learned something from last time."

"Let's pretend like nothing happened." She wiped her tears. "Let's forget not only our quarrel, but everything else too."

"Pretend like nothing happened? What about your injuries? I won't press you to tell me anything because it's your life, but if someone would do something like that to me, I wouldn't be able to forget." I spoke candidly, believing that if she is to do that, she's just putting another item on the shelf of belongings that symbolize trauma from her past.

"The injuries, they'll heal." She uttered with conviction.

"Don't you think you're trying to bear a load that might turn out to be too heavy for you at some point?"

"We only have to pretend for a couple of days until the semester is finished." She grew silent, knowing the truthfulness of my response.

"It's your choice."

◆

Outside, I checked my watch to find out that it was 3:48 PM. I must have been there way over two hours. In front of the door, there was another one of those flowers I found last night. I disregarded the coincidence. Sun was now shining luminously as I walked down the stairs. My legs felt a little numb from the uncomfortable sitting on the floor. Before leaving, I looked once more at Heather's apartment. I felt guilty for thinking that her request was, in fact, a blessing. I didn't want to continue, and she offered a splendid alternative. Feeling guiltier and guiltier for my take on the matter, I thought.

"Looks like one of my classmates deserves some punishment."

The News

HOME, I WAS greeted by a thousand faces, staring at me from every corner of my almost barren home. The walls were covered in paintings. I didn't postpone my search for answers. I quickly took a hold of my laptop, opened it up, and turned it on. I remembered that I haven't checked my voicemail for over a day. I walked to the answering machine and listened. A monotone voice stated that I have seven messages. Over half of them were just those mood-ruining advertisements spoken by an automated voice. Even in a place like this, advertising tried to affect, persuade, and influence people. Skipping messages, I finally arrived at my destination, the final two.

The first one was from the library. Apparently, they were sorry that I quit, but it wasn't an attempt at to get me to return. It was a message personally from Fredric, the man who got me the work. He said he had a job opportunity and was wondering if I would be interested in further cooperation. I deleted the message without a second thought.

A prolonged pause commenced before the next message.

"It's me, Aidan. I guess you might be debating how I got your number, but that's not important. I tired finding Marcus, the other thug, but he's nowhere to be found. I'll keep looking, but I think it might be a good idea to meet and discuss this issue because I have a feeling that he might be dead. I'll make sure of this before we meet. I'll be present in front of the Scarlet Snake at 8:30 PM." Aidan said.

"Looks like I won't get a good night sleep." I said to myself. It all seems fine, but there is something that stood out. If he believes the other thug to be dead, wouldn't I be the primary suspect in his eyes? This might be a trap, so I shouldn't go.

The next three hours went by in a flash. The searching has consumed me whole, so it felt like the outside world didn't exist. I forgot to eat and drink. After I was done for the night, it almost felt like I was short of breath. Maybe if breathing was a conscious effort, I would be suffocating midway through.

My hunt was hopeless. I tried using various key terms, ranging from transfer of pain to reflecting pain. No luck. No matter what I inputted, the search came up with meaningless topics on meditation and psychology. Although I was done with finding answers for the night, one thing sparked my interest. I found a website. The homepage read, "Chosen by the Will of the Universe." There was something mystic and bizarre about the site. It consisted of only two pages. One of them was the homepage, which had a black background and text further below. "Those chosen by the universe, those needed by the universe, they give back what was given to them." On the very bottom, in the corner was a link to the list of members. There were only 27 members. At first, I thought about signing up, but there was no sign-in link. I gave up, closed the window, and turned my attention to the case.

The information on the case was fairly limited too, but I was rather successful in gathering what was of importance. So far, there have been 23 deaths. I found out that all of them happened at night, somewhere between midnight and 4AM. I was hoping to get the names of all the victims, so that I could inquire to their relatives about any info, but more than half of the names were kept secret by the police. Luckily, the names of the first two victims were announced on the news. The two names were Nicholas Archer and Isabella Wright. In such a small village, it shouldn't be too difficult finding out where those people resided. I predicted that I might be unaccepted and uninvited by their family members. I decided to dedicate my tomorrow to investigating those two individuals anyway, but I had my doubts.

It might be a little too early to speak with them. If I talk to them, they might feel as if someone is pouring salt into their newly-opened wounds. Should I really go?

I turned on the TV to listen to the news.

The announcer began speaking in an excited voice not fit for the matter he was addressing. "We have some breakthrough news. The terrible incident took place last night in an alleyway near Griffin's Bar. A male in his 30's stabbed himself in the chest multiple times, resulting in death. What a horrible way to go. Furthermore, that same night, a second horrific event happened where a lady in her late 40's jumped from the roof of her apartment building near View Point Ave. Yes, that's right, respected citizens, we are here to report two suicides. The plague is not letting go. Is this the work of an instigator? Is this the work of an ominous force? The detectives are silent."

I was lost in thought.

They did group the two indicants together, but I'm sure the detectives have their suspicions. After all, who would choose that kind of a death for himself? I have no way of knowing how the other incidents looked, but I have a feeling that if there is someone pulling strings behind the curtain, he would be obsessively careful and diligent, making sure everything fits in. That would mean that either I'm extremely lucky, or the detectives disclosed fake info.

A thunderous knock on the door derailed my concentration. I wasn't expecting anyone, so the only feeling I was surprised. I calmly walked to the door and intended to look through the peephole. My heart ran wild, telling me to do otherwise. When I did, there was no one on the other side. I reached for a knife. My imagination took a full swing as I didn't know what to expect. I was at the mercy of it running rampant. The outside was empty, but my doormat was filled with those red carnations that I kept seeing throughout the day. It was the very flowers I kept ignoring.

"Who would go to this extent to get my attention?" The thought raced through my mind reminding me of despair.

If someone was aiming to make me feel uneasy, they surely succeeded. I felt a tinge of fear amass as stress begun to pulse through my veins. My mind went blank as I couldn't think clearly, and the only thought that kept coming back was the idea that I might not make it out of this place alive. I recalled the last 24 hours in my mind, and I came to the conclusion that I was naive in believing that no one could have witnessed the events in the alley. I scream inside my mind as I cleansed my body of the unwanted. Angered, I changed directions. The one and only way I'll make it out of here is by becoming tranquil inside.

I kept contemplating about what this whole thing could mean. I knew for a fact that there were no witnesses before I passed out. Afterward, I must have been out for only a couple of seconds, and based on what Aidan said he didn't see anyone. Of course, he could be lying. Once I returned to normal, I am sure that no one saw me. There were no cameras in the area either. The building across the street is deserted, so that's out of the question. When this whole thing started a day ago, my priority was to keep attention to the minimum.

It was obvious that someone knows. There is no such thing as a coincidence.

I stumbled into my bedroom and reached for my bed. Feeling drowsy because I haven't slept for over 48 hours, I fell into a deep state of sleep. It was the first time when I didn't travel to the dream world since four months. I had no dreams, but I had everything I wished for during the night, a peaceful slumber.

Historia's Flowers

THAT SAME NIGHT, clamor forced me out of my sleep. The radio transmission was coming from my living room. The incomprehensible exchange of words put me in a state of restlessness. Yet, this time, my mind was way too clouded from sleeping that all emotions seemed dulled. I grabbed a hold of the knife and made my way to the adjacent room.

The noise ceased, and someone behind me uttered, "I confirmed that Marcus is dead."

"Is that so important that you have to break into my home, Aidan?" I asked.

"It wasn't you, was it?" He had a firearm in his hand.

"If you would practice rational thinking, you would know the answer already."

"D-Did you kill him? And why didn't you show up at the b-bar?" He shouted while his stuttering returned.

"Keep it quiet," I said. "Or you'll wake everyone up. How could I have killed him when I didn't even see his face?"

"I b-broke into his apartment. His wallet, his money, and everything else is still there. But your phone was nowhere to be found. No one would have left like that. I b-bet we won't ever find him."

"He could have thrown the phone away, and now, he's hiding somewhere, but that's a little unlikely. Where else could he be if not next to his lifelong treasures?"

"Now that you mention it, if he was looking for help, he could only turn to three people in this town. One of them is Michael, who's dead. I'm the second one. The last one kind of disappeared recently as well."

"It's a little far-fetched, but if there was no one at the scene, maybe Marcus told someone he shouldn't. That someone believed him, and then killed him. That could explain why the phone is gone."

"If that's true, it means someone is searching for you." he said, his face blocked by the darkness.

Heavy stumping on the floor shook the entire room. "Shut up down there!" The landlord shouted.

"Keep your voice down." I went for a glass of water. "If that's true, you're next in line." He gave me an angry look. "That's why you're going to help me."

"W-Why would I do that?"

"It's the only option you have in reclaiming your normal life."

"W-What are you planning?"

I took a sip of the water. "We are in no position to

make a move, so return to your life. Soon, you'll stumble upon the murderer. That's when things will become clearer."

"Become clearer? Are you not worried?"

"I am." I gave an indifferent shrug that didn't disclose my true emotions.

"I have a feeling you welcome that idea," he said, "of getting rid of me."

"Soon, everything will be back to normal."

He seemed to reluctantly agree. "Everything? Wait, you're not t-talking about the suicides, are you?"

I kept silent, letting his mind run wild. He gave up on any further inquiry, and after a final exchange, he left. The night grew still, and I was able to sleep again. I debated if I should change my locks, but figured he could probably get in anywhere.

This might come in handy sometime.

The following morning, I felt restless, but it wasn't the type of restlessness where you can't wait for something to happen. It was a feeling that you desire a future event to come and pass by quickly, so that you can get it over with. When I finally made my way outside, it took me quite a while to locate the homes of the two victims. One person, despite being home, never opened the door. I saw the woman in the window, staring, checking who was intruding. I even made eye contact, but the woman immediately hid behind the curtains like an immature child. I understood her. I didn't blame her for not wanting to talk. I chose against pestering her anymore and aimed for the second person on my list.

When I got there, I waited before the red wooden door. I was hesitating. Standing there, it felt like the person knew that I was outside. I felt like he could sense my presence even though I didn't hammer on the door. When I was finally motivated enough to come in, the door was abruptly opened by an older man.

He looked around 70 years old. He was almost completely bold. He wore a flannel shirt, and both of his hands were held behind his back. Despite his age, his posture was absolutely straight. He had the aura of someone who was in the army, a dedicated soldier. "Reporter?" he asked.

"No, I'm not a reporter. I'm sorry to invade, but as you know, we only have a single policeman, so the idea came up that citizens should look into cases to see if any details were missed."

"Is that another brainchild of the sect?" he asked. My excuse was brutally similar to those ideas I detested. I grimaced and observed as the old man begun whispering to himself. "They're spreading really fast. Almost a quarter of the residents are members already."

"No, it's not. I ..." Before I could finish, the man yelled.

"Then get out and never come back!"

I forced my shoe between the doorway to prevent him from closing the door and spoke in a hurry, "I realize I know nothing about your son, Nicholas, and I apologize for coming here, but the police labeled this case as a suicide. I believe it is not. If there is a chance that you have doubts, provide me with any info that might help. People don't kill themselves just because they have simple problems." During my speech, I slipped in a piece of paper with my name on it in hopes that he might reconsider.

The man closed the door in rage.

With no other leads, I gave up on the matter. I considered asking around town, but I concluded that I'm not the most liked person around here. At home, someone called me. I was familiar with the number, my cell number. I answered. The other side was mute, waiting for me to speak.

"What kind of a madman does something like this?" My tendency to provoke others surfaced. The person on the other end hung up. I felt like I jumped into his trap. He probably wanted to confirm the voice of the cell phone's owner. If so, he's probably very close to making his move. I debated if those red carnations had anything to do with it, but I couldn't find a connection.

I felt like the whole situation got out of hand, and again nothing went as planned. The television buzzed in the other room, concerning an official police statement. Dench claimed that an instigator is behind the wave of suicides. When asked by the reporter if there are any solid leads, he asserted that it's too early to say. Checking my kitchen, I found out that I had no tea, which was my favorite drink, so I jumped out to take a walk.

◆

The streets were absolutely desolate. To some extent, people were scared, but I didn't think that was the reason for it. There was a different meaning to those lifeless avenues. People were falling into despair. Life was leaking out of their buddies because of those recent events.

The mailman rode his bike, whistling in the opposite

direction. A lady in a rocking chair gave me an irritated glance. Someone sounded their horn behind me. It was Fredric, the librarian who was a village-life-loving, young man. He was moderately energetic, but very formal. Unlike most, he had extremely long hair that stretched to his waist. All the strands were tied back by a lone piece of cloth. Upon putting down his window, he said, "Looks like you didn't get my message."

His comment was rather friendly, and it didn't have even an ounce of malice in it, but I had no doubt that he knew I did get his message. He knew I just chose not to reply.

"Yea, I was really busy."

"I wonder what you do as a pastime. You're completely free now."

"No one is perfectly free." He matched my pace. "Is there anything you wanted?"

"I would like you to meet someone." He gestured his hand, welcoming me to jump in.

"Now?"

"If you have time, I don't think I can let you escape this time."

Speechless, I reluctantly got into his car. I didn't want to continue this farce, but he would continue pestering me until I complied. We drove down the avenue though the not-so-busy Main St. In the distance, the towering multi-floor brick building of the sect was monitoring our travels. The sect's headquarters was a place on the western outskirts of town, one that was fully surrounded by an electrified fence, which was disguised as a pure green hedge. The compound was a collection of three buildings that encircled the garden in the middle.

Being here made me uncomfortable. The first thought that my irrational-self posted in my mind was that they knew about the incident. Sure, that was plausible, but if that was the case, why would they wait for me to agree to come here? I was surely here for a different reason. Could it be that they want me to join the sect? Why? The more we traveled, the more vivid the notion of suspiciousness became.

We drove in through the gate. After parking the vehicle, I was led to the garden. The garden was wholly green, but a few lilies were here and there. There was a man sitting on a bench, perusing a book page by page. His face was hidden behind the hard cover. A buzzing sound make me look up. I noticed that there were multiple bees flying in the air, but apparently, Fredric didn't fear being bitten. However, I couldn't say the same. Once, we reached the other side of the garden, the main building stood before me. Multiple staircases had to be ascended for us to reach the top, where the leader's room was located behind a mighty, sturdy door.

Fredric gently knocked. He was greeted, "Come in!"

Inside, the spokesman was seated behind his bulky desk. It was the first time seeing the man up close. His excited pupils were slightly covered by his black eyebrows. His pointy nose, and bulging cheek bones made him look much older than he really was. The thin strip of mustache hid his welcoming smile.

The room itself was ordinary. It was filled with bookshelves, office equipment and such, but it had an exceptionally peculiar window. It was one of those tall and narrow ones that gave me the impression that the man was cautious of putting in a larger window because he was scared for his life. The rest of the room was a landscape for countless pictures from the air force. The man must have been passionate about planes to say the least. A solitary picture that stood out was an image of three best friends. The spokesman, although much younger, was stationed in the middle. He was holding the other two individuals by the shoulder, but there was something creepy about it. One of his hands was planted firmly while the other was loose, almost propelled backward like he disliked the guy. The face of the guy was similar to Fredric, but the shades obscured his face, so I couldn't be sure.   The spokesman must have been unaware of the issue because I'm sure that if he was, the picture would not be hanging on the wall.

"Take a seat." He gave me an analytical look. "My name is Maximilian Waye, but you already know that. Fredric is a friend of mine. We go way back before I created this beautiful thing." Waye spread his hands, full of pride. "He told me about you, and I think we might have an interesting proposal for you."

"I'm not sure I understand why I was led here in the first place. Fredric knows I'm not looking for work." I pretended to be ignorant of what was going on. There was a newspaper on the table which I was eyeing. As soon as the spokesman noticed, he flipped it over. The gesture was almost unnoticeable, and its aim was to deter my interest, but my desire to see it only grew. I thought that it might be something important.

"Well, I was told that you have a very unique personality trait."

"Which one is that?"

"You mind your own business; you can keep a secret."

He combed his hair once. "We have concentrated on putting this town back on track. We now have around 350 members. More are on the way because of how depressed people are."

"Why do the people rush for this place?"

"We give them hope. It have only been 24 day since the suicides started, and in a bigger city, people don't easily notice deaths, but here, they're weak. Any sign of dread, and they automatically break. That's why it's so important to find the culprit."

"I don't see how gaining members could aid you in catching this culprit."

"Each member that joins is interviewed by one of my trusted guardians." Waye argued.

"People lie. For all you know, he might be a member."

He grinned. "In addition to that, the majority of members stay in this compound. They want protection, and they're easier to monitor. No one can leave between 10PM and 6AM. Once more members join, we plan on forming a group of people who would oversee the streets during the night. We plan to search every home. We are interviewing those close to the victims as we speak." Waye continued with a pompous explanation.

"So you know all of the victim's names?" He must have somehow acquired the police records.

"Yes, the end justifies the means. We have to take steps in order to help." He smiled.

"Some people still see you as vampires sucking blood out of the weak." I retorted anxious to see his reaction to the assault.

"Let's not go in that direction. I dislike rumors, gossip,

and other stories. It's best if we put all those preconceived notions on the side lines. That way we can understand each other better. You see, I know what people say about you, but I don't care about that because all rumors enlarge our problems, issues, questions, and pasts." He remained as kind as ever.

Someone banged on the door. A young woman peeked inside. She took his loud response for a calling. She had a tiny posture and kept her head down, observing the ground. Her black long hair obscured her pupils, preventing eye contact. Her name tag read Veronica Williams.

"What do you want?" Waye asked. "I didn't call for you."

The girl lightly tightened her left hand into a fist as if jealous or angered. She apologized before closing the door and leaving.

Fredric spoke without any regard for the event, "So, we are offering you a position as a guardian. Guardians are the fully trusted individuals within this group. Their work consists mostly of overseeing various happenings, but they have great liberty. They also have access to any and all of our resources. Would you be interested?" He stared at me.

I was uncertain of what my response should entail. I wasn't confident I could simply decline.

Fredric added, "Of course, you can leave freely if you're undecided."

"I think I need some time." I was quickly showed to the door. I sat on a bench, waiting. Fredric remained within Waye's office. Most of what they said was inaudible, but I was fairly positive that they already knew my answer. Across the hall someone walked into a door. It was my first time seeing a member of this place. They wore dark blue robes with hoods that covered their faces almost completely. The sleeves, however, weren't very long, so you could see the hands up to the wrist. Thin yellow strips traced the outer edge of the hood, the sleeves, and the base of robe. This particular member sported a tennis wristband. After an extended wait, I was dropped off at home. There was another red carnation at my doors. I sighed with frustration and worry that the culprit knows where I live. I watched Fredric drive off.

When day grew a little bit cooler, I made a trip to the store and picked up a copy of the local newspaper, Enlightened Messenger. Upon finding the exact page, nothing seemed suspicious. It was full of ads from local businesses and people searching for help. At the very bottom, there was something else.

> *Lamenting the indisputable grief,*
> *Harassed with a terrible resolution,*
> *Existence devoid of consequence,*
> *Attendance of raging disappointment,*
> *Open 6PM-11PM. 132 Red Doves Dr.*

The poem had a vibe favoring the current situation in town. It was a depressing read, without any exits. The location in question was an enticing lead. In my mind, I recalled the entire situation I was in. I imagined that maybe I could leave all this alone and move out as soon as I'm finished with my degree. That would mean I could escape within mere days, but something was keeping me here. Was it the awful desire for answers, or the adventurer within me? It was a sensation of thirst for knowledge. I needed to know.

A blow on the door woke me up from my adventures in the land of thinking. This time, with my mind in control, I jumped out of my seat and ran for the door, my fingers caressed the handle of the kitchen knife. When I opened the door, there was someone present outside my place. It was a woman. Her eyes peeked out of her face, which was surrounded by lengthy white hair. Is she the joker behind the flowers?

"Have you got my flowers? I hope it's of no surprise that I'm here. May I come in?" The woman tried to pass me and walk in to my apartment. I blocked her entrance heavily leaning my hand against the frame of the door. The knife was hidden behind me.

"I certainly got the flowers." I could hear my heavy heart beat slow down. "So what is this all about?"

"Everything you need to know was symbolized by the flowers." She insisted on coming.

"To tell you the truth, you're speaking nonsense."

"And if you could tell me a lie?" She teased me. Her playful nature reminded me of someone.

"I would probably say that I am pleased about your visit." She walked in. Her footsteps had an atmosphere free of discomfort despite invading my home.

"Your home is quite different from other humans." She looked around, taking in the sights. My presence was completely ignored by her. She tiptoed around the whole apartment, which was quite small. I didn't know if she was doing it deliberately to anger me, but she seemed to stop and pause at a few pictures, lost in thought.

"You have one minute to explain yourself. Did you see what happened in the alleyway?"

"The short answer is yes, but I'm not sure if seeing, in the sense that you're considering, is the right word."

"Were you present at the scene?" I reiterated my question.

"That's a definite no." She finally returned, circled around the sofa, and took a seat.

"Elaborate."

"Well, let's just say that I saw the event through the eyes of my soul, but don't worry, I mean no harm. My interest in the world is limited to observing, teaching and recording."

"What's your goal then?"

"As I said, I just want to observe a little. I'll be here for a day or two, and once that time passes, I'll be on my way."

"If you think I'll let you intrude into my life, then you're out of this world." I tried to regain my cool, but my heart kept beating faster and faster, fueled by my anger.

"What if I am?"

"You said that you can see through the eyes of your soul, right? Couldn't you just observe from afar and never disclose yourself to me?"

"Yes, that's precisely how I usually go about my business, but it is much more interesting to have a conversation. Dialogue is like a tasty meal for the mind, but if and only if two people take active part in it, and they're both passionate about the subject."

I was carefully thinking about my next question. The situation turned into a bizarre conversation. I wanted to ask her about the ability. I probably shouldn't have. "What do you know about the ability?" I disregarded her response and changed the topic, with the aim of testing the waters of her knowledge.

"It's rather complicated, but I might be willing to answer some questions if you ask me specific ones." She put her index finger to her mouth as if lost in though. "I think I owe you that."

"What is the point of this ability? I mean, there must something more to it, right?"

"I think people believe that the Exchange of Death is given to those who the Will of the Universe deems useful in some way, and that if they're kept alive, they might do something that benefits the universe as a whole."

"Exchange of Death? That's what it is called?"

"That's what they call it, yea."

"They?"

"Far too complicated and time-wasting."

"I have time."

"Ask one last question then."

"Can you get rid of it?"

"I haven't heard a question like that in a long, long time. There might be a way, but I haven't heard of one." She clearly didn't want to provide any valuable info. "End of tonight's trivia." She applauded.

Forced to realize that I can't make her tell me anything, I was left with even more question. My safe heaven was lost. I was once again fighting. "Whatever, I'm done for tonight. Take your things and get out."

"That's not exactly how you should treat a lady."

"A lady doesn't visit someone when she's uninvited."

"That's true. Guess we're both guilty."

"Speak for yourself."

"I'll leave you alone, but I could really use a bath-room."

"Right behind you." She took off her purse, tossed it on the sofa, and left. I figured it was done on purpose to see if I would dare to rummage thought it. I scrabbled in the bag blindly with my hand, hopeful I would find something about this woman's identity. I felt absolutely nothing except the texture of the bag itself. The woman had no cell phone, wallet, perfumes, or anything else as a matter of fact. Losing my motivation upon finding out that the bag was empty, I stopped my search before the woman got out.

"I guess I don't need to thank you for the nonexistent hospitality."

"You didn't introduce yourself."

"Call me Historia, Sebastian." She smiled.

"Fine, would you be interested in some cooperation?" I kept myself from inquiring how she knew my name.

"What would it involve?"

"Just a simple errand." I decided it would be for the best to follow a new road as today's investigation failed miserably.

"In return, I'll get?"

"To watch humans."

She paused for a second, facing away from me.

I wasn't sure how she would respond.

"Sure!" She started walking, aiming for the exit.

"Wait, we're not finished."

"Are we not? If you're talking about the details, I came to the conclusion that you are talking about the newspaper advert."

"Yea, I would like you to go in my place." How does she know all that?

"Are you not surprised that I knew your intentions?"

"That's the least surprising thing that has happened in the past two days."

"Goodnight."

"How will I reach you?" I threw last resort question.

"My address is 94 Augustus Dr." The door closed silently.

Watching the news, another suicide was reported, but this one was described exactly like the one in the alleyway. The gruesome stabbing was deliberately spoken about to invoke disgust in the viewer. Was this a message? It almost seemed like someone was mocking me, imitating me. Was this his intention? I couldn't decide what to make of the occurrence. I was interrupted by a call from Heather, who, in a disturbed voice, uttered the words.

"You received that weird text message too, right?"

The Beheading

I CLEARED MY throat. "I've lost my phone. What message are you talking about?"

"Supposedly, Kasper wants to meet today, claiming it's something important. Are you going to go?" The suggestion seemed peculiar in my mind. I quickly realized that this whole idea sounds dubious. Yet, I wasn't sure if I could completely ignore it.

"I might. He's probably just seriously talking about compiling the project." I was trying to persuade her that it was nothing meaningful.

"Just don't tell me I have to go too."

"I'll take care of it."

Setting my foot outside, it was already completely dark, and the streets were empty. The town didn't have very good lighting outside, so it was quite scary walking in the darkness. From time to time, when you were in a shadowy passage, the walls begun to gang up on you, and it felt like any second they might collide with each other. I soon closed in on Kasper's home. The wood squeaking on a nearby porch brought to my attention a lady, who was watching the street. She was preparing to take her bike for a spin.

When I eventually chose to go in, I was surprised that the doors were open. I walked inside to see Heather kneeling over a headless body. There was no way of knowing whose corpse was resting on the floor, but it was presumably Kasper's as it had the same stature. The whole room was dark, and there was only a tiny lamp working, which illuminated the scene like in a play. The floor was covered in blood. Kasper was wearing the same clothes he had in school. His head was severed from his body as if somebody struck him in the neck with a sword. The head was nowhere to be found, and any attempt at a search would be meaningless, for the place was wrapped in darkness. Kasper's shirt was pulled up to reveal a tattoo of a lizard which Heather was looking at. I walked up to Heather and pulled her away. Her attire was entirely soaked, making me doubted her sanity a little. She seemed to be smiling madly.

At the same time, I wasn't sure if she was not the one responsible. However, I was sure it wasn't the one who was behind the suicides. This was a cold-blooded murder. I didn't know anybody who would be capable of something like this. The only thing I could think about is that I don't want to ever meet that person. Conversely, I didn't regret that this happened. A click was heard in the background which I ignored.

"If this is your work, I want you to know how happy this makes me." Heather's eyes were blank.

"Don't label me like that, I detest meaningless violence."

"But violence served a purpose dealing justice." She smiled while tears of trauma dripped down her face.

"Are you sure that's him?"

"Positive." She pointed at his tattoo.

I tried taking her outside, but to my surprise, the main doors were sealed when I remembered for a fact that I left them open. They were absolutely jammed, locked. The key gone. It seemed like this whole situation wasn't getting to Heather. She was completely spacing out as I searched for a way out. It only took seconds to search Kasper's compact residence, for it wasn't only small, but most doors were locked. The only door that was open was to Kasper's dim bedroom where I found the only plausible exit, a back door, but it was protected by a combination lock. The bedroom walls were covered in wallpaper. The floor was littered with CD's, video games, and other small items. A big 50" HDTV had fallen from its stand. It was broken. There was also a board for playing a game called Go on the floor. The item was so out of place that I immediately recognized it wasn't his. What's more is that a typical board like that isn't numbered, but this one was. The numbering was done with a cheap black marker, so some numbers were losing their shape. The Go board illustrated an almost finished match. Only two spot were empty.

I bowed closer. That's when I saw it. I was startled by an image of Kasper's detached head under the bed. I retreated in disgust. It felt almost like staring into an abyss of death. The situation was outside the domain of my ordinary life which made all the stress congregate in my chest, forcing my breathing to became a chore. The lifeless eyes weren't closed, so it felt like the head was staring at me. The acrid smell reached my nostrils forcing me to fight the need to vomit. Yearning to rush out of this place, I took note of the numbers: 2, 4, 9, and 10. I quickly put in random combinations. After several fruitless tries, the lock released finally letting me out.

I fell onto the grass and saw a note which contained a time and address.

21 Heralds Boulevard. 10:15 tonight.

Faceless Madness

I WASN'T FAMILIAR with the location written on the note, so I was slightly amazed to find a dilapidated two-floor house. The building was made of wood. The wood was rotten, so it gave me the feeling that the home must've been abandoned centuries ago. It was surrounded by weeds. Timber planks for blinds, there was broken glass on the porch. The front door was wide open. Inside, it was silent, but it wasn't a portentous silence, it was a serene silence that gave me the feeling that this place is purged of everything—good and bad. Walking further in, the whole place was filled with cobwebs and many bugs which was not to my liking. The staircase before me led to the second floor. The corroded wood made me extremely cautious of going up. At the summit was an old-fashioned door. I knew I arrived too late, so

I quickly walked in. The antique door wailed, signaling my appearance. I saw Aidan confined to a chair. A man resided behind him in the shadows which obstructed his face.

"You're late, so there has to be punishment." He pointed the gun over Aidan's head and slightly angled the gun before firing. Aidan deafeningly shrieked in pain as the bullet pierced his hand. I was unable to take action. "So what took you so long?" The calm voice sounded from within the shadows.

"Besides your little trap, I actually had to watch over one of my classmates as she almost lost it." I said, thinking about my sudden leave after Heather called the detectives.

"Well, you're here now. You can't even imagine what it took for this meeting to happen. Before we get into any other details, let's play a little game, shall we?" He waved his gun. "I'll ask you a question, and you'll reply to the best of your ability. Those questions will determine the outcome of today's meeting."

I was in no position to decline. I promised myself that he'll pay for toying with me.

He continued. "Let's take this situation for a second. A witness to something you want to keep secret can die. You can give the execution order. What do you do?" Aidan begun to shed tears in terror.

"I abstain from voting."

"Wrong!" The man firmly pressed the trigger of his gun, aiming at my chest. Just before he fired, his hand quivered breaking his aim. The bullet hit my elbow. I screamed feeling it tear thought my bone. I leaned forward. The pain was extremely overwhelming.

"Guess you are one of the good ones, or maybe not." The man spoke frustrated. It seemed like he truly aimed to kill, but he couldn't. When blood begun to drip down his arm, he looked at me and smiled. He seemed to have no trouble ignoring the pain. "So it's true. What that guy said was true! Magnificent. But I'm really disappointed that I can't have some fun after finding someone so special. I can't kill you after all." He ripped a piece of cloth and tied around his arm to prevent unnecessary loss of blood. "Let's try again." The man moved his weapon over Aidan's head.

Considering that my reply might determine if Aidan lives or dies, I reflected on my decisions. Again, my tendency to not get involved spoke in my head, telling me that it would be beneficial to let him die. I dismissed the thought. I'm bound by morality after all, so one's life should take priority. Sickened by the idea of being bound by another chain, I tried to look at the bright side and argued that he might be useful later on.

"Question number two. You have a gun in your hand. In front of you, there is a victim and an attacker. Three people, one has to die. While the victim has never taken a life, you are responsible for three kills, and the attacker for only one kill. Which one should go and why?"

"I should be the one."

"Because?"

"Purely based on statistics you've given me."

The man smiled, took a syringe, and stabbed Aidan in the arm. Aidan's screeching became softer until he fell to the ground sound asleep. "He's just going to suffer some temporary memory loss when he wakes up."

"So are going to finally conclude this charade?"

"This is yours." He threw my cell across the room. "I stumbled upon a fellow who was an acquaintance of Marcus. I was there in the club when Marcus told him that story. That's how I learned everything. Of course, I didn't believe it right of the bat, but I was bored, so I chose to investigate."

"What happened to Marcus and the other thug?"

"You shouldn't worry about it. No one else will hear the story. I figured that it's for the best. Beside they were too barbaric and violent to live here." He said convinced of his own words. So he eliminated them, at least one thing is put to rest. Now almost everyone who knows is in this room. "You're not going to ask about that thug from school, are you?"

"Kasper? No, I'm not curious about the reason for his death. I'm more interested to hear about his relation to all this?"

"There is almost none. It was pure coincidence; I saw that you were the last person to call him. The numbers matched, so that's how he became a part of the plan, but he died of his own fault. He was a savage." The man spoke, leeching energy from the ominous atmosphere. "And the girl was only there to spice things up. She was stalked by the thug."

"Wait, you don't feel any sympathy for him," he said, watching me. "And here I was considering that you're going to complain and accuse me of being cruel and a monster."

If I said that, I would be a hypocrite. I wanted to say that, but I didn't. He wasn't like me.

Satisfied, he turned his back to me, thinking to himself. "They're existence was hurting this town. In essence, they were violent fiends fueled by greed."

"And you're the white paladin?"

"I'm just killing time in a way that benefits others. Your classmate, Kasper, assaulted a girl."

"Why didn't you stop him?"

"Why should I? The girl managed to escape with mere bruises and a broken bone."

"And if she didn't?"

"Kasper would die a day early."

"Why didn't you just confront me without this farce?"

"It would be way too boring."

"I think I can find something to sate your hunger for entertainment." I tried to get him on my side, deciding that it would be advantageous. "What if I told you that I know for a fact that there is someone behind the suicides? Not only that, he is using the same power I have—to kill."

The man looked at me enthusiastically. "That sure has upped my mood." He listened as I told him the details. He then proposed a mutual aid.

"What are you thinking about?" I asked.

"I'll help you, but only if you have something of equal value in exchange for my help, and you can provide it in a timely manner. I'll do the same. This will be for the best."

"Perfect. We should also pick a meeting place, and I'll dispose of the cell you returned."

"In the southern woods, there is an old graveyard. Travel west from there, and you'll reach me. Three days from now at midnight. You should probably bring him along" The man pointed to Aidan.

"Fine, what about emergencies?"

"Phone booth at the intersection of Mill Street and Lake Road. The number is saved in your cell." Without another word, the man disappeared in the shadows. Knowing nothing about him, I was unable to predict if he'll uphold our deal. I felt a hint of defeat as another azure depiction flickered in my mind. The picture was of a man on the floor, viciously trying to grasp something with his hand that seemed broken. His eyes defeated. He was shot countless times.

Before returning to the crime scene, I took a detour to dispose of the lock and the note. I was hesitant about keeping the phone, so I tossed it in the sewers somewhere along the way back. I was sure they would question my odd behavior. It was suspicious to say the least, but I should be able to brush aside any accusations. I remembered that someone jammed the door. It was almost as if someone locked me in, so if I'm lucky, there should be a hint of another person at the scene. In addition to that, Heather was there first, so she can vouch for me. On the other hand, I don't have an alibi for the time before that, so that's troublesome. If anything, they can only speculate. I came to find out that the crime scene was already cleared out when I made it there.

The house was isolated by the police.

The street was empty.

I was alone.

Scars

———

IT WAS NOW the next morning, and Historia was plundering my mind, asking questions. She woke me up early, slamming and kicking the doors with extreme verve. I had no choice but to let her in when she proclaimed that she won't give up. My initial conviction to never let her inside my home vanished quickly.

"So what's it like?" she asked.

"What?"

"Not feeling scared of dying? That's what most people with this power feel."

"How should I know? But if you were to ask about not being scared in general, I would say that dying is the least of my worries at this point."

"What are your worries then?" She took a stroll through the kitchen, and poured herself a glassful of water.

"Despite the idea that my life is more durable, I can still feel pain for example."

"You know, the majority of people with this power die within a week." She chuckled. "Most feel godly, thus they're not careful which is why people notice things. In the end, they're usually labeled as fiends, and they're executed. At least that's how things were in past, but people don't change."

"Thank you for trying to cheer me up. How did you come to know about this power?" I asked, eating my breakfast.

"Well, I am a scientist of the mystic, a scientist of the divine. I'm a writer for a magazine about those things too. They're my passions, so no wonder I know quite a bit about this stuff too." For some reason I felt like she was outright lying about her unearthly profession. "I'd like to consider myself a teacher too."

"You know, last time you said you could see with your soul." I looked her in the eyes. "I wonder if you saw last night's events, if so, you could draw what that man looked like?" I made an honest attempt at questioning, despite not counting on any help.

"Wouldn't that be cheating?" She smiled. I wasn't sure if she was seriously considering the situation, or if she was just weird and loved to fool around.

"Today, let's head to that place."

Historia glared at me, as if she was consenting to the ordeal as planned. A polite knock on the door echoed through the room. It was a very humble tap that wouldn't even wake me up. It turned out to be Officer Dyer and Detective Gregory Dench. They were here to know why I left the crime scene last night. Their visit was not surprising. The only question was why they didn't come quicker. After all, it was a hideous incident, yet they seemed to be fairly relaxed.

The officer's full name was Nicholas Dyer. He was a fairly tall individual, who currently wore the standard policeman apparel. He had countless heavy creases on his forehead and hair loss as well. People say that he is quite a coward in the face of danger. One might think that bravery should be required of a policeman, but it isn't, especially in a place like this. Most of his work until now was made of cliché things, such as lost and stolen goods. On the other side of things, he is well-liked around here and always tries his best.

When I opened the door, Dench asked, "Sebastian Snow?" His voice was annoying. "We had a couple of questions, may we come in?" He was dressed in a classic black suit. He had a short brown haircut. One might thing that he used to drink a lot because of his mildly red face, which looked worn out and harsh. He had his hands in his pockets.

"Sure. What's this about?" They waltzed in, oblivious to my question. Without my consent, Dench took a seat at the kitchen table where my meal was located. Despite multiple free chairs, Officer Dyer seemed to be more respectful and took a stance against the wall.

"Yesterday a gruesome crime took place. The victim was Kasper Mason. The one who alarmed us of the offense was Heather White. Were you present at the crime scene with Heather?" Dench spoke with an aura of someone incompetent. His words bore a sound of heedlessness which made me a little uncomfortable.

The first thing that came to my head was if they knew

that I was there. No, they must know, I immediately reiterated to myself. Heather told them, otherwise they wouldn't be here. This is a test question, so I must tell them the truth. Am I a suspect?

"Yes, I was there."

"Heather won't talk, so we can't get anything important out of her. No wonder, the girl saw a nightmare come alive. Yet for some reason, she's motivated enough to try to tough it out by herself in silence. So step by step, tell us what happened?" Dench asked, blazing through his notepad.

"Yesterday, all of the sudden, Heather called me to tell me of a message she received. She said Kasper had something important to discuss. I told Heather I'll go by myself. When I arrived, she was already at the scene. She was kneeling near the headless body. She seemed to have lost it, so I decided to take here outside and call the police. The main doors got jammed, so I had to use the window to get out. Outside, Heather called you while I saw someone hiding behind one of the houses. Not thinking rationally, I chased after them. I ended up chasing shadows."

"Chasing someone? Who?" Dench pressed on.

"The situation got to me. A classmate died after all. I must've been seeing things."

"Well, why didn't you come back to the scene after all that?"

"I did, but there was no one there anymore."

"We checked Kasper's phone, and if I'm not mistake, he sent you a text as well." Dench gave me a glance from behind the paperwork in a comfortable manner that was aimed to make me relax and put my guard down.

"I wouldn't know, I lost my phone."

"Don't you think it's weird that Heather arrived first?" He stared at me with cold eyes and an ambitious smile. He looked like he just caught something.

"No idea." I chose against voicing my sincere opinion. Heather had a reason for confronting Kasper, but she didn't have the mental fortitude to commit such a crime. The lead would yield nothing for the investigation.

"Lastly, where were you between 7AM and 9AM yesterday?"

"I was here at home."

"Anyone could confirm that?"

I called for Historia, who was concealed in the other room. Surprised, she replied, "Yes?" She gave me the look of someone who doesn't like to be used.

"Officer Dyer, give here all the necessary paperwork and get all her contact info." Dench directed.

"I think it might be in the car." Officer Dyer nodded. "One more thing. Care to explain this?" He held the phone in his hand which I head disposed of last night. "I thought you lost your phone. Why is it here?"

"Historia found it and returned it to me, but as you can see, it's practically broken." I responded noting that the phone has spent some time in water.

How did they get it?

The questions sprung into my mind. I tried to conceal my shock as I thought about the trouble someone would have to go through to retrieve the phone from the sewers. Who would go to these lengths to get me into this mess? I imagined that it might be Historia, whose cheerful personality echoed with joy the moment I lost my confidence. Seeing the corners of her lips rush upward into a smile, I was sure it was her.

The officer confiscated the phone and gave up on further questioning me.

"I have to leave soon. Can I come with you and sign it outside?" Historia smiled at Dyer.

The only person left inside was detective Dench. He loosened up his tie. He quickly found a glass in the sink and washed it before pouring some liquor into it. He gulped it all in one go as if he knew that it's forbidden, but couldn't suppress his desires. "I heard about your little encounter with Judith." He exclaimed, entertained by either the glass, or the thought. "She's always like that. She takes everything so seriously: the job, the rumors, even a simple discussion. But that's to be understood after what happened to her, so don't worry about it."

He shot another glass down his throat. "A lot of people want to put their past behind, but everyone needs to realize that the past will forever long be right in front of your eyes when you look in the mirror. The past is who you are. That's what my old man would say. I hate the idea, but I can't argue against it." He grimaced. "The past allowed Judith to be the most determined and the best in what she does. That's why I took her with me. She is as determined about finding the culprit as I am."

"Unfortunately, it seems like we don't have the necessary paperwork." Dyer announced, peeking from behind the door.

"They must have been left behind. Looks like you'll be forced to come to the station." Dench said. "Anytime works within the next 24 hour."

As the doors closed, I heard their idle chatter. Detective Dench roared, "I forgot to tell you that you did a good job yesterday at the scene. I know, not everybody is use to these gruesome things, so it'll take time, but you're working on overcoming you weakness which is good."

They let me go, so that means that they don't have any concrete evidence, or it could mean that Dench's infamous ignorant side kicked in, making him apathetic to this particular case. Either way, I was suspicious of the lost paperwork. Was it coincidence? Was this an initiative to make me lose my cool? Or maybe I'm just overthinking this? Thinking about this for hours to come, I aimed to finish my morning chores before heading to school. I decided that I should be cautious since the detectives might attempt to follow me around.

The lecture hall was as vivid and lively as ever. Every person that I didn't know was here, and every seat was occupied except two. Taking my place, there was still time before the professor would arrive. Behind me, I overheard a conversation between students, who seemed to be relatively nervous.

"I heard from my neighbor that someone died, but it wasn't a suicide. It was a murdered." The girl whispered almost inaudibly. She bowed her head, hiding behind a row of seats. It almost looked like the discussion frightened her so much that she would like to sink into the seat, turn invisible.

"Yea, rumors spread like crazy. It happened yesterday. At least that's when the police found the body. Can you even imagine that it could have been someone from this school?" Her boyfriend frowned, oblivious to the truth.

"This town is getting really sick." The girl said. "Who would have thought that I once called it home, right?"

"We'll leave this place once and for all in only a week." The boyfriend reassured.

"Before that happens, thing will probably get even weirder. I mean, look at it, the suicide haven't ceased, they have gotten more gruesome, and now this!"

"Yea, what kind of a madman would stab himself in the chest, huh?"

Another professor, possibly a substitute, walked into the lecture hall. It was a mature lady dressed in formal clothes. She wore a pair of large glasses. She took a piece of red chalk and began writing on the black board in big letters. She then clapped her hands as a way of pronouncing her authority and illustrating her tough resolution. At this second, the class's debate was brought to a halt, and all the heads turned to the front of the room in an attempt to show respect. The woman remained silent, and she looked down at her feet like she was deeply saddened, unable to articulate a word. Without looking up, she stood there. She wanted the class to fill in the blanks and figure out what is happening. The words on the board read, "Class Dismissed!"

People as a whole didn't leave happily. They left, lost in thought, depressed, sad, irritated, anxious, and feeling every other negative emotion. Despite the fact that the students had no idea if this is just a random occurrence, they instinctively linked it to the curse placed on this town. A foreigner might believe that this is just a coincidence—that maybe the professor is sick, or he had an urgent family matter—but people felt it deep down inside that this was not the case. There was a void within them filled with despair and hopelessness. An empty space filled their mind, and the brain was yearning for a thought that it could swallow. Emotions fuel thoughts. Today's emotion fueled only a single idea, a notion of despair.

The hallways were livelier as the souls were rushing for the exit. While some remained ignorant of the things around, most had only one thing on their minds—the heavy weight of dread. There was a conversation next to me as I was pacing my way down the hall.

"When they took me into the station last week, Detective Dench was mumbling something in the restroom. It sounded like he was freaking crumbling with guilt. It sounded like a recording or something."

"Really? But if that was the case, why won't the higher-ups confiscate it and use it as evidence."

"Obviously they don't know."

Outside, I saw Heather arguing with some teenager. Behind her was a little kid crying. It appeared like the teenager took the ball away from the kid and stabbed it with a sharp object. The ball was flat by now. I slowed my pace down, trying to be as late to the party as possible. Before I made it, the ordeal was over, but the teenager walked away without correcting his actions.

"There is no lecture today, and there might never be." I found myself unable to pick a phrase that would be suitable to start the conversation. All the usual greetings were downright inappropriate considering our history together.

"Yea, I heard. I had no intention of going anyway." She looked at me, still very serious.

Behind her an undergraduate uttered, "You look well, Heather." An ignorant statement to the point of being disturbing. Heather turned around and made a successful attempt at forcing a smile, making it all seem like nothing happened—like time was reversed. To all outsiders, it seemed like there was no malice. To me, it seemed like it was only temporarily subdued. I couldn't believe how Heather forced herself to return so quickly to normal life after yesterday's events.

I considered myself quite proficient at dealing with stress and other emotion, but this situation made me realize how adept Heather was herself. She was a masterful actor, playing on the panorama of life. She was able to conceal all the spite caused by the past—all within her.

"This is my portion of the project." She handed me the flash drive. "I'll be there to present next time. By the way, I can't say I'm doing fine, but you should not burden yourself with what happened. You do know that?"

"I'm not troubled by the situation, but by the lack of words that I would deem appropriate." I said.

"That's because you're troubled." She saw through me before going her way.

Officer Dyer was stationed outside the school gate. He was standing awkwardly, pretending to be busy, but he couldn't think of anything to do. I wasn't sure if he was following me around or not, so with a lighthearted attitude, I walked closer and joked, "In such a small town, it's not so easy to tail someone, don't you think?"

He looked at me surprised. "I'm sorry. I know it's a difficult situation, but try to understand we're just trying to tie up all the loose ends." I once heard that he had a lot of trust in this town's citizens. To some, he was like a father, who wasn't harsh but sympathetic. On a daily basis, he tried to educate and help those breaking the law.

"Don't worry about it." I made a friendly face. "This just proves how strong-minded all of you are about getting to the bottom of this. That means a lot to me."

After the encounter, Dyer lost all his motivation to continue his pursuit, so I stopped at a phone booth and made a call to the station. The one who answered was Judith. I said that I wanted to speak with Dench. She handed the phone to him, and I was sure that no one else was following me.

◆

I made my way to the location of yesterday's madness, the deserted building on Heralds Boulevard, where I met with Aidan. Downstairs, he was sitting on an armchair. His right hand was bandaged up to his elbow, speckled with red dots. Seemingly, the blood leaked from his wound.

"Couldn't you pick a better meeting place?" He made a fist with his injured hand.

"Well, I thought this would be the perfect place."

"So what now? We should find out the identity of that man, right?" he spoke tapping on the wood. His tired look reminded me of how much I yearned for it to be over as well.

"You read my message, so you should know what's next." I remembered the note that I left with Aidan after that maniac vanished the other day. It contained the meeting coordinates, and the detail of our next goal—finding the identity of the murderer.

"So you're planning on using my trauma?"

"This is a small town. Of course, he could be hiding somewhere, and we won't ever find him, but we know he's wounded. His voice was drilled into your memory.

It's time to use that to our advantage." I said, slanted against the nearby wall.

"So? You w-want me to explore the t-town in hopes of finding t-that guy?" He raised his head with his brows high up. His stuttering returned.

"Not exactly. He did say that he hunts for criminals. It would only be natural that he would conduct his searches in public places where they hang out. You should start with those."

Aidan made a face. "Fine, but after we find him and settle t-this, I'm done. I am n-not doing this because you told me. I know you must have ulterior motives, but I could have died yesterday. I didn't." He paused. "It's probably because of your choices. Michael always said that when someone saves your life, he become like family. At that point, you have a debt. That's why I'm doing this."

"To be honest, I helped you twice already."

"You t-think so? And who is the person that endangered my life numerous times?" He turned to me.

"I thought you had realized that you have gotten yourself in this."

Aidan walked to the exit, looking straight down. His spirit was at a low level. "You have once asked me why I don't f-feel anger and why I'm not looking for revenge. You see, revenge is very foreign to me, but I think that's only true to a certain extent. I have never felt it, so I can't be sure, but I think that I would be longing for vengeance if someone were to hurt me in a permanent and irreversible manner. You see, this wound hurts immensely." He gestured with his hand. "But in a couple of months, I won't remember I had it."

"What about the scar on you face?" Listening to his speech made me feel like he was giving me a word of warning. He was speaking words that were easy to misinterpret.

"I wouldn't know what I felt back then. It happened when I was a child. Probably the fault of my parents."

"Shouldn't you blame them for it?"

"You got me there, but I think I have enough of other things to blame them for. They're just not here, but somewhere else—I have no idea where." He walked outside. "I'll let you know if I stumble upon anything. Too bad the wound wasn't deeper; that why there would have been a chance that he would have to go to the clinic."

"I doubt he would be that careless."

The Crumbled Defense

HOME, I WAS debating on what to do next. Dyer's childish behavior revealed that they are indeed doubtful of me. I considered that I can rest assured they don't think I am the culprit, but I also believed they are considering the fact that I might have something to hide. By forcing me to come to the police station, they're probably hoping that I would make a mistake, so it would be wise for me to stay home today. On the other hand, if I can't clear all their doubts by tomorrow, I'll be unable to move freely. I'll have to improvise once I get to the station. Tonight, I'll postpone my move.

I was anxious about the situation I was in. Thoughts raced in my head until I ended up on the conversation I heard during the lecture. The students were thinking of leaving this place; I might do the same. But I don't really like to leave things unfinished. As things stand now, this place is on a collision course. The more people leave, the only ones left will be those that have deep roots here, those with a family, and those that in some way hope to benefit from staying.

My apartment was quite barren to begin with despite my numerous paintings, but I started to gather anything of use. I really was expecting to be forced to move. Very soon, I gathered anything of importance, and I started packing. This same night, Historia arrived, and I explained that we will investigate that ad tomorrow. I didn't tell her the reason, but I had a feeling she already knew.

First thing in the morning, I found myself in front of the police station, determined to shed light on every bit of doubt they had about me. Every day now countless people from the Unity were stationed in front of the station. The horde appeared to be vigorously increasing in numbers like bacteria multiplying. They held banners and were armed in screams, motivation, and steel willpower. Over the course of the week, they argued about many things, but all of those had one thing in common— distrust of the law. They argued that the detectives should bear no secrets, and that the information about the suicide case should be open to everyone. Their screams were fueled by the ever-growing power of the Unity.

Today, the spokesman was missing, but the people were in his full control. He didn't have to oversee any of this to know that they will follow his beliefs.

Unable to pierce the crowd, I went around to the back. The rear of the police station was a dirty place, occupied by garbage mostly. Cans filled to the very top with rubbish and recycle bins with their main purpose lost over the recent years were used to dispose of anything and everything. The weighty smell was unbearable. It was a scent that wouldn't propel you to vomit, but one that seemed to bring in much less oxygen to your chest. I took out a handkerchief and placed it against my face as I made my way to the door. It was left unlocked.

The inside of the station was very much modern and up-to-date in terms of equipment. Regardless of being used by a single man, it was a workplace designed for a whole team of people. Over a dozen workstations, cubicles absorbed much of the otherwise free space in the back. Each workstation had a phone jack, but most were empty of absolutely everything. There were no stashes of paper-work, no phones, no desktop computers, yet some had laptops most likely brought by the detectives. Moving to the front, I passed a narrow corridor. Five chairs were lined against the wall near the exit. They were designated for people waiting, but the chairs were wooden and rigid, which made them very painful to sit in over a long period of time. The sunlight coming in from the large windows was blocked by curtains. I could still hear the Unity's cries which penetrated the thick glass. Opposite the entrance, there was a small desk where the policeman was usually seated, but today it was occupied by Det. Judith Page. The desk had the only fully operational desktop computer as well as a sign-in sheet.

"You'll need to wait for a second." She stated giving me a grim, bored look from behind the reception desk. "You know, when I first saw you, you had the aura of someone who would go out of bounds."

"I could say the same thing about you."

She smiled annoyed. "Let me see if I can find the document you need to sign. I actually had some more questions."

"What would they involve?"

"Your guilt?"

"Of?"

Det. Page ignored my question. Once she found the paperwork, she led me to an empty room. I was uncertain of going in, but I wanted to familiarize myself with her character a little bit more—I gave into my curiosity. The room strongly resembled an interrogation room in that it contained a single desk and two chairs, but it lacked a two-way mirror. She slammed the door with all her strength. I took a seat behind the desk. Page was seated across from me. On the table were the documents and the pen. Before I could carry on with reading, I was interrupted with some question.

"Based on initial reports, we know that Kasper died over 12 hour before you and Heather found him. Heather was practically broken in the beginning, but she confessed that she wanted to confront him about what he did. That's why she got there first. Do you have anything to add?" Page finished her verbose statement.

Either I overestimated the situation, or she wasn't as forceful. "No." My answer sounded too obvious.

"She also stated that when she called you, you told her that you had lost your phone. Yesterday, Detective Dench and Officer Dyer visited you, and they found your phone. Did you just find it overnight?" Her tone was serious, yet it had a sarcastic side to it.

"As I stated, Historia returned the phone to me." I

doubted that she would believe my statement. Detectives shouldn't and don't believe in coincidence, and this was no exception. This situation could get out of hand, yet the notion that she had no proof kept me calm. Too much has happened in my life over the past four days. My silence grew, and she continued her assault.

"You were also the last person the victim got in touch with. What's more, I would like to hear about what happened regarding the death of Michael Bailey?"

The Liar's Truth

I SAT THERE unable to voice a word as my mind was flooded by anger at my foolishness. I disliked how sure I was. I hated my previous point of view. I detested my past and that I wasn't more careful. I imagined myself defeated, falling from a bridge into the dark cerulean waters below. As I was enveloped by the water, my whole body felt cold. I envisioned all of the last events and judged them one by one. Over the course of these last few days I took many risks. I took the easy way out by going with the flow, but that's not why I'm here today. I'm here because I made a grave mistake. I must've overlooked something minor, yet so significant. Seating here with Judith Page, I realize that it wasn't Gregory Dench who was pulling the strings; she was the one stubborn about finding the truth behind each crime. Page was the one who took the paperwork and send the officer after me.

Dench was uninterested in what happened behind a gruesome death of a meaningless person. All he cared about was his success, and he knew that it won't come from spending time on something like that. Yet Judith was a total opposite. She cared not about what people think about her, or what the law might think and how it'll react to her actions. She did this for herself. Yes, that's right, she's not doing this for anything but her yearning for the truth.

No! She doesn't know anything. She's just bluffing. She's hoping she can force me into a corner and get a confection. All I have to do it play innocent. I became more confident about not giving up. "I'm innocent. I didn't hurt anyone."

I was still standing in awe when I regained myself in the real world. My eyes were wide open, and it probably seemed like I was losing. I prepared my response when I heard banging on the door.

"Wait, what are you talking about? I never heard of that guy." I continued in utter panic, but not the guilty type—the innocent type. I looked her right in the eyes and kept constant eye contact as I confessed "I know it seems like too much of a coincidence, but the phone was returned to me by Historia. I'm innocent. You don't think I had anything to do with Kasper's death, do you?"

She seemed to be a little startled. She wasn't sure how to react to my swift comeback. She stared at the rusted metal desk, where the worksheets were located. She looked at me again agitated that her provocation didn't work. This made me a little calmer, and I realized that her accusation about Michael Bailey were without basis and evidence.

She was ready with her newly crafted come back when Dench busted through the door with Officer Dyer just behind him. "What is going on here?" he roared, looking at Judith.

"I just needed some clarification regarding some facts about the case." Judith said.

"Well, that's over now." Dench stated with the paperwork in hand. He then asked me to reread it and finally sign on the very bottom. "We're done here!"

"Wait, I'm not finished! You can't just let him go!" Judith's protests had no impact on Dench. I handed him the newly signed formalities ready to leave. We walked out into the lobby when she lost her cool and objected to my leave again "Dench, you can't let him go!

"As I said, he's a dead end, we already have a new witness." Dench retorted.

"But this liar is just as guilty as anyone else! His hiding something! It's obvious." Judith lost control, her emotions run rampant.

"This is unacceptable! Detective Dench take control of your subordinate." Officer Dyer jumped in as I stood to the side watching.

"Page, get yourself under control. What do you think you're doing? He has secrets, that's for sure, but he is not the culprit." Dench flung the paperwork to the side. "There was an older lady who saw someone lock the door behind Mr. Snow. We'll be going to see her right now. That's why you won't be the best detective because you let your emotions get in the way. You judge people based on predetermined ideas."

"You know why you won't be the best detective? Because you don't care about finding the truth. All you are troubled with is solving the case and shining like a star!" Dench tried grabbing Judith by the shoulder, but she brushed his hand off. Judith tramped for the exit. She had the pace of someone who would stop at nothing to reach a goal. Her face imitated that look when I offended her the first time we have met. She felt conquered and livid, but not ready to give up.

"Hold on." This was the opportunity I was waiting for. I could use this to my advantage as a way to clear some doubt. "I want justice to triumph over this case as much as all of you. I'm disgusted by the idea that I was regard as the one to blame for this. I also realize that Det. Page is a very ambitious person, but her work will really suffer if she is dwelling on something else. I think it would be best if I stayed and answered any other inquiries." My words reached Judith in an instant, and her face had a trace of both antagonism and glee.

"You don't have to do this." Officer Dyer said.

"Fine, but if and only if you consent to this, and in case you want to leave, you can do so at any time and she can't stop you. In the meantime, I'll be heading to meet the witness." Dench said indifferent to the escapade that just took place. He had different matters on his mind.

Office Dyer protested and tried to persuade Dench to do something about my proposal. Voiceless, Page walked to the back and took a seat in one of the cubicles. I took a seat across from her and wrote a note. The silence didn't last long.

"Did my charming words not reach you?" I joked, but on the outside I was really stern, dealing with stress.

"As they say, 'Flattery works on puppets and fools.' Anyway, why would you do something like this? You were practically free."

"Not from you."

"That's for sure." Her mood didn't change a bit even with her blithe response.

"Well, since we have a little discussion to do, why not head outside? This place is mentally claustrophobic." I stood up.

"There is something about you. Despite our tremendous loathing of each other, we might be quite similar. We play our cards in life differently from everyone else. You don't like to be anyone's puppet as well."

After she checked that all doors were locked, we left through the back. She didn't say a word.

The Pool of Blood

THE WEATHER IN the open air was mystically downcast. The whole sky was covered in gray, and all the different shades of blue vanished overnight. The thick layer of clouds blocked out all the sunlight, so it didn't feel like a morning at all. Even if a ray appeared, it was only for an instant as the clouds restructured to block it, reacting to the warmth of the sun. We headed to the park, where we spotted a lone bench to sit on.

"Enough walking around. I know that you don't intend to give out any detail for free, so state you price?" Judith was agitated.

"Take a seat. We'll get to all the details." She swallowed all her fury, and she listened closely to what I had to say. "How about this: I'll answer every question honestly, but in exchange, you'll have to agree to three requests."

"What three requests?"

"First, you make a vow that you won't shadow me around."

"So in other words, I have to play convinced that you're not the culprit?"

"Play? No, nothing like that. Just open your eyes wide enough to see that you're hunting for someone else." She nodded unconvinced. "Second, everything that I'll say here will be kept between the two of us. Of course, you can consider it when you're investigating, but not a word to anyone else."

"And lastly?" She sat with her legs crossed.

"I'd like to hear you story." Initially, my last request asked for data on the case, but I judged that it's too early to ask for something like that. Changing my mind at the last second, I started thinking that a different question would help me gouge her character.

"What?" She stood up, but she didn't leave. I think her curiosity gave way to her obedience. She ingest her pride, anger and every single one of her predetermined ideas about me and the world. "That's my story and mine alone. What makes you think that I would talk about it with someone like you? Besides, how can I trust you? What makes you think you can trust me?"

"You said it yourself; we are very different than most people here. Our ideas differ from those of the majority. Our character upsets those of the mainstream, and we think for ourselves." She looked at me for the first time without dislike in her eyes. "In essence, telling someone something important is like investing in them in hopes that they'll pay you back. I think you'll consider my payback a worthy one. Or we could just go our separate ways, but from what I heard, the suicide investigation is in a standstill." I gazed at the clouds.

"Fine" She took a seat again, eyeing the panorama of the park. She was looking for someone or something. "Four years ago, I was working on an investigation. It was a mass murder case. The man we were chasing picked out his game from people who were proud—too proud. When he caught them, he humiliated according to their so-called faults. He recorded their fall from grace on tape, and our investigation team was the recipient of those tapes. We found a promising suspect, but he was a sly one. We had no proof." Her hands trembled positioned on her knees as she shed a solitary tear.

I felt a faint sense of discomfort bottle up within me, and for a second regretted making her do this.

It seemed that it was easier for her to make the confession if she wasn't looking at me. It looked like she was pretending that I disappeared—that she is alone and the only one who is listening is God himself.

"I was chosen to play the role of a new victim. The other two people from my team were supposed to oversee the operation. They were carefree. Every day they giggled, and they chuckled even though the situation was grim. As planned, I slowly befriended the suspect, and soon I was invited to his place. A small hut in the woods, that's where I was caught. Of course, the other members were close by and were listening to what was happening, so I wasn't that scared but ..." She was unable to speak about what happened.

A kid zoomed past us with his two friends, playing soccer.

"That's alright. You don't have to continue. This is

taking too big of a toll on your psyche." I said, feeling a bit guilty after seeing how she reacts to recalling these events.

"No, you wanted to listen to the whole story." She paused briefly and looked at her phone. "He tied me to a chair. He laughed, screamed, played, and mocked me. I started panicking because the team wasn't reacting to my calls for help. He spilled something filthy over my head. When he took a knife and begun cutting my hair, I began crying. When he started making small cuts to my body, I knew no one is coming for help, but I had a tiny knife tied around my wrist. I managed to cut the rope around my hands. Before I knew it, he was the one on the floor, bleeding. They found me covered in blood curled up on the sofa." She wiped her tears.

The story was ghastly and dreadful. It was a very heavy burden so much so that even listening to it I felt like something grave was poured onto me. Was this the reason she wanted to conclude the narrative? I stared her in the eyes. For a second, it felt like I understood her a little better. I was unsure if I could trust her, but I had an obligation toward her now that she has opened up. "Can I see your hand?"

She loosened her grip on her clothes and opened up her palm. The trauma from telling the story made her hands feel cold, almost to the point of being lifeless. I put a small packet knife in her hands and made her grip it firmly. "What are you doing?" I grabbed her hand before she could retreat.

I made her point the knife at my upper arm and draw blood. Blood spoiled her sleeve. She eagerly rolled it up to reveal a tiny cut. By now, my arm was completely mended, so I looked at her. With a solemn tone, I said, "I think this is how the culprit kills."

To my astonishment, she didn't panic, nor did she ask if this was some sort of a trick or magic. She had a look of someone who understands something very well. Countless blocks have fallen in place right in her mind to make things clearer. After she analyzed the innovative take on the case, she said, "You're not the one, are you?"

With no intention of honoring the question with an answer, I fell silent as a final question was thrown my way; "Do you know the identity of the one who killed Kasper?"

"No, I don't." After this confrontation, I think I understood a fragment of her better, but this fragment shined on the darkest elements of her psyche. My original objective achieved, I felt troubled as I realize that she really was on the tip of her toes right on the margin of psychosis.

◆

Resting home on my sofa, the day past quickly as the warm sands of time fell between my fingers. Recently it felt like time sped up, like it was gaining momentum. Events happened and after they were over, several fresh dealings swiftly zoomed over my head. An unstoppable process happened where it felt like I couldn't stop. It wasn't just the time that sped up, but my whole life did too. Back in the day, I was dragging life right behind me tied to my ankles while now I am being pulled by life, and I could trip any second.

I made a call or two, slept, ate, and before I knew it, I

was stationed on a catwalk. The place turned out to be a tattoo shop. Before arriving, I had to purchase a new phone as replacement for my old one, as well as a pocket knife for defense. Crouching, I was close enough to hear any exchange of words below and spy from above. Although once Historia walks into the shop, she'll be on her own. She was crossing the street into the grim backstreet. The sun delayed the night's arrival. The murkiness of the night was nowhere to be found, hiding behind the corner for the right moment. However, with each second the sun was shining dimmer and dimmer like it was dying. The night that was awakening felt like a long one. It was a never-ending ordeal where all you want to do is look at the light in the hopes that a miracle will happen, and you won't have to suffer anymore.

The tattoo shop was a very obscure place, where no ordinary person would stroll by, especially after it gets dark. The logo of the store read, "Honorary Darkness." The logo was illuminated by violet lights, and the face of the store was glass covered by various pictures. I couldn't see of what, but I assumed they were of former patrons. The outside was illuminated by a single streetlights, which was very weird in its own right, considering that it was a very out-of-the-way street. In this town, those had no lights at all.

Historia was just about ready to go in when three gen-tlemen walked out of the shop. Each dressed in a fine suit, but they were no office works. They each had this weighty pace, like someone who had done many wrongs in life and was carrying a surmountable burden on his back.

The first one to pass Historia was head and shoulders

above her. He was a towering individual of unprecedented height. He had a frown for a face that only amplified his boldness. His head was shaved closely to the skin. The expensive suit combined with his character created this intense aura around him that forced anyone into a turtle-like position of terror.

The second individual had a lazy attitude. Both of his arms were in the pockets of his dress pants. His head bowed forward, which could be interpreted as a lack of confidence, but that would be a wrong conclusion. He seemed to dislike the work he was doing. The gel in his hair kept them tidily back, away from his face.

The last one gave of an impression of overconfidence. He was beyond any other emotion. His step was lighter than the other two. Could it be that he coincided with all the wrongdoings he did? Could it be that he accepted all the hurt that he cause? He was free of remorse. He bore a light, self-satisfied smile. His mid length, light brown hair loomed over his face. His eyes were like the eyes of a predator, enjoying his life.

"So we have wasted another day chasing ghosts, huh, Jude?" The one with the lazy attitude kicked a rock while aiming his words at the bold man.

"You might be right, Dorian. Does the boss even know what he's doing? He seemed to have lost his cool. Could it be that the one we are searching for is just a figment of his imagination?" Jude responded without showing any feelings.

"If that's so, who killed the other five that arrived here with us?" Dorian's lazy look was altered into one of misery. "I know his girl died, but the boss could just find another one. We wouldn't have to suffer coming to this place."

"You two, shut up for a sec!" The confident one turned around. He was allured by the irrational idea of a girl walking into an intimidating location such as this one at night. The man couldn't resist striking a conversation. "Are you looking for something?" The man uttered in a kind voice.

"Just sightseeing." Historia made an idiotic remark.

"Sightseeing? In this town where there are almost no foreigners? Plus it's getting dark soon. You heard that guys." The other two didn't care; they didn't show any emotion. They were use to his nature and knew exactly what he attempted to do. "Could it be that you saw the message in the newspaper and decided to check it out too?"

"Yea, you caught me. I'm a writer for a supernatural magazine."

"Supernatural magazine? That's a first in my lifetime. Would you like me to show you around?" The man bend forward, making an effort to see Historia's face closer. As the conversation picked up, I shuffled through my backpack, looking for my cell.

I called Aidan. "It's time."

"Fine, I'll make the call, but why won't you do it?"

I spoke with him just before coming here, and he asked the same question. Again the whole idea was irrational; he would be much safer and more likely to live longer if he just wouldn't plunge deeper into the grim side of this town. Was it human nature? Does curiosity take over even in the face of fear? "As I told you before, the less you know, the happier in life you'll be."

"Alright, suit yourself. By the way, no luck with finding that man so far, but I have a feeling which tells me that I have met that person before. The voice sounded familiar."

"Well, keep on looking." I noticed the sun escape behind the horizon line.

By now, the man was much more eager to pester Historia. He was tagging on her purse like a dog. The man was like an annoying fly, which was magnetize to Historia. The other two watched as Historia made a firm attempt at getting rid of the man. As I watched, something seemed very wrong. To a bystander, this view was standard affair; a man hitting on a girl, and more often than not, the girl feels awkwardly, embarrassed, or scared. In this case, none were true. Historia showed no fear, no interest, and definitely no panic. I couldn't see her face, but her gestures were caused by pure irritation and will to fight back. Right now, there was only one attacker, but two were standing by, and I bet that they would jump in if the leader commended them to do so. A girl should feel helpless and definitely frightened as the streets were almost completely covered in murky shadows, obstructing even my view from above.

Historia felt none of that. She gave of an impression of someone beyond life.

Down the street, I saw Judith driving her car, arriving at the future crime scene. Aidan's call summoned her. I called the cell phone I put in Historia's purse. The man, ripped the purse out of her grip and found the phone. She fought back, trying to keep a hold of it, but he was stronger. The man opened up the flip phone.

"Hey, Historia," I said. "How is your article coming along? Oh, yea, what did they want with you at the police station?"

No words came from the other side, but the man's pyramid of comfort crumbled. I could hear the other two asking, itching to know what he heard, but he kept his eyes on Historia. On the other end of the passageway, Judith arrived at the scene. The man knew that something was up. The whole place was inked black. Visuals were dim, hazy, and dark, so one could say that this place was an auditory world   He could not see who was walking, but he instinctively grasped Historia attire and viciously twisted her around. She pivoted until her back was against his chest. Despite using her full strength to fight back, there was a huge gap in power. The man took out his gun and pointed it firmly against Historia's head. He was aiming to not only kill but also escape. Judith reacted with upholstering her gun as she saw them. The man held the gun steadily in his hand as if he had vast experience.

"Hands in the air!" Judith said.

The place stood still in a life-and-death gamble. The conflict escalated into a killing provocation. The murky lane was a perfect place for a confrontation such as this; it was the ideal location for getting rid of someone. Not only was there no witnesses, but at night, the place was covered in shadows, and the only light that was present persisted with flickering impatiently. The aiming was difficult—almost impossible. As the two looked at each other, they couldn't see each other's faces. Their hands grew tired, and muscles tensed from the constant, extraneous motion of aiming. The two fellows that came with the man took a rest at the side of the alleyway as if they had not a care in the world. As the game spiraled into its finale, breathing ceased between the players.

Historia was still wrestling against the man's grip. The

man seemed to stir her left and right, trying to impair Judith's careful aiming. As the man took a final breath, Historia trampled his foot, loosening his hold of her, and she docked down. Judith shot him in the arm. Historia fled west into an alleyway. Judith closed in and made an odd gesture of pointing her gun up. She waved her hand, turning her back to the man, and signaling him to run. The other two recognized Judith as they seemed to lack discomfort.

"You aright, Leon?" Dorian asked the confident man.

Leon, attempting to stop the bleeding, gave an order. "Find the girl! Fine her!"

This should give her a good scare, although I'm a bit unsettled by her inhuman behavior. All her emotions, gestures, and reactions felt like she had somehow escaped from the most terrifying aspects of this world. Going west was practically like boxing yourself in as the passage had no outlets. A couple minutes later, the men returned announcing, "She's not there."

"Keep looking!" Leon was in the process of bandaging his arm.

"You see, it's a dead end, we searched every inch of it." Dorian said.

"If it's a dead end, how did she run away, huh?" He asked irritated. He grabbed his gun and fired a shot.

As they left, I walked down the catwalk.

Unfortunately, the shop was closed down, so no luck there until tomorrow. Walking into the west end of the alleyway, there was a stench similar to those found in locations populated by everlasting drunkards. There was a disgusting odor of vomit. The floor was filled with papers, broken bottles, and other trash. The way had no branching paths—no intersections—but it twisted left and right, back and forth until the very end where there was nothing. No visible proof that something was ever there until I turned on my flashlight.

What appeared was a shocking discovery.

There was a perfectly circular pool of blood on the ground.

A Normal Day

_____

THE RECENT EVENTS regarding Historia had sparked my curiosity, but I wasn't sure how to form a complete rational picture out of the bits she left me. She was always spouting nonsense and was keen on playing mind games as much as a specific person that resides within my imagination. Her behavior was bizarre, and almost out of this world. Thinking rationally, I reluctantly dismissed the idea that she was literally out of this world, although based on my recent experience, the thought could very well be true. The events that happened in my life for the past week have been everything but logical. The power, all the events related to it, and even the idea that someone is using that very power to kill were all absurd separately, but together they made me question rational thinking, and I haven't even considered the idea that someone was hunting my dreams. All of these, were not examples of coincidence. I rebuffed the idea that things just happen without a meaning. By now, I was convinced that they're all interconnected. They're all related and significance resides behind each one.

Historia's disappearance didn't go as planned. I was truly counting on getting rid of her from my life. The problem is that the pool of blood is nothing in the face of evidence. The group that she met declared that they didn't find her. She disappeared, but can I really be sure that she vanished permanently? No, that would be too easy, but if I'm lucky, she might not come back. It's probably safe to assume the ridiculous idea that she melted into a puddle of blood as a way of escaping the thugs. Nonetheless, what-ever the truth is, I got rid of her for now.

I debated what happened to the Mankind's Most Per-severing Teacher before drifting off into slumber. Lacking sleep from yesterday's happenings, it was only a matter of time. The white hallways woke me up in an instant as I entered the room.

"Where were you all this time?" I asked not counting for an answer.

"Close by. You just didn't realize it. Weren't you hap-py that you got some breathing room?"

"Breathing room? I was gifted with an exact copy of you, only a bit more malicious. Ready to speak the truth about the power?"

"The suicides are keeping their momentum steady? Who'll be next? Heather sounds like a perfect candidate."

Not only did the teacher dissolve my inquiry, he also struck a galling topic. "What are you? You don't value life even slightly. More so, you like death."

"And so do you?"

"No! I might be emotionless toward death, but it doesn't please me or make me laugh. Don't you have an ounce of respect for life? Oh, what am I talking about? Of course, you don't. You're literally not human. You're invigorated by death."

"Humans died, they die, and they'll keep dying."

"And you won't?"

I was kicked out after ruining the mood of the dweller of dreams. His face showed a tinge of remorse. Something in my attack seemed to bring out whatever was still human within him. I came back to the land of the living as class was about to end. Today was the last formal day of class. All that was left to do were formalities, and that chapter of my life would be concluded. To my surprise, Heather arrived on time to present and with all her work. No matter what was born within her at the time Kasper died, it seemed to be dormant for now—or maybe I was too much of an optimist. We presented at the opening of class, the professor was back from being sick and everything seemed back to normal.

Outside the school building, sun seemed to be shining vibrantly as I walked with Heather. She was pretending to act her former everyday-cheery-self because there were a lot of people and she didn't want to draw attention. She held her books tightly to her chest, but as soon as we were outside the gates, her look reverted to the serious one.

"Finally the end. We won't have to continue this farce." She signed.

"Do you have any plans on what to do next?" I asked still mildly uncomfortable by her presence.

"I sold the family restaurant." People were habitually

unobservant, so they wouldn't hear any difference in talking with her, but I knew she changed. Who would have bought out a restaurant in a place like this? The people currently leaving don't color this town as a first-class investment.

"Are you going to be moving out?"

"No, not yet. I still have my nightmares to cope with. You don't even know how the Unity helps people."

"I can only imagine." I quickly responded with the cynical part of me.

Continuing our walk down the gradient, there was a scene taking place on the other side of the road. An older man in a trench coat was on the ground. Looming overhead, two youngsters, with beer bottles in their hands, were expressing amusement at the situation, making an occasional attempt at sipping snifter. As the laughing grew louder, they begun stamping and kicking the man still on the ground. The elderly man imitated a turtle—or fetal position—as he endured the barrage of monstrous attacks. None of the other people seemed to react as the massacre soared in the domain of torture.

Heather, who was usually the first on to jump in to save someone, was now standing, watching. Her eyes were wide open as she stood in fear. Even though she looked like she couldn't take it anymore—like she shouldn't stare at it—she continued to watch.

Sickened by the meaningless violence, I crossed the street. I made my way closer and shouted, "That's enough!"

"Who do we have here?" A thug spit on the pavement.

"Aren't you the one the people call inhuman? If so, why do you care what happens to this old geezer?" The other youngster turned to me, his bottle empty.

"Just because people say something, doesn't mean it's necessarily all true." I made a silly comment as their attention turned from the old man to me. One of them smashed his bottle against the pavement, aiming to forge a weapon. I was just about ready to take out my knife when a heavy shout came from behind me.

"Fellows, what are you doing? Cease this at once?" The one yelling was Officer Dyer. Hearing the sudden arrival of police, the thugs fled.

I turned to face Heather on the other side of the boulevard, but she wasn't there anymore. By the time the policeman sprinted into the vicinity of the assault, the old man stood up thanks to his own strength alone. As I tired leaving, I looked at a photo left on the edge of the sidewalk. It was a picture of a family of three: the parents and a son. It was one of those professional pictures taken on a sole color background. As I took a closer look, there was a huge resemblance between the father on the picture, and the bloodied man bend forward next to the wall. The man was much older than the one on the picture. He was mostly bold now while his former self had a short cut. The ambiance he gave off now was different. He was defeated. I made a gesture, trying to hand him the picture he dropped.

He was gasping out of pain when he took it and shoved in the pocket near his heart. "Thank you for stopping them."

"Shouldn't you be blaming me for not jumping in sooner?"

"That would be ungrateful of me."

Sure would be, but it would be an honest answer. I kept this to myself as I saw that the man didn't look angered.

"Are you alright, sir?" Officer Dyer returned after giving up on chasing those smalltime crooks.

"Just leave me alone and go help other citizens of this town."

"But, sir, you're hurt. I should get a doctor." Dyer insisted.

"Look, you should be enforcing the law around here, right?" The elderly man took a seat on the floor. "Well, if you want to follow that believe, you should truly go help someone else."

Dyer was perplexed but left obediently. He kept turning to look over his shoulder every once in a while.

"Young lad, I have a question for you?" The man called out before I could leave. "The picture, you don't even know how much it means to me. It's a symbol of family and tradition. When a man loses tradition, he loses himself. That's what happened to those that attacked me. They're controlled by their primal instincts, wouldn't you say?"

"That's true."

"Let me guess, my behaviors was weird?" The man spoke in a soft almost sleepy voice. At the same time, there was a hint of overwhelming power dwelling somewhere inside the void within him.

"After so many kicks, most would end up in the hospital, but you stood up, which made me think that if you really wanted to, you could have defeated them."

"You might be right. Does that make me a masochist?" The man didn't laugh at his own comment.

As the conversation drew to a close, his escort turn up—those same three, I saw yesterday. They must have been visiting someone, in one of the building around this area because a young girl looked out her window and in a blithe attitude announced, "I'll call you if I ever remember anything."

"Thank you so much for all the help!" Leon made a soft smile that emancipated his kindness. It was a face very much unlike the one I remembered from last time. Unlike the populace of the town, he didn't force a smile. It came naturally as if it was an unconscious reaction to his emotions inside. Yet at the same time, I had some misgivings. He wouldn't be the first one to fake emotions.

The crew was still far away, but their discussion was one full of involvement and participation, so I could hear the strident clamors of their voices from across the street.

"Look at that guy, again staring at the pitiful photo of his family." Lean avoided the sight.

"Well, I consider family a big burden too, but everyone should live as they see fit. Besides not everyone is like you." Dorian stretched his arms out to the sky.

"What is that supposed to mean?"

"To say it lightly, you're manipulative and narcissistic, and the only way you'll submit to someone is for you own good. Your sole desire is to be revered by those below you."

Lean laughed as if enjoying their little chatter. "Claims who? The person who is pro freedom, but at the same time, an utter hypocrite, who's a lap dog with no liberty."

Leon's comment hurt Dorian in the most painful of ways.

"Leon, you can't comprehend the ideas of family and I understand that, but there are beautiful values behind family. There is sacrifice, complete trust, and most of all, unity. I for one can't wait to leave this town. My family is there waiting for me." Jude spoke based on his untainted feeling of homesickness.

"Waiting? Didn't you once say that you don't get along with that prick, your son? Did he have a sudden change of heart?" Dorian commented.

"No, but he's 26, so it's only natural that he wants to do things his way. I bet that once I'll be a grandfather I can mend that relationship."

"You're a complete fool." Leon had no sympathy for Jude's blind feelings.

Dorian eyed the street ahead, stopping the conversation midway before it would turn into a clash of views. "Is it just me or is Kazuki bleeding?"

"What's more important is the identity of man standing next to him?" Leon announced as they finally made it to where I was. He stood there with all the friendliness gone, and whatever was left crawled out of the depths of the abyss, where all the darkest emotions dwell. He had a nature of a snake combined with the abilities of a chameleon. "Kazuki, what happened?" Leon asked the elderly man with a face created of antipathy.

"I was attacked, and he helped me." Kazuki pointed at me.

"I'll be taking my leave." I said.

"Kazuki, couldn't you have defended yourself for once? That way you wouldn't look so screwed up when we return?" Leon took out a handkerchief and tossed it at Kazuki, implying that he should clean himself up. "As for you, here is your reimbursement." Leon explored his wallet. He took a hold of some paper cash and carelessly shifted his hand in my direction, letting go of the bills. The wind carried them up and down like paper planes across the road. They scattered covering a big portion of the concrete.

"You can keep your cash. Next time, how about watching over your subordinates? May be that way things wouldn't have gotten out of control?" I commented involuntarily hurting Leon's pride.

"Leon, you're really hurting your image by being so disrespectful." Dorian joked, and Jude chuckled at the insightful remark. "We're not going to be in town much longer, but in case you need help, come to this place." Dorian spoke tagging a piece of paper into my sleeve that would open up a door for me to find him in case I needed something.

◆

When I finally got home, the apartment stood empty. The place never reflected my persona, but after the recent clean up, it was ready for someone else to move in and fill it up. My time in the village has been slowly but surely used up as I was just waiting to get out. In all honesty, I haven't decided when I would leave since this case did trap me into a world like no other. At first, I was dreading the thought of participating in this case, but right now, I quite frankly begun to enjoy some aspects of it. A part of me surely wanted to leave, oblivious to the things left undone, but a bigger part awoke with a hunger for curiosity that couldn't go on famished. As the day was still bright and young, I received a call from Aidan.

He was startled as he spoke in a voice stepping into the boundary of whispering, "He's here. I'm in the dinner. He walked in with a group."

"Did he see you?"

"I think so. He defiantly saw me, but he didn't have a hostile gaze. He's here with two other people: a girl and a guy." Aidan spoke almost too quietly to be heard. His voice seemed to vanish as his heavy breathing prevailed. "Wait, they finished eating. They're packing … walking out." I heard clatter on the other end as Aidan rose from his chair. All the voices and tones merged into on seemingly indistinguishable sound, an antithesis to white noise. After waiting for what seemed like forever, I think I heard Aidan speak again. "Excuse me, you saw the group who sat over there, right? I think the one with the long hair lost his keys. Do you know where he lives? I'd like to return them to him."

I waited as the phones speaker muttered sounds from the restaurant.

"I'm here. I think I have got his address. That's the beauty of living in a small town where everybody trust each other." Aidan's panic was subdued. I could sense a hint of satisfaction from him.

"We got lucky. Anyway, there is another business to be addressed. Meet me on 94 Augustus Dr. in an hour."

"Look, I'm not your servant?"

"Maybe that'll be true soon, but right now, you owe me two favors. Today is time for number one."

Time flew by until I was on Augustus Dr. where Historia's home was supposed to be situated. It was a place like no other in this town, for it was a four-story building as oppose to two-story like most in the area. A good number of structures in town were frail-looking and they almost seemed wooden, but this building looked like a stronghold. It was a red brick building with numerous apartments. In the front of it were five steps leading up to the entrance where a grass door was located. Inside, I smelled a weighty reek in the corridor. An old, cobalt, soiled carpet stretched through the hall. In essence, the carpet was there with the aim of looking elegant, and maybe that's how it was when this place was first brought up, but the rug was filthy and distasteful by now. Air conditioner hummed in the background as I climbed the stairs until I was on the third floor. I saw Aidan. He arrived before me.

"You made me wait." Aidan scratched his nose.

"Sorry, but I did say we're meeting in an hour."

"No one in there."

"That's what I need you here for. You'll pick the lock on the door, so that we can go in."

"Watch the hall." Aidan, without much fervor, knelt beside the door and took out his working equipment. A lock pick in his hand, he began playing the doors like a musical instrument until his symphony was complete and it opened.

The inside was almost identical to what my habitat looked like today morning, but this place went further than I did with the cleanup. While my home still had some furniture which was there when I moved in, this one was absolutely vacant. Not only that, but it seemed as if there was no furniture here to begin with since the dust covered the space evenly without a question. The walls looked newly painted, which gave the impression that this place is destined for a brand new owner. The pallid color also made every room look the same.

After a second of probing the site for clues, I walked

over to a piece of paper. The room, where I first found it, looked unoccupied since the page dissolved into the color of the floor, so it was only when I stumped on it that I became aware of its existence. It was a letter from Historia.

Dear Sebastian,

Regrettably our acquaintanceship came to an end, or did it? Overall, I must say that I enjoyed our brief conversations in the real world. I hide no loathing toward your recent action since you probably attached my name to that joke I pulled. Nonetheless, your journey hasn't come to an end, so I'll be watching. Good luck, and I will be waiting in person at your journey's end. Who knows, we might even meet in the real world again.

Enjoying humankind's every lesson!
Historia

"What is that?" Aidan walked into the room where I was reading.

"Well, what can I say, it's a farewell letter from someone I met." So she's alive. She can watch all she wants as my story unfolds as long as she doesn't get in the way. Could she have a connection to the dream world?

"Are we done?" Aidan asked when someone called his cell. A woman's voice sounded unclearly through the speaker.

I couldn't understand a word, but from her bitter voice I concluded that she's sick.

"I have to go." Aidan said in a hurry after hanging up.

"Same here, but first, give me that address."

"Are you going to go see him now?"

"Agonize about your own business." I folded the letter into my pocket. "I'll be concerned with this issue."

He wrote the address. His writing was very sluggish and sloppy, but it felt like he could write neatly, yet subconsciously, he didn't want to. Before we went our separate ways, I made a last comment, "How about writing down the real address now?"

My provocation seemed to work. Aidan turned around with his head bowed down. He looked defeated when he begun to write what seemed to be the genuine address. It was on the opposite end of town from the previous one. He left without a word.

Outside, the day's mood turned heavier and heavier as the time adapted to my pace. On occasions that were difficult and problematic, it seemed to run at a pace slower than a vehicle getting pushed uphill, but when a pleasant moment took place, it hit boost and soon it was gone. I was watching the view of the sunset as I planned my next strategy.

I knew that I'm might have to visit the woods depending on how things play out. I picked my bike as a form of transportation. The ride down hill was a pleasant one since the afternoons had this warm yet refreshing atmosphere. The breeze blew lightly against me, slowing me down just a tiny bit as I was pulled down hill by the force of gravity. The roads in this town were especially well-made when it comes to riding bicycles, so I was using no external force. A smooth travel it was.

At first, I wondered why that person would pick a

location in the woods south of the graveyard, but it soon became clear. His house was one of the last ones on the southern end of town, so even without a method of transportation, it would be a brief journey to walk there. Standing in front of his two-story house, the steps extended to the front door. The grass around the house was neglected, yet at the same time, there was this thick, green smell that stretched around the whole place. Right in front of the door, I realized that only one window had the lights on. It was the room on the very top floor, the attic. Thinking of what I would say at the instant the door sprung open, I realized that I felt somewhat tense. I wanted to leave this place. Before my state would get out of hand, I knocked on the door to prevent myself from doubting my decisions.

I heard footsteps on the other side, lightly rushing for the entry. A girl, with long auburn locks with traces of red, opened the front door. She smiled, but her eyes spoke otherwise as she had not a touch of bliss in them. Her wardrobe consisted of dark blue jeans and a loose blouse. She also had a pearl necklace on.

"I am here for …" I began speaking to find myself unable to convey a plausible excuse. All my preparation vanished the moment it was to be verbalized. The flash of idleness spread through the air for only a couple of seconds. That's when I heard the voice of the man from that night.

"What is it, Bridget?" The man soared down the steps leading up, his angered-lunatic demeanor absent. It was exchanged with a depressive ambiance. He slowly strolled closer as Bridget backed off, almost appearing as if she was repelled by him. This must have been the girl's most honest feeling when compared to her warm welcome.

The girl swayed her head, telling the man, "Take care of it."

"How may I help you?" The man asked. He was wearing a plain white dress shirt as well as jeans. His dark hair resembled the color of the night sky. It was awfully long like it was grown out, but not because he liked the style; it was because he didn't care. The cut seemed to have no concise direction as it went every which way, nearly covering his eyes.

"Well, I was hoping you could recall the night of May 3rd for me?" I said.

With just this solitary question, I now had his complete attention.

"Let's walk outside." He slammed the door behind him without being careful about alarming anyone upstairs. "He did something again, did he?"

His question made me confused. "If you omit one death, two detectives, and a game then I would say that you did nothing more."

"Wait, you want payback? But you don't understand? It's not what you think it is?" He said, waving his arms in front of his face. His body was a vessel empty of ruthless and destructive emotions. He lacked the feeling of distress from my sudden arrival and the spark of lunacy in his eyes. His hands came together like he was praying.

"I don't understand? Yea, I don't understand what you're playing."

"Listen, I want no trouble. You don't understand."

"Then make me understand."

He looked at his house. Bridget was standing in one

of the windows. "Let's take a walk." The first ten minutes was packed with an annoying silence that made me wary of the man. He sure knew what I was talking about, but I was positive that he is not the one I spoke with that night. The man had no confidence, nor strength. He carried a feeling of desperation like he had given up on himself, people in general, and the world. He was very different from the one I was hoping to meet.

"My name is Chris. As you probably figured out, Bridget is my girlfriend. Two months ago, there was an incident."

"What does this have to do with anything?" My comment seemed to have no effect on Chris as he continued his monologue.

"One day, we were attacked by four thugs. I was nearly killed. As for Bridget, they made her watch as they massacre me, although she was pretty beat-up as well. That was the first time in my life that I wanted the world to die." Chris took a big breath of fresh air, followed by a breathing exercise in quick succession. It was an effort to relief the trauma. "Bridget always blames me that I'm not dependable, that I'm unreliable. She believes that if I really cared about her, I would protect her. She bestowed this idea onto me that I could really have done something. Before long, I wished I was a different person."

"Don't tell me that ..." I felt outraged by the implication of the story, the irrational idea of an alter ego—a metaphor of a dual personality disorder.

"Yes, he is my creation, or maybe he is just a part of me. I try to believe that he is the embodiment of all my memories. He calls himself Magnus."

I chuckled at the puny man. His depressed eyes didn't change, yet his face was more and more bleak. His face muscles were striving to hide his frustration.

"That's a pathetic excuse."

"I should have known you will never believe my story."

I stared around until there was no one in sight. I slowed my pace down. I rested my hand on the man's shoulder. As he turned around, I gave him a heavy punch in the face.

"Shit! What is wrong with you?" Chris uttered as blood spilled out of his nose onto the pavement.

"I can't be certain, but the man I met that night would kill me for something like this. More so, he would never allow me to land a punch. He would fight back, and ultimately, he would kill me for even trying." I said after my little experiment.

Chris randomly threw a punch, but I leaned back effortlessly, avoiding the blow. His careless attack wasn't the least bit intimidating even for me—a complete amateur at fighting.

"So does he only surface at night?" I chuckled.

"Not really, as soon as I fall sleep." Chris sighed in an effort to cope with the story. "He surfaces. I wake up as a different person."

"But that means you get no sleep?"

"It does. Countless times, I wake up in the morning minutes after he had just came home. I'm tired, sleepless."

"He told me he takes out the evil of the world. So what exactly is his goal?" I still doubted the matter at hand.

"He claims that cleansing the world of rotten exist-ence is his goal, but he is just doing it for fun. There is nothing more to it. He is bored and bloodthirsty. He has his own priorities and his own beliefs. If I met him in real life, I would probably end up detesting him."

"So you can communicate?"

"No, we can't. But we are connected. That's the whole reason he can't kill those that he hasn't witnessed committing a crime—those that aren't totally broken. I think my consciousness and moral code still have a very strong effect on him, but only when it comes to taking a life. Everything else is left to his judgment, so in essence, he could use torture if he deems it fit."

So that's probably why he didn't kill Aidan. That's also the reason why he missed when he fired at me. If that assumption is true, then I'm safe for now. At least, that's what I would like to think, but as Chris said, he can do everything else. Death is the least of my worries. I ended up taking the story into consideration.

"I have to meet him today." I checked the time.

"Good luck. You should probably hear this too. Magnus once told me a story about a thug that he was searching for. One day, he finally found him with his girl in a hotel, but he realized that he can't shoot him. That's because of my hold on him, but the story doesn't end there. He asks the thug multiple questions upon which he will decide if the thug has the right to live. He told the thug that if he sacrifices the girl, he gets to life. The thug complied and took her life at which point he sealed his doom. Magnus was now free to take a life."

"So he tricks people." I spoke, recalling the questions he put me through.

"He feasts on them. For all I know, he has no respect for anyone, but at the same time, he is above all the emotions that torment me." Chris fell into the land of thought. He wiped the last trace of blood from his face and asked, "Do you know if he had any syringes? A couple different substances were stolen from the local clinic?"

"You might be right. When I met him, he used one to put someone to sleep."

By the time our conversation was over, we made a big circle around the whole block. By now, the sun has diminished, and the only thing left was the soft, unblemished light of the moon. Despite the summer heat, days have been going by quickly which only strengthened the feeling that my time here—in this town—was running out.

At Christopher's doorsteps was a man chatting with Bridget. The man had a deep green dress shirt with the sleeves rolled up to his elbows and black dress pants. He also had a pendant with some unknown design. His slightly long bluish-colored hair only inflamed his unique style.

"Hey, Chris, where have you been? Who's that person by your side?" He asked in a light and subtle tone, pointing at me with his gaze.

"I had to take care of something. He found something that I've lost."

"Call me Virgil. Pleasure to me you." The man jumped from the steps to take a closer look at me. The whole endeavor gave me a feeling that his goal wasn't being polite, but obtaining more info.

The inquiry made me realize that I have not disclosed my name. "My name is Sebastian Snow. Nice to me you."

"Chris, it looks like we'll have to continue tomorrow. It's quite late, so I'll be going." Virgil exclaimed before disappearing suddenly in the distance covered by fresh darkness.

"I'll be leaving too."

As I turned my back, Chris grabbed me by the shoulder and leaned forward, uttering a word of caution.

"You know, if he hasn't killed you yet, he's just waiting to corrupt you. He is just waiting for the right moment. When you make an immoral move, he'll be there to take your life."

Bridget called him home in an unhappy manner, oblivious to the gloom of the situation.

The Poem of Suicide

THE NIGHT WAS still young as I dreaded the idea of dealing with Magnus.

The scheme that he is killing out of a sense of justice wouldn't be so problematic if it wouldn't be twisted so much. I don't know what he deems immoral or wrong. There is even a chance that he just uses justice as an excuse when it works in his favor, and other times dismisses it all together. He is most of all unpredictable, and he doesn't have any chains that fasten regular human. In other words, he is living in his own little world, despite walking on the same earth everybody does. As long as he needs help on finding a new prey and info on the ability, he won't kill me, but that same thing can't be said about Aidan. Oh, well that's not my problem, I thought.

With plenty of time left, I deviated from my path, took a detour, and aimed at getting more info.

I was stationed in the spot where I last saw Historia. The place didn't bring up any strong feeling, and any sensation that I felt was quite mellow. The light kept flickering right in front of the tattoo shop. The light was a magnet for all the various moths and bugs that flew around near the garbage cans. Turning around, I could still see the catwalk where I was stationed during the incident. At the end of the day, there has been no change here except the doors were closed. I had no idea if the store was closed down or not, but I knocked trying to press onward. The light inside vapidly turned on, but my view was heavily obstructed.

"Who is it?" I heard a voice on the other side. Some-one had a sore throat.

"Usually at this hour the tattoo shop was open. I was hoping to speak with the owner."

"Store is closed! Get out!"

"I actually intended to pay but whatever." The en-deavor at picking his greed worked as the door opened slightly. The chain holding it closed was still there, but at least I could continue.

"Pay up first." The man announced as he stared from behind the door. He had really big black circles under his eyes as if he hadn't slept for months. I took out a couple of bills and threw them inside. The men walked back deeper into the room to collect his incentive which gave me enough time to unchain the door and walk in.

When the man noticed me, he inched backwards. His cowardice spoke voicelessly. He then screamed. "What are you doing? Get out! Now!" The light illuminated his bruised face. His shirt held a tag with the name Jason Fisher.

I paid no attention to his blubbering, locked the doors behind me, and took a seat ready to interrogate him. The room had a pretty simple blueprint. The back had a stool next to a cashier where the owner would probably sit, waiting for his next client. Behind the cashier was a wall with a set of big black doors. For some reason, today the doors were wide open which gave me a chance to peek inside. The open area had four specialized chairs, as well as two tables. It a professional tattoo shop. Most of the walls were decorated with sample tattoos, as well as enlarged photos of actual customers showing of their new skin. Despite the initial professional look of the place, the inside was dirty and squalid. It answered my question why the shop was only opened at night.

I grabbed my pocket knife which made him shriek. "What do you want?" he said. "I'll do anything!"

I noticed a few syringes and a couple of bottles on the counter. The idea was evident; he was a drug addict.

"You know the poem in the newspaper, right?" I asked, and he nodded. "Well, I'd like to know if you wrote it, and if there were any other people involved in its creation."

"I did write it, but it wasn't my idea. There was this man. He came in and requested that I write something about the suicides and post it in the newspaper. He told me that it would surely get me more customers. After I finished, he came in once more and approved it." He shook his head happily as he told the story.

"Describe him." I stepped to the counter to take two bottles from the man's stash.

"I don't remember. It was a long time ago. My memory is blurry! It's short-term! But many asked about the poem."

"Is that why you have those bruises?" He nodded again. "Who else came to look at the poem?"

He scratched his head, his muscles tensed as he attempted to recover some long-lost fact from his head. "I know! I know! The one that came first had a really long cut and a calm mind. He showed respect."

Is he talking about Fredric? I can probably assume that's true because that's where I found out about the ad. Waye wouldn't come on his own. He would send someone he trusted to do the work for him.

The tattooist stretched, leaning toward the stool. He tried to climb and reach the top of the counter where the drugs were located. I stepped on his clothes, stopping him. I flung a glass at the two tiny bottles where his delight was located. The sound of glass shattering emptied into the quite space of the room. The man's eyes widened, and his pupils disappeared almost completely. The man was filled with unprecedented rage. He screamed. "What did you do? What did you do?"

He turned to me, ready to show aggression which dripped from his eyes in the form of tears. He was completely consumed by his only purpose of filling himself up with this poison called drugs. He had no qualms about anything else he did in the world as long as he could get his fill. Before he could unleash his rage, I waved three bottles right in from of his eyes. It seemed to calm him down. He eyes were filled with tears of bliss, and he seemed to diligently listen. His whole attitude was disturbing which only inflamed my desire to shatter his joy. "You'll get this once you answer a couple of final questions. You did describe one person that was here. Was there anybody else?"

"A day or two ago, the police came. They closed my shop, but they did not see the poem. It was taken by the man with long hair. He wanted to own the complete version."

"They closed the shop? Why?"

"Because of my addiction. Scumbags, how dare they do this to me?"

"Do the names Leon, Dorian, and Jude tell you anything?"

"Recent customers, they left me a hefty tip."

"Did they ask about the poem?"

"They did, but I didn't have another copy. They then tried to make me remember." He pointed his hand at the bruises. His eyes were firmly placed on the bottles in my hands. I wondered if he was truly listening, or if he was just pretending, or worse, making it all up. I decided that my final question is the most important, so I tried getting his attention.

"Do you have a copy of the poem?" He shook his head. I dropped one of the bottles to the floor. The velocity forced the glass to fragment into pieces. I reiterated my question. "Do you have a copy of the poem?"

The man hesitated, his eyes wandered about calculating. "Yes, I do." The man screamed. He crawled to the back and took down a photo from the wall to reveal a miniature safe with a combination lock. Upon opening it, the man gave me the poem.

"It's the only one left."

The title read, "Poem of Suicide."

Lamenting the indisputable grief,
Harassed with a terrible resolution,
Existence devoid of consequence,
Attendance of raging disappointment,
Advancement futile,
Improvement oblivious to pointlessness,

The poem wasn't out of the ordinary, and any hope of finding a secret message was gone in an instant. I recalled how Fredric took a copy, and I decided that it needed closer examination. Tagging it into my pocket, an intense bang on the wooden door made the room tremble as if an earthquake was coming. The tattooist had no intention of coming close to the door and only scowled, moving backwards. The banging ceased, allowing me an exit. At the mouth of the alley, I was greeted by Fredric.

Ambitions

FREDRIC SMILED TO me. "Of all places, this was the last one where I would have hoped to find you."

"I could say the same about you."

"Care to talk?" You didn't seem flattered about the proposal, huh?"

"I guess I'm just not a fan of the Unity. But I had a question for you." I walked slowly. "I'm sure you noticed that there is more to the spokesman than meets the eye. I'm sure you don't approve of all his views, right?"

"Where did that question come from?"

"I don't know. Just a feeling."

"You see, my story with Waye goes way back. My father loved to hunt in the woods, and so did Waye's. One time, we met. I still remember the tension when the two strangers faced each other. I was standing right next to my old man as he tried to calm the situation down. Waye was nowhere to be seen yet. As the two hunters aimed to go their separate ways, he jumped out, startling both of them. Instinctively my old man lifted his rifle. That's when he was shoot by Waye's father, who only wanted to protect his kid. My father died in those woods. After that, Waye's father took me in. Sorry for the long exposition."

"That's alright. That surely explains the bond."

"Don't misunderstand me. I am not helping him because of some notion of family. I was just reiterating why I would associate with a person like Maximilian in the first place. What about you? What's in your past?"

"My past is lost somewhere in the never-ending stream of disappointing memories." I joked at which point I was reminded of the constant travels with my parent at a young age. My father's spark for the mystic has swallowed my past whole. The only reason why I hid the matter was because I thought so little of it. There was never any point in explaining.

"This town sure has changed." Fredric altered the subject as if showing respect for me, as if accepting that I wouldn't talk about my past. "It kind of seems like everybody that is different from the usual crowd searches for the one behind the suicides in order to acquire something."

"Like Detective Dench who yearns for prestige?" I inquired fascinated by this new revelation coming from Fredric. At that time, I had a feeling that he didn't come up with this comment in mere seconds but intended to spark the discussion a while ago.

"That is an example, but I know of two others, so who knows maybe that statement is truly right?"

"On the other hand, anybody from the 'different from the usual crowd' could be the one behind it."

"Exactly, you fit the description pretty well." Fredric grinned.

"As do you." I said.

"Now, on a more serious note, if we are right and there is an instigator behind the events, all is well. But what if there really is something wicked, nonhuman that is enveloping this town, and we are just pawns running around, chasing our dreams and mind creations? What if we are just doing a lunatic dance?" He grew a little desperate.

"I don't know if a mastermind exists. It would be very difficult finding a victim every single day, but what if it actually got easier to find a victim each day. The village is getting more depressed and devoid of happiness each day."

"That someone would have to be quite charismatic and fluent in persuasion to accomplish that."

"Just my take on the matter."

"Say, how did you like the poem?" Fredric inquired, his tone brutally serious. The friendly discussion was over. Throughout the conversation, it felt like we saw through each other's veneer of pretended emotion and suspected each other. Now, the curtains have been slightly blown away by his comment.

"So, you realized that I noticed the article. I'm just a concerned human being about the town I live in."

"That tattooist is quite a nasty fellow. I actually made him open that vault, and there was no copy of the poem. He must have still remembered it and wrote it down again."

"I wouldn't have acquired it if it wasn't for his weakness to drugs."

"So what did you think?"

"Dark, empty, emotionless."

"I was more concerned with any clues. You see, I have a feeling there is something in the poem that only a chosen person would notice. I mean, someone left it there for a purpose, and that purpose isn't to find victims."

"What makes you think that I would know anything?"

"Well, you got this far. Let's just say, that I am a firm believer in faith."

"Is that why you don't feel down about the suicides?"

"I try to look at the bright side." He looked a little sad when he said those words. In an instant, all his emotions evaporated, leaving only a husk of a man. That man would only climb higher and reclaim his happiness.

I looked at the watch. It was time to go, but before I could utter anything, a car flew by the alleyway and the door opened. The voice of the typically, reticent assistant was firmly yelling, claiming her domination over Fredric. "Where have you been? We need to go back! Director has a vital announcement."

"Another sorry excuse just to get me back to his side. Guess I'll be taking my leave. Thanks for the chat, and do let me know if you figure out anything with the poem." Fredric said away from the girl, so that she wouldn't hear a word.

"You know, I never thanked you for the work in the library."

"No need to thank me. Looking back at those peaceful days brings nostalgia." Fredric left in a hurry.

I decided it's time to meet my enemy.

I got on my bike and begun pedaling. After a while, I was finally able to loosen the muscles in my legs as gravity did most of the work for me going downhill. The clouds seemed to be eating at the moon tonight. Each second, a fraction of the moon was enveloped in a cloak of cloud which caused the streets to get more obscure and murkier. Thankfully, the road was a pretty basic one up to the cemetery, where I would be forced to toss my ride and walk into the woods.

The cemetery was a place owned by the funeral services nearby. Unlike most, this village had no fancy assortment of gravestones. There were no grand, overly large memorials that only a select few could afford. Most of the monuments were in the shape of a small cross, or a rectangle with an oval top, but the most prominent feature was that all the tombstones were of equal size, giving the place a feel of equality.

Passing through the graveyard, or rather following the fence on the side of it, I became conscious that there are actually two graveyards in this town. I once heard a story that a long time ago there was only the one behind the church, but as it increased, it became obvious that the church would have to cut out some of the woods to provide space. The woods are owned by one of the village man, Maximilian Waye. He harshly protested tearing apart his land, and so the church had to find a new place. The southern portion of the forest, close to the funeral services, was the perfect place and the debate was soon settled.

I started my trip west into the ominous forest. At

night, the vibrant green color depleted into a lifeless dark olive where the creatures of the night hid. I was forced to run on my flashlight as soon as I made a couple of steps. The light gave way to a moderately lively-looking grass and tree trunks. The animals, although mostly quiet, were making sounds. Especially the owls who fixed their eyes on me, making me feel as if the forest itself was watching and evaluating my every step. Those big eyes without a body bulged out of the darkness. They didn't blink. They constantly observed the life of the forest, recording every ounce of info for future generations. Any peacefulness spawned by the hunters waiting for their pray was disturbed by the working insects. They were attracted to my flashlight, making my life harder by blocking the light. Just as I was beginning to have enough of this trouble, my light was completely wrapped in pests. I heard a discussion coming from the southwest. I run with full force in that direction while listening to the dialogue.

A man wept feebly as Magnus stated, "Just keep digging, and it'll all be over very soon." There was a pause. "Sorry where did we left off, Aidan? Oh, I know, you were condemning my methods."

"You think that you are judging evil? But you're just as rotten as they are! If you're so determined to take out the trash, why not point that gun at your forehead and press the trigger!" Aidan said. For some reason, fear didn't dwell in his heart tonight.

Magnus was mildly amused by the morality talk.

"If you so wish." A shot was fired. "You talk as if you know how this world works. You talk as if you are the good guy, but are you not a pitiful thief? Wasn't extortion a weapon of choice for your former teammates?"

Aidan bit his tongue. His line of questioning crumbled. He had no argument against what Magnus reminded him of, but at the same time, deep inside, he detested what he has become. He stood there with a face that could convince anyone that he never wanted to be a criminal. It was the situation he was in that compelled him to develop into a mugger. He contemplated with no apparent line of defense. The sweat poured over his face. He was at the edge of his mind as if he couldn't bear the situation.

"The world made me into who I am!" He uttered lacking conviction. The night allowed his response to reach deep into the woods.

"That's quite wrong. Everybody has a choice. Do you think that you're the only one whose life isn't covered in flowers? Do you truly belief that life is a cakewalk for everyone else? You want know what I think? You feel guilty for what you have done. Deep inside, you know it's immoral, and so whenever an opportunity presents itself, you educate others about morality, but not because you want to help them. You preach because it helps you cope with your past. You do it because of your selfishness. You feel better doing so." Magnus looked disgustingly joyful.

The words punctured Aidan's head. A seed was planted in his head that made him doubt his former self. He never looked at it that way. He believed that an honorable deed counteracts a malicious one, but it doesn't work that way. He went out there trying to do little praiseworthy things in order to help others, or so he thought, but Magnus's words perforated him like little stakes, making him concentrate on just how pure his intentions were. He got angry at himself even more as the thought bore fruit. The anger made Aidan reflect that doing something for self-satisfaction negated all the good that came from it.

The talk hushed as I reached the edge of the woods and arrived in a somewhat open area in the middle of the forest. Aidan was crouching on the grass, slamming his muddy fists repetitively in the ground. On a moderate incline where grass came to an end, stood a man with a shovel. His lower half obstructed by the pit he was in—a pit he himself dug.

On the lowest branch of a tree nearby sat Magnus. His leather jacket zipped up to his chin, the cuffs of his sleeves covered in dirt. The dark jeans were torn around his ankles where his sport shoes met the cloth.

"Oh, you finally made it. Fortunately you haven't missed anything important." Magnus announced in a full-hearted voice.

"What's happening?"

"Not counting a man at his road's end, I just exposed Aidan to his true self." He waved his revolver.

The men in the hole repeatedly plucked the shovel in the ground, slammed his foot on the end of it, and heaved the mud out. He was a muscular man who was quite adept at making his way through life, forcing his domain on other people, but here, he was just a disgraceful man with no vitality and vigor whatsoever. He cried like a little child who lost something dear. A favorite toy perhaps; this man's favorite toy was life. With every motion of the shovel, he was taking a step on a long way toward death, but unfortunately for him, he was almost there. "I have a child." The man sobbed.

"So did the majority of people you killed."

"Look, I don't know what I ever did to you, but I have people waiting for me."

Magnus pointed his revolver which made the man trip and fall on his back into the hole.

"You have people waiting for you? Would you like to listen to your comrades before you'll be on your way?" Magnus tuned in on the radio receiver, and I heard a vivid conversation between Leon, Dorian, Jude and one other person.

"Who would have thought that this town would be so …" Dorian was at a loss of words.

"I would have advocated leaving this town if it weren't for the fact that we have lost six members already." Jude stated in a grieving voice. Even though it sounded like most of them wanted to go home, he was the only one truly feeling miserable about being here.

"Hey, boss, considering the circumstance maybe you could enlighten us about the purpose of coming here? I know she was your girl, but who cares?" Leon inquired without an ounce of discomfort, speaking to his superior.

"We didn't come here because of me relation to her. For all I care, she could have just disappeared whenever she wanted. We came here because of how absurd her death was, and if it really was murder, we should find the culprit in order to preserve our authority." Hearing the boss's voice, the man in the ditch showed a look of admiration.

The moment the man forgot about the current situation, his body splattered blood from three spots as bullets left the chamber of Magnus's revolver. The thunderous trio of blasts remained in the air condensing into death.

"I find it suspicious as well that Sarah would commit suicide. She was too immersed in the thrill of life to do something like that." Dorian commented. A sound of pages turning filled the room.

"I found out from the police that Sarah jumped from a roof—a classical suicide case." Leon stated.

"Fine, boss, but the question is; is the person that killed our companions the same one who is responsible for Sarah's death." Jude drank something.

"I think it could go either way, but my personal opinion is that these are too different cases. After all, our companions vanished while the suicides have continued to occur although in different ways." The boss explained.

"It was a really good idea befriending that detective." Jude continued drinking.

"I don't trust her one bit, but I can't argue against her usefulness. Does anybody have a light?" Leon was yearning for a cigarette.

"Catch." Dorian threw a lighter around the room.

"Woman these days. Can't they understand that they should keep their feminine side? I mean, that's who they are. Yet they keep adopting men's customs. She is an example of that, and so was Sarah. You, my friend, are lucky to have found a true housewife, Jude." Leon complained.

Before the conversation could continue, Magnus turned off the radio and soared from the tree.

"The theater is closed now! Who's going to do the cleaning?" Magnus pointed at the hole behind him, turning down the noise from the transmitter.

I made my way to Aidan. "What happened?"

Aidan pushed me to the side and stood up. His body

was up, but his mind was still cowering on the ground. "How can you be so calm? How can you not criticize what this man is doing? One day, we'll be in that ditch!" Tears dripped down on the ground. His soggy eyes showed no sadness which was now replaced with ferocity.

"He's right. You should listen to him, or maybe not. After all, you know that already." Magnus announced, giving of a smile as if he was above everything that is happening. "Anyway we'll have time to address that later. For now, who'll volunteer to bury the gangster in the gully?"

"Why not do it yourself?" The words escaped without me even knowing. I was too concentrated on other matters.

"Yesterday while hunting, I met someone who rivaled me in a fight. While not a good shooter, she was proficient with using a knife. She even postponed my hunt." Magnus unzipped his jacket and pulled up his blue shirt to reveal a bandaged stomach. The work was unprofessional. The bandages were carelessly wrapped, so he must have been the one doing the job. Blood pierced the bandages.

"He's wounded. Why not deal with him now and bury him in that ditch too." Aidan's thought developed in words. He kept looking at the ground.

"Says the person who panics at the first sight of blood." I mocked Aidan which only infuriated him more.

He was dead serious.

"Go ahead and try if you want to get hurt," Magnus waved his gun. "But don't count on it that I'll be defenseless."

The discussion was finished. Magnus sprinted in our direction. His worry of the wound opening up disintegrated as his bloodthirsty-self gave way to violence. Once he was right between me and Aidan, Aidan tried to punch him, but Magnus effortlessly duck down and uppercutted him. Blood splashed from Aidan who was falling backward in slow motion. Magnus turned his attention to me even though I had no intention of fighting. He took a quick step onward as he grabbed his gun, pointing it at my face. I dodged to the side as the bullet passed my head, missing. My right side noiseless, astounded. Magnus lunched another attack and buried his knee in my stomach. Slowly falling on my side, He kicked me once more with all the force he had, his wound begun to bleed plentifully. At last he turned his attention to Aidan who was on his knees, still recuperating from the last blow. He pointing his gun at Aidan's angered face.

"Shoot me." Screamed Aidan.

Magnus pulled the trigger, a click sounded. Aidan fell backwards scared. The gun's chamber was empty.

Since I didn't bleed, it seemed that the pain was going to last, and it had no intention of going away. This sudden revelation made me consider that the power triggers with blood. Although annoyed by the turn of events, I was satisfied with learning a little bit about the power.

Magnus was now finished. His hunger for bloodshed quenched until he head Aidan's final comment.

"You … both of you … you're both the same. You think you're better because you can point out how I don't know myself. You think you can preach. A man with the power of a fiend and a man fueled by vengeance for how brutally he was treated. When I saw you in that restaurant, I was certain I knew that face." Aidan tried getting up, but he fell. "Now I remember, you were in the newspaper a couple months back. Supposedly, you and your girl were cruelly assaulted by a bunch of criminals. Is that why you act so tough? Because you think that you should have done something back then?"

Without another word, Magnus's memories swiveled in a spiral where the degree of hatred is the deciding factor in which memories will triumph. All the pleasant ones drowned below, and the ones filled with hatred climbed to the top. He held his revolver as he forcefully attacked Aidan with its chamber. Aidan fell to the ground, losing orientation of his surroundings. He struggled, trying to stand up, but was locked into crawling. All was in vain. Magnus kicked him to the side and began booting him viciously. Blood escaped Aidan's jaws as he lost any strength he had left in trying to fight. Even though he was in an unfavorable situation, his face showed no signs of regret for what he had done. Magnus pummeled him without a care in the world, and all he was concerned about was letting out his anger. At one point, it seemed as if nothing else mattered to him.

I slowly stood up, put my hand on his shoulder, and said, "Enough."

His torso soiled with blood was aching. He brushed me off and walked away. "I'll kill you before this place dies—both of you."

Our meeting ended there and then. Magnus begun the burial, but because of his incessantly leaking wound, I decided to help him. We finished while Aidan still rested on the ground covered by the grass. Once we were finished, without a word we went our separate ways. I found out nothing from Magnus that would be of value.

Furthermore, we did not settle on meeting again. I felt satisfaction from the notion that Chris was telling the truth. Magnus was so furious that I could bet a hand that if he knew that I met with Chris—that I found out his secret—he would truly kill me. His acting was the truest because he wasn't really acting.

The day ended as I arrived home.

Tired, I was lost in the whirlpool, heading to the dream world.

Someone Dear

———

THE WHITE WALL lingered blindingly. I felt like something was pulling my consciousness away, and this vibrant white was keeping my attention—keeping me awake. I always felt that. No matter how many times I've arrived here, I felt the same. I went thought the same process. Mankind's Most Preserving Teacher was stationed at the window. Something was different about the room. He was watering some flowers. The light, cherry-color flowers were very much in contrast with the room. The soothing rhythm of pouring water made me dizzy.

"Didn't see you back there? You must be surprised about the flowers." He grinned. "Where I come from, they're viewed as a symbol of death. Not only death, but ambition as well—ambition to die. The light red carnation reminds me of memories I once had. Did you know

that within the town it only grows behind the cathedral?"

"Why can't you just cease with the small talk?"

"Alright. I must say your last words shook my inner
self a bit so I'll tell you about what dwells within you."
His face evolved into seriousness. It was the first item he
dropped the insolent, mischievous attitude. "To understand the power you need to realize that there are many
forced within the universe. One of such forces is the Will
of the Universe. You can call it the force that flows
through everything, or God if you prefer. The other such
force is death. It's the eternal notion that everything
dies—the clock that ticks wherever you go. The Will can't
interfere with life directly. It lingers about, overseeing
everything humanity does. Many times, humans tried to
change the world for better or for worse. When that
happens, the Will picks an individual who'll, without a
choice in the matter, make a pact with death. The Will
chooses a human being based on who that person will be
in the future. If it decides that the person only needs time
and a bit of protection to protect the universe in some
way, he'll be granted the power. In essence you have been
granted the power to do something. You'll be driven by
the Will of the Universe into completing your task. Only
then you'll be free."

The only convincing fact that influenced me into believing the teacher was his serious nature. I kept all the
info to myself and asked, "For using the power, what
does Death want?"

"Lives of those who'll strive to hurt you."

"If the Will is there to help the world, how come the
one behind the suicides is like that?"

"Maybe you're just imagining things, or things are not as you see them." He dropped the serious act. "You sure have made a lot of new acquaintances."

"Things happened, but I don't know what you're talking about."

"Oh, come on, there isn't a single person that you are fond of?"

"None."

"I bet there is one. It's the only person that you willingly showed your power to. That's the one that had your full attention."

"Maybe so, but I'm not in the mood to talk today."

"I'll let you get back to sleep then. Disappointing."

The next day I was awakened by the beeping of my cell, a call from Heather. She asked me to meet here since she had something to discuss. She was completely secretive about it, so I didn't question her and decided that it would be best left for when I get to her place in the afternoon. Her call left a bad taste in my mouth as I knew not how to deal with her. Her personality made it hard for me to address any issues since all she yearned to do was to put the horrific to the side.

I was eating my breakfast. The morning meal consisted of a simple slice of bread and scrambled eggs. Since I woke up, the only thing that pulsed through my mind was the eagerness to find something in that poem. No matter how I looked at it, the only thing moving me forward was the belief that I'm right—that there is something in the poem that will show me the way.

The day was a sunny one. There were absolutely no

clouds whatsoever, so people should be happy but no, that was not the case. Everybody at all times found something to complain about. Outside of my home, I was met with a moving truck. Someone, trying to leave this place, was packing. Distinct from the usual service, the workmen tried their best to speed along, packing everything with unbelievable speed.

I overheard the mother.

"Kids, hurry up! Pack only the essential stuff! Everything else will be taken care of later." The mom screamed from outside, waving her hands at the twins looking out the window upstairs. The father was aiding the workmen in packing and supervising them at every turn about how thing should be done.

On the main street, there was a huge upheaval about something I didn't know about. Assuming that I might meet Judith if this is crime related, I stopped by and gradually shift through the swarm of people. The crowd had formed something resembling a semicircle around the corner of the block where the grocery store was located. There was a black, four-door Chevy parked at the side of the road. The sun was smoldering the paint.

Dench was escorting a young man, his head was bowed in shame and his hands were cuffed behind his back. Out of the grocery, run an old lady, who was the usual worker behind the counter as well at the owner of the place. Her drained and tattered legs gave in, preventing her from advancing. She fell and buried her face on the ground, weeping, "My boy hasn't done anything. He is not a killer!"

Judith was there, making her way to the scene. She must've arrived late. She stooped next to the old lady. They spoke for a brief moment before she rushed to Dench who was now unlocking the door to the car. They were far away so any words spoke didn't reach me.

Dench yelled in a tone composed of authority. "He is the one! I'm sure of it! A lady saw him and his car at the crime scene." No argument accomplished anything as Dench was sure of the youngster's guilt.

"There he goes again … that blind fool." Virgil suddenly appeared behind me.

"Oh, it's you. We've met yesterday."

"Certainly. I didn't want to say this with Chris around, but it's good that he found some friends. So far, I think he only had me and Bridget."

"How long have you known Chris?" I posed a random question, trying to hold up the conversation after deciding that walking away would be inappropriate.

"A year or so. Before his life fell apart." Virgil lacked sympathy.

"So what's this game you talked about yesterday?"

"Curiosity sure is a wonderful thing. I mean, it's the essence of living. Without it, no dialogue would last, and no discovery would be made. Anyway, it's a little difficult to illustrate, but you should visit sometime. We do it every other day. The basic idea for it came from preserving our friendship. I think that if it wasn't for me, Bridget and Chris wouldn't be together anymore. I'm the adhesive that holds them together against the magnetic forces of their problems." Virgil smiled.

"Overestimating yourself?"

"How is that?"

"Well, they surely are living together, but are they really together?"

The man made a helpless smirk. "We're still working on it. What about you? When did you meet Chris?"

"Only just recently. So what do you do?"

"I'm a psychologist. I'm trying to help around town. Humans are really a helpless species. And I love hypnosis."

"Alright. I'm sorry, but I must be going."

"Remember every other day we have that game." He left after the mass has dispersed. By now, Dench had drove off, and Judith finished her conversation with the old lady. She was walking outside when we made eye contact. I ran to catch up to her in an abandoned alley.

"He took that kid. With just one small fragment of truth, he decided to close the case. They might be right about him. He might have framed people for something they didn't do." She confessed as a method of releasing negative sentiments. "Sorry, I'm not one to complain."

"Everyone is at some point in their life."

"Guess, you should be in high spirits. Any doubt toward you is now gone."

"I'll be in high spirits once you'll trust me." I snickered. "Anyhow, I'd like to hear something about the case. It started with people jumping from buildings, and I know that there were a couple cases of stabbings. Any other, different incidents?"

"There was a case or two of someone suffocating almost like they hung themselves. The victim even had marks from the rope around their neck, yet there was no rope, nothing. That was one of the weirdest things I have ever seen. That's why I think that you are right."

"Thank you."

"I didn't ask last time, but why trust me?"

"I was hoping our collaboration might bring an end to this sooner, or maybe, I considered that you would believe my hypothesis."

"I want to know more about what happened and how you relate to everything. Care to give me any clues?" She crossed her arms in front of her chest.

"May 1st."

I stated and walked off. I dug into my pockets. I checked all of them; my phone was nowhere to be found. I had no idea how much time I have spent here. I switched from a relaxed pace to something in between a walk and a run. I stopped at the university and found out that, with how things are going, there won't be any ceremony for the graduates. I gave them my family's address, so that they could send me my diploma, thinking that I was just too uncertain how my life will play out here in this village.

The morning solar rays were not at full strength but portended an extremely sizzling day. Unlike in movies where the weather reacts to the scene and adjusts itself to set the right mood, this didn't happen here. The sunny days persisted like never before in this town despite the rotten mood. To me, it felt as if the astral beings were laughing at us, enjoying this spectacle. If my superstition was right, they were chuckling full strength almost to the point of choking.

I truly wandered if this village was cursed? I looked back at the days I have spent here and my recent past. I was not one to reminiscent, but I couldn't understand what went wrong. Was it something the people did? Was there something terribly wrong with this place that it needed to suffer this much? This isolated land where everybody minds their own business succumbed to something malevolent, a force like no other that can't be judged by human standards and has to be extinguished.

The stairs leading up to Heather's apartment had a shine to them, the rays reflected of the metal. The parking lot was full. All spots were taken—occupied. The ever-lasting blue sky gave of a happy feeling like everywhere else. The dread didn't get to me. It didn't catch up yet, but it was only seconds behind. Still standing at the very bottom, a person mirrored my stance from the very top. It was an awkward situation as he seemed to stare at me, but when I began to move, so did he. I scaled the flight of steps as the person descended. The metal reacted to my every step, echoing in a dull sound. My pace seemed to synchronize with the person above. We passed each other at exactly the half way point. I didn't see his face which was shaded in darkness by his hood. He's breathing was heavy as if he had just overcome a time of mental and physical trauma.

At the top, I noticed that the door was wide open. Wary, I slammed on the door as if alarming everyone that I'm about to come it. No response came from the inside. The idea made me feel uneasy—empty. I carefully made my way inside. The place had undergone no change. It was still as messy as it has ever been. My eyes widened to see Heather unconscious on the floor. My heart stopped for a second. It was a reaction I had never experienced, and one that I could not prepare for. I felt as if I carried a load for too heavy for myself. Mentally, I wanted to rush forward and help, but physically, my body resisted. I fell to my knees and painfully stretched out my hand to check her pulse. It was gone. Her body was empty of a soul. For a moment, I was lost, lying to myself that I must be dreaming. I had never practice adapting to a situation like this. I was a newcomer to despair. People full of emotions would instantly cry out, but it seemed like my body lacked that function as if it prioritized other things over this very basic idea of mourning.

Shaken to the core by the turn of events, I picked up a note of the floor. I had my name inscribed. Opened, I was welcomed by a letter from Heather. I examined the handwritten memo signed by Heather.

I have no idea where to start or what to say. At the time of writing my mind was only containing anguish, yet I want to do something good. I have always loathed your idea of inaction, but I have recently learned something. It was at the time when we watched that old man get beat up. I wanted to rush out, but couldn't. I was scared, and the only thought that I stumbled upon was "I'll let someone else take care of it." At that moment, I realized that I shouldn't have judged you. We are all the same. Although for different reasons, everybody has inaction written into their minds. The thought that I'll let someone else do it is always there, following us around, but it's up to the person to struggle against it. I'm not saying that everybody should be a Good Samaritan, but we should all fight against out imperfections. Please keep this in mind. Please keep a piece of me alive by trying to do what's right. Please try to be a better human being. I know I'm asking a lot, so this only strengthens my idea that all humans are the same—selfish. I want you to know that I cherish the time we have spent even if it was a very difficult time. When you read this, I'll be in a better place, and you'll be vengeful, but don't search for the one behind this because of revenge. Search for him because of a different feeling—a positive obligation.

The letter pierced my strong outer layer and dissolved into my arteries. My body felt excruciating, yet much more alive in a way that I disliked. I securely gripped the letter in my hand and stared at the clock. The time was 9:10 PM. The melody of tragedy played as I was surrounded by death of someone dear. Heather looked as if she was asleep. Her now pale cheeks devastatingly stroke a chord of death. Something bitter welled up in my heart.

Poignant tears poured down my face, and for the first time, I cried.

Change of Death

THE SIRENS RESONATED with the arrival of the police. The first and only one at the scene was Officer Dyer. Seeing him back then, I notice just how frail of a heart he possessed. A heart that was so sensitive and sympathetic that it thwarted his intentions of hiding his intense feelings. Today's sadness was written all over his face caused by a death of a stranger. By the time we disembarked, I salvaged my composure, but only on the outside. Within, my serenity has shrunk to an unnoticeable size.

"I realize that this is not a good time to go to the station, so if you want we could postpone the discussion until later, or we could settle it here in the car since I have all the necessary paperwork." Dyer attempted to be understanding as this death seemed to touch his heart as well.

"Let's get it over with." I said, unable to get rid of the feeling of sadness. We entered the vehicle, and Dyer drove away from the scene of the crime. I watched as the members of the clinic went in. We drove into a parking lot a little ways from Heather's former apartment. Dyer parked facing away from the scene. He opened his notebook and asked a serious of question before posing a basic inquiry which made me stunned.

"Was there anything suspicious or important at the scene of the crime?"

I gave Heather's final memo to Dyer who read it to himself before stuffing it into his bag to take for evidence. After taking a pair of final notes, he declared. "That letter, it's beautiful. I could learn a thing or two from it. People say that I'm a coward when it comes to dangerous cases, and surely there is some truth to it. It's just that I have never encountered any barbaric cases like those of recent times. I act more like a civilian than a policeman. Because of that, I can't look at all those horrific things calmly and with a cold-heart like those detectives. The first think that comes to mind when I look at something like that is 'What kind of a man would do something like that?' I feel nauseous, and my head spins. I lived in this town for years, and that's why I'm regularly fighting to be a better police officers. However, many times I leave the crime scene because deep down I'm scared. I'm scared that once I'll be able to look at brutal crime without any emotions, I'll be closer to becoming like the wrongdoers. In the future, I plan to overcome any cowardice inside, but not by becoming accustomed to brutality, but by risking my life for my precious town." Dyer made a long clarification that was possibly sparked by the letter and the recent death. The notion of fighting one's weakness reached deep down into his heart.

Before leaving, I asked a question myself. "Did you know Heather?"

"Not really. Although, a long ago I was the one who supervised the case when her parent and sister died. Back then, there were four policeman her in this town, but you know how youngsters are. They wanted to make it in the big world, so they moved to a big city. I was the oldest, so I stayed. Heather's case was just a one big accident."

"Once you're done. Could I get that letter back?"

"Yes, I'll make sure to get it to you."

With a farewell, the talk came to an end, and I was set to go home. Once there, I found my phone on the counter. I must've truly left it there. Without a moment of refuge, the phone clanged reminding me of the time when Heather was the only one to call me. Despite my dislike of the usual small talk—without even knowing it myself—I came to accept Heather into my nonexistent circle of companion. She was my only connection to a normal life, and now she was gone. The phone cease ringing, but only for an instant as someone persisted with the sound assault. The small screen indicated a random number. Flipping the cell open, I answered.

"We have to talk." Magnus declared in a serious voice.

"Now? Now is not a good time." I explained without waiting for his response in a downcast voice.

"Let's just say that it's something pertaining to a life-or-death situation." he said, trying to attract my curiosity and force me to come.

"Where?"

With that my evening was consumed in a spiral of violence.

◆

Although I didn't want to see Magnus, I decided that it would be best to concentrate on something else until the sour taste in my mouth vanished. The meeting location was a roof top. I jumped on my bike. Just as described by Magnus, the catwalk was fully open and functional which allowed me entrance onto the roof from a passage behind a building I wasn't familiar with.

The panorama of the street was clearly visible. Opposite the rooftop, where I was station, was a small two-story motel with only a single floor open. I was most likely because the number of visitor was not only low to begin with but dipped down even more lately. The fragmented drizzle that suddenly appeared made using an umbrella almost compulsory. Fortunately, the roof had a partially protection from rail. Down below, an argument was taking place right inside the main lobby. A man was waving his hands anxiously, trying to vent off. He was fighting his urge for violence. Walking outside, his face was concealed by a black sunshade. Before he could take a step, multiple silent blows were stroke to his chest.

The scene ended when Leon run out of the lobby to see his dying companion. Unaware of the location from which the blow came from, I run down the catwalk after making sure that no one saw me. The taste of hate for Magnus was stronger than ever. My phone rang once more with a message, and a new set of meeting coordinates of the abandoned house where our first meeting took place.

◆

I entered the house in a hurry. I couldn't tolerate the ordeal that I have just been put through. In a straight up fight, I had no chance of winning, but there is something that was my forte in difficult situation—concealing my true emotions and having a mask for every occasion. More and more, I begin to wonder what will come in the near future. At this moment, I swallowed my anger and walked upstairs only to wait for the right moment to strike. At the tip of the staircase, I was greeted by Magnus.

"Sorry about the regrettable change of plans."

"Change of plans? Is that what it was?" I noticed that Magnus wasn't his usual self. He was serious, filled with lifelessness. His body, like a cadaver, leaned against the frame of the second-floor window.

"My absence on the rooftop and that kill were spontaneous, but it all happened in an instance. It was a necessity. Before we continue, let me listen to this." Magnus turned the dial on the radio catching the signal of the bug—Leon's crew were unnerved in the deepest meaning of the word. Despite only having the audio, I could judge with sureness that the situation was bleak and deadly on the other side.

The doors slammed open, almost sounding like someone kicked them full force to break in. Leon shouted. "Boss! Millen is dead. He's dead!"

"Do something with those hands, or you're going to dirty the entire floor." The boss retorted. Leon's hands were covered in blood as if he drank from a blood-spattered stream. Small almost muffled drops were heard in the background.

"Here!"

Leon thanked Jude for the towel and began cleaning the stains that were destined to come off from his physical self, but the mental side would be forever scared by one more death. A stranger's death is very much different from a comrade's death. Lean has just learned that lesson.

"The motel where he stayed—" Leon scowled. "Someone shot him twice in the chest. I was right there, but there was no helping him."

The boss was consumed by a feeling of losing, but not a loss of a person—a loss of a game.

"Boss, if you don't mind me asking," Jude broke in. "When we came here, there were twelve of us, excluding you. Right now, we are down to five. I believe that if we want to live, we should ditch this place at once."

"I second that vote. This cursed place will consume us in a bloody massacre before we can do anything." An unknown voice of a simple thug ascended with a brave argument.

"We're not going anywhere. We have to win, don't you get it?" The boss roared. "Either we stick with the game and win, or we're dead!" His demented voice filled the room. No one said a word as fear dripped down their throats. Despite having the strength of number in a majority vote, for some reason, no one made any more remarks. Not a word of objection traveled through the air occupying the room.

"I'll speak for the rest of us." Leon said. "We respect

you as a boss, Earl. After all, we have known each other for 17 years, but this place is like no other. We have families. Our lives are not about winning or losing, but staying alive to see the beautiful things in this putrid world."

The other members in the room tuned in, agreeing with Leon's words.

"So you're just going to bail out? Leave everything behind and run?" The boss tossed something against the wall. "What about the members that were killed here? Don't you think that we need to honor their death by killing their murderer?"

"I can't speak with certainty, but I think that if they would be able to pitch in here and know, they would have told us to go home." Dorian stated, leaning against the wall and loading his gun.

"That's right, boss. Sometimes we just need to back off for a second and value life." Another member said. The tension rose, and it felt like any second now someone would grip their loaded gun. The boss had no chance in a violent act. He would surely be dead before he could kill two of his subordinates, let alone four.

"I'm sorry. Anger got the best of me." He took a seat. "I don't know what I was thinking, rattling on about winning. I just believe that honor and respect are the most important things in life. It's not just about killing, but more so about finding where he buried them, so that we could take them home. I think you all agree that having a proper burial is a must for our comrades." Everybody agreed, yet Jude was filled with indecision. "We already have a sketch of what the culprit looks like. I believe we can succeed. We should never walk alone just as I previously said. I have also picked a place for our new hideout."

The bosses sudden change of heart was not an unconscious shift do to emotions, rather it was a deliberate change out of necessity. It seemed as if the morals of the entire crew were breaking down. He knew that he can't keep them by force, so he aimed at their sense of comradeship. Every member knew each other well which gave of a feeling of brotherhood. Their greatest strength turned out to be their downfall as the lunatic boss consumed by his ego led them toward death. "Oh, yea, Dorian. Remember that you spoke about a man who defended Kazuki, find him too. For all we know, he might be the killer."

Magnus turned off the radio. "I have been picking them off since they arrived the day after the third death took place. At first, it was easy, but now it's getting harder and harder. That time when I fought that woman, I think one of those members took a good look at my face. As the boss said, they have my portrait now."

"Is that way you rushed for the kill when I was on the roof, to weaken their numbers?"

"I was planning to take him into my car and bury him like all the others, but someone would have seen me, so I had to drive away. Anyway, I have a request. I want you to confront them and find out if the picture matches me. They might knock on my door any second." Magnus spoke in a dismal voice, very unusual for him.

The request astonished me. At first, I would have turn down the offer instantly, but on seconds thought I decided otherwise. Sure there is a chance I might confirm that none of the gangsters are the culprit, but at the same time, I might find out some valuable info on the case as well as Historia. This is an opportunity, but the risk is far too great for the reward. On the other hand, I am in the same situation as Magnus. What's more, the crew is near desperation which can put me in real danger. Still, I retained my reserved self. "If you think I'll comply, you're crazy."

"I do because you're the target as well."

"It's not like they'll set me free if I confront them. It's practically suicide."

"With the power in hand, you'll figure something out."

"As you said earlier, we only do something in exchange for a favor."

"Name your price."

I had no answer for his question as there was nothing he could provide that would ensure my future survival. Still, I recalled that Chris told me about the clinic. The thought raced in my mind. I contemplated what I would do if I were to confront someone like myself. I speculated if poison would work. I speculated if it would be possible to put someone like that to sleep. "You have easy access to the clinic, right? I'll need a couple of items." I took a pen and wrote down the necessary items.

Magnus smiled in a disgusting way. His white teeth inscribed a hint of amusement into his soul. "Chris told you about that, right? I figure that might happen. Anyway, I'll get them by tomorrow. I just want you to understand that I'm not doing this for Chris. For all I care, he could disappear. I'm a completely sovereign entity. Surely, Chris would have wanted me to bring justice to those that hurt him, but I did nothing like that. They're still wandering the street."

"I have to meet your second half tomorrow. Virgil invited me to that game. Let's meet right after it's done. I already have the address of their hideout, so I'll be there."

"Fine. I'll be stationed around the phone booth just like always, so come there once you're finished with your task."

"No, I'll go there first to check if you've done your assignment."

The day came to a close. The night developed into a good sleep opportunity. Shocked by the recent turn of events and disappointed by not being able to decipher the poem, the meeting with Magnus allowed me some free time from my mind wandering.

Walking down the street, I watched a cruel prospect. An overly large man, dressed in overalls, dragged a youthful woman by her black hair outside and threw her at the trash cans. By the time I was close to his home, he commenced his assault. He violently stumped her abdomen with his shoes. Again and again, the girl squealed and yelped out of pain. He began yelling about her worthlessness.

The event didn't pick at any of my emotion until I got closer in and saw the girl's sad expression. The letter from Heather sparked in my heard as every word was recapped in my head. All those thoughts bunched up to shut down my typical self.

My hearing couldn't interpret her cries, the man's nonsense even more so. The light from the windows and the wide open doors didn't illuminate me or the violent scene. My eyes closed, all that was left was peace on my mental monitor. There was a man eating inside, his back turned to the scene as if he knew what was happening, but he didn't want to watch it. Clenching my fist as if gathering all my strength to fight, I aimed at the man's skull. Unaware, the man was an easy target as I dashed ahead landing a punch. Echoes filled the space as my knuckled crushed his skull. His balance broken, his massive body fell to the ground. Before he had the chance for a counter attack, I stretched out my hand to the girl. Helping her up, I dragged her off.

The Killer's Voice

———

THE SLIGHTLY COLD air brushed around me. The enormous male tried to give chase, but his endurance was particularly low, so he soon gave up. The night turned life into nonexistence as all my senses were put to sleep. The girl wrestled against my grip on her hand as if trying to escape back to her captor. Letting her free, I ended up right in front of the gates to the church where the light bulb was extinguished and vision wasn't particularly good.

"What do to think you're doing?" The girl attempted to put up a fight and argue, but catching a breath took priority, so her voice was solemn and calm at the same time.

"Saving a damsel in distress would probably work if you're looking for a description but—" The girl interrupted me before I could finish.

"What do you think I should do now? That's my home. I have nowhere else to go!"

"Here. I tossed her my pair of keys to the apartment, knowing that I have an extra somewhere home. "You can stay there. Those are the keys to my apartment. It's pretty vacant, but I'll be there for some more time. So until I leave, you can use it."

"I don't know what you're pulling, but this isn't funny!" She was grasping her ribs. "What are you one of the good guys?"

"My first time trying to do good, and I stumble upon the most unthankful person whose not familiar with my detestable past."

An awkward silence hummed as the girl stared at the keys in hand. She grappled against her inner demons and tendencies. "Thanks. I'm used to getting beat up, but today was something else." The girl changed perspectives as the pain was finally getting to her and the bruises surfaced. I had no idea what to talk about, and neither did she. The night ended as she agreed to use my home for only a lone night.

Unexpectedly, Heather influenced me with her character and her beliefs. What started as a chore, turned into a mission of some kind. From the beginning, I was searching for reasons as to why I would torture myself staying in this town and hunting for what might be a ghost. The most basic of motives, and one that has kept me going this far, was my hunger for knowledge for why I was stuck with this power. The sole belief that at the end of the road is a messiah who'll rip down all the curtains to divulge the truth is what fueled me, but tonight, I found another reason, a reason with a force to keep me going and never look back. It was composed of pure yearning to stop this mad man and put an end to the decay of the town. Heather hoped that I would promise her that I won't be looking for revenge, and I can say with certainty that I'm not. Her death surely touched my heart, but if there is a motivation behind why I claim the culprit has to die, it is to heal this village.

The smell of flowers from last time sent me into the lair of dreams. I avoided the indistinguishable hallways, where I could get lost for all eternity, and faced the teacher. The anonymous man had almost no emotions today. He was lost deep in thought as if something was irking him. He looked like he felt an obligation to do something, but it was too late. The burning fire of regret sparked within the empty cast.

"Last time when you told me about the forces, I forgot to ask something. Could it be that the blue hallucinations have something to do with repaying death? I mean there is a meaning behind them, right?" I inquired thinking that most of the time when I was severely injured I was forced to watch the azure scenes.

"The indigo hallucination, huh?" He closed his book. "Most people who I've known believed that they are one of three things. Some consider it our thoughts hidden deep within. Ones that we don't want to disclose. Others thought that they are just mirages based on our past. Then there were those who thought this phantasm is a premonition of what's to come."

"Which one do you believe in?"

"Does it matter?" He stood up peacefully from the

chair and waved me goodbye. "You have to find the answer for yourself." His uncomfortable stance made me think that I'll be forced to watch these barbaric visions every time I use the power. I considered them a currency to pay off my debt.

◆

The following sunrise, the girl was gone. The extra keys I gave her was on the kitchen table. The couch where she slept looked exactly like before her visit. She left a note to thank me. Apparently, her name was Shannon. Today, I slept until early afternoon which was quiet refreshing, considering my recent sleeping habits. Eating an overdue breakfast, I faced the soar reality that I didn't decipher the poem. On and off I kept looking at it, but no matter what, I couldn't hit upon the hidden meaning which I hoped was there. Taking a one final look at it, the words jumped out at me. Crossing out the definite articles and aligning the words into a column, I was left reading the initial letters down.

Light red carnation.

A name that meant completely nothing in the face of recent events—except it stood for the flower that Historia pestered me with—evoked a memory in the dream world when the mysterious man told me the flower's sole location within the village confines. It grew in the backyard of the church. Fervent about the find, I rushed for the church. I was convinced that the suicides had something to do with the dream world and the power.

In no time, I watched from outside the gate to the church. The metal gate was locked, preventing me a typical entrance. I jumped over the rocky hedge. Rushing to the back, the row of graves led me into the very back of the cemetery. The church lingered above, picking at the clouds with its daunting tower. Its gothic flavor beating strong. Being led by possibilities, I found a tiny garden of flowers. However, I saw nothing out of the ordinary before I decided to blindly put my hand into the flowers. I searched around, but the only thing I felt was the soil pulsing with the life of the reaper. In the very back was a phone.

It was one of those gray flip phones. One owned by a careless possessor, or maybe the scratches and marks just accumulated overtime from many unfortunate events. One of the hinges holding the screen and keypad together was broken. Upon opening it, I could hardly read the screen as it was cracked—not working—but the phone was running. I selected the phone book and called the first number. The beeping made me wait uncomfortably for someone to pick up. I doubted that my journey would end here as finding the culprit wouldn't be this easy, yet at the same time, I was eager to collect my reward. The beeping seized as someone answered. There was no response welcoming me, but I was sure that someone was listening.

"Do you know about the exchange of death?" I inquired, thinking that it would yield a curious response.

"Finally a winner. So you must have met that man, huh?" A bland voice sounded through the microphone. It was one of those computer generated voices that sounded like an AI. The person took percussions not to be recognized.

"Unfortunately."

"You must have a lot of questions?"

"You have no idea."

"It's not every day one meets a brother, so it's only natural I should welcome you to my brotherhood. Are you familiar with Ox Drive?"

"Yea."

"Be there on the roof at 11:30 AM today. Based on your reaction, I'll judge if you're worthy."

Considering that I might not make it there because of my other plans, I took the phone with me. Unable to find a suitable response, I wondered how to react.

Going to meet the mob is probably perilous, so I decide to consider how I would react to certain scenarios. The one that irks me the most is if they suspect me of being the suicide mastermind. I wondered if Judith told them anything about me. I thought that it would be best to have a diversion in order to escape in case they suspect me or something goes wrong. The only one I could depend on was Officer Dyer. I still had his phone number from when I spoke with him the other day. I'll have to send him a message, or someone has to do it in my place.

By the time I made it home, I was just equipping myself to head out. Thinking if I should waste time with Chris, I considered that solving the dilemma with the mob is of utmost importance to my survival, and because of the unstable nature of Magnus, I should probably check up on his alter ego. I grabbed an illustration of Historia that I drew in advance to inquire to the gang about her. I packed up and opened the door to meet Shannon. She said that she had to go home to pick up some of her things. I confirmed that she can stay as the TV sounded in the background.

It was one of those talk shows. Today, they were interviewing the spokesman, Maximilian Waye.

"So I realize the tough situation in your hometown. I also heard that your influence is increasing." The reported stated trying to begin a discussion. The show only just started.

"Yes, you can say it that way. Our society now consists of 713 members, but my power isn't the one that is increasing. The authority of the people is increasing with each member." Waye leaned back into his arm chair.

"How so? I heard that member have very little rights. They're locked up inside the keep. They're literally prisoners"

"You see, you're telling me that they're prisoners, but so are you. We are all prisoners of our emotions. In this case, the emotion is fear—true fear. Staying in the keep is a way of freeing yourself from the prison of that emotion." The spokesman looked relaxed. "Members have a big say in all of our decisions. They take an active role in all our politics. Alone, they're week, but united under one banner, they can take back the city and return it to how it was."

Shannon listened to the conference as her fists trembled. An emotion brought up by the things on screen. She voiced her opinion with her back still to me. "You know, I think what you did back there, gave me a chance to live a life. It gave me a chance to confront someone."

"I was wondering if you'd be interested in a deal."

"What are you talking about?" She looked over her shoulder, letting go of her troubled thoughts.

"Let's just say that I have a mission to complete in this town. I might need some minor help. Would you be interested in being my guardian angel?"

"What makes you think I'll help you? Nothing is free in this world."

"That might be true. Judging from your reaction, the broadcast made you relive some terrible thought. Your fists clenched in anger, they trembled out of despair and hatred every time the spokesman said something. Your quarrel is with him, I'll be dealing with the Unity in the very near future, so I'll be sure to take you along if that means anything."

The girl disliked my response. She didn't want me to know anything about her, but the behavior made her a wide open book with easily read chapters of her most hated events. "I could just go there right now if I wanted to."

"I doubt that the spokesman would see you, especially if he knows who you are."

"What do you want in return?"

"A couple of minor tasks until the confrontation. There is a number on the sofa. I'll be busy between 10PM and 11PM. If you don't hear from me, call that number and ask Officer Dyer to visit the place below it." I stated after writing all the necessary info on a piece of paper. Shannon halfheartedly agreed to my proposal. Considering other scenarios that might happen in the near future, I noted down secondary directions that included Aidan's coordinates and a numbered checklist of tasks. I slipped it under the TV.

◆

The second floor of Chris's home had lights on just like last time. I began climbing the stairs before I was interrupted by the presence of blood on the railing. It was a minor amount, so it would be practically invisible for a standard human being but once noticed it seemed very much out of the ordinary. The doors were unlocked by Virgil since he was probably awaiting my arrival. "Good evening, it's great that you're here. Although, we started a little earlier, but that's no big deal."

With a simple greeting, I walked inside. It was my second time here, but on my initial visit I wasn't inside. The spacious living room gave me a feeling that the place is alive because of their extremely large TV, the slightly bluish couch right in front of it, as well as a ton of pictures dwelling on the walls. The place had no sound-proofing since I could hear every word coming from upstairs. Bridget and Chris had a fight.

"You can never do anything right! You mess up even the most simple of tasks!" Bridget assailed Chris in a bias tone.

"Are you any better? Guess what Miss Perfect; you don't mess up because you don't even move your little finger! Everybody else runs around to serve you since you're depressed!" In spite of his calm behavior, Chris was fed up with the infuriating comments and rebutted.

"I apologize for their behavior. Could you wait a second? I'll work this out." Virgil looked at me disappointed about my first impression. He went ahead leaving me stranded in the enormous living room.

Bored, I begun walking around and taking a peek at all the various pictures. Multiple of them showed Bridget and Chris embracing and hugging. Who would have thought that such love existed between them? The primary feeling that I got when I originally met Chris was a feeling of loneliness and being lost somewhere in the darkness. Despite having a beautiful girlfriend, there wasn't even a spark of love within him at the moment. If I didn't know to begin with, I would have guessed that Bridget is Virgil's loved one. Whenever she glances at Chris, she has a look of disdain.

"I'm sorry. I think it would be best to suspend your visit as they have no intention of stopping their quarrel." Virgil had trouble hiding his grin that sparked from out of nowhere. To him, tragedy was comedy.

"Shut up, shut up!" Chris screamed annoyed at Bridget's continues accusations.

The whole thing seemed to gain momentum.

Blood of TriumPh

THE MOB'S QUARTERS were a not-so-elegant motel on one of the side streets. A couple minutes ago, I had a talk with Magnus who showed me that he gathered all the things I asked for. He had not a care in the world for what happened to Chris. He seemed to be excited at the idea of making a move on the boss. I told him that I might have to disclose some info about him if my life is on the line, so he should be prepared to adjust for what's to come.

"Chris is so pathetic." Magnus commented.

"I wonder what will happen if he ceases to exist. How will you hold up?" The question sent Magnus down the step, plummeting into nothingness as he had a change of heart. It wasn't the time, nor the place for sentiments, yet my question stuck him like a spear.

Standing outside, I finished typing the message to Office Dyer in case Shannon won't do her job properly. I whispered into thin air believing that Heather was listening. "I know that I promised to strive to save the ones I can. I will follow morality. I promised you that I will do what I reckon right, but I also want you to know that from now on there might be a struggle in which I'll have to use force. I can't promise I won't dissatisfy you. Although I felt a little lost after your untimely death, I think that I straightened out my priorities. I decided that I'll fight until the end to finish and dissolve the darkness that surrounds this town. I am not doing it because I need to do it, but because I think it's righteous to bring the one responsible to justice."

I made a step forward.

I knocked on the heavy metal door of the old-fashion motel. It was almost midnight, so human presence was absent. The door handle chose not to cooperate as I tried opening the door. In the right corner, there was a secretly placed camera. It must have caught a glimpse of me when I stared into it. The darkness persisted, yet the doors unlocked as I heard a snap coming from the other side. The doors release by themselves, inviting me inside. The room had no light as if it was blinding which was terrifyingly unpleasant. I carefully stepped inside. The lights glimmered insecurely until they had enough power to turn on.

It was a reception room, the lobby of the motel. The multiple dirty and diminutive black rags which were on the floor added the feeling of obscurity to the place. The reception desk which reached above my waist had one of those golden bells used to call for assistance. The back door was opened, but only slightly, shedding light on the pile of magazines inside. On the left was a staircase, leading the guests to the dirtiest of rooms. Behind me, a slam awoke me from the land of thinking.

Leon locked the door, asking. "What do you want?" He was holding a gun unsteadily.

"Dorian said I could come if I needed assistance."

"Did he? You're that guy who prevented Kazuki from his masochistic games." Leon had a wicked smirk as he brushed his eyes with a handkerchief. He slipped out some eye drops out of his pocket. A drop or two, and his itchiness was gone.

"Give the man a break. If the assault persisted, Kazuki might have sustained wounds that would take weeks to heal thus impeding our progress." Dorian stood atop the staircase, leaning over the balustrade as if tempting death to come and get him. He had all the enthusiasm just like last time, but it was lightly washed out like he was lacking a vital source of energy. "I'll let the boss know that you're here, but you might be forced to wait for some time."

"No rush." I said.

Leon gave up on his offensive attitude and walked upstairs with Dorian. I was left to my lonely self without knowing what they might be planning. I took a seat opposite the clock that hung over the entrance as I prepared mentally for what's to come. How will they react?

"What's it like, knowing that the evil that scurries in this village right now was born from the same place as you?" Jude had a serious tone in his voice. His peaceful step made me oblivious to his presence until he reached the entrance where he relaxed on a chair next to me. It was a maneuver to keep an eye on me, but his attempt at sparking a conversation was sincere.

"I wouldn't know. I moved to this town because it was peaceful, but now it's … mad."

"And it's about to get worse." He took out a pack of smokes and scavenged for a lighter. "I have a daughter. Smoking is forbidden at home, so the only thing good about these trips is this." His stretched out the pack, inviting me to take one.

"I don't smoke." I waved my hand. "I could never understand family. To some it is a gift and to some a curse."

Jude chuckled. "You don't even know how often I heard people say that. Yet many of my now diseased comrades had families that they deeply cared about. I don't know if you realize this, but there are very few people who can be classified as purely white or purely black." He took a look at the clock as the tiny hand was moving toward 11 PM. "People think that one deed defines us, but it's a set of deeds that defines us."

"Moral of the story?"

"Is the supposed culprit behind the suicides really evil?" Jude finished his smoke. "I don't have an answer. I'm just speculating out of boredom."

There was an uproar going on upstairs. Presumably the boss was upset that Dorian gave me the location of their hideout. He was suspicious of just about anyone, but that was to my advantage. In normal circumstances the boss would never choose to talk to me, but now his curiosity was attacked, and he wants to know what I'm here for.

Jude strolled upstairs. Leon gestured with his hand. "Come on."

I was led into a larger room where the boss sat eating dinner. He had a napkin tacked around his neck, as well as utensils in both hands. He was an old man, around the age of 75 or even 80. He had a long beard and lengthy hair. The color has long fled from his body as his pale skin gave of a feeling of weakness. The man was of mixed origin. He had a tinge of Asian mixed with Caucasian ancestry. He gave me an ominous stare and ordered me to take a seat. My first impression was shuddered and swapped with that from the radio. Regardless of his age, the man had strength of huge magnitude.

"What is it that brings a visitor to our place at this late of an hour?" He wiped the sauce dripping from his chin.

"I was searching for someone. The police are helpless, so I was hoping you might be able to help."

"A gentleman introduces himself promptly."

"I apologize. My name is Sebastian Snow." I detested the idea of being pushed around, and that's just what this old man was doing. I swallowed my pride and played the game.

"First of all, I would like to thank you for aiding Kazuki. My old friend has emotional problems. In simple terms, the being that he hates the most is himself."

I remained quiet as I was unsure if I could speak.

"I once had a friend who was a martial artist. One day, he was asked a favor. Unfortunately, he condemned the idea which led to the kidnapping of his wife and son. Nowadays, he wanders around serving his new master in hopes that he will be able to buy back the life of his family." He took a big piece of fish and swallowed it whole. "You see, he is a fool since he never once thought that his master might be merciful. His wife and son are not in captivity. They live freely far away. He is a fool because he stares at only one side of a person. My friend has only one person he hates more than he does me … himself."

"You like that story, don't you?" Jude interrupted.

"It speaks of human nature in more than one way. So, young lad, what is it that you are willing to sacrifice in order to achieve a misunderstood goal?"

I was puzzled, my heart anxious to beat harder and harder. "There was a woman who spontaneously arrived to return something that I lost. Three days later, she was nowhere to be found. This is a picture of her." I pressed the sketch of my creation against the table top, tempting the boss to take a look. His fragile hands reached for the photo, and he firmly grasped it. He seemed to know something since he stared at the picture for quite some time, but he wasn't merely observing, he was analyzing something in his head while his eyes run around the picture. In essence he was blindly staring while he was in the land of philosophy.

He took the napkin from the table with the inscribed name Earl Winters. Putting it lightly to his mouth, he cleared his throat before voicing his opinion. His high and mighty spirit dwelled in a brittle human body. He was callously coughing. Age has taken its toll, and the man could only pretend that he was well. His hands shivered, but was it from being tired or something much more wicked? He took a lighter and burned the image at which point he uttered. "Do you know why this town is fixated on every aspect of art? Because the creator of this place believed that the creative side is the one to use when speaking with the heavens. Even the erratic, tall contraptions around the village are a proof since architecture is an art as well." The boss commented, staring at my art work. "Anyway, Leon, you remember that girl you met in front of the tattoo shop, do you?" An affirmative response came from the other room. "Care to tell your take on her story?"

Leon brushed against the wall, his drowsy eyes told me that he wasn't sleeping for what could be days. "I stumbled upon a girl in a back alley. Her name was Historia. Supposedly, she was a reporter for a supernatural magazine, but you already know all that, right?"

"The gist of it."

"Taking into consideration her youthful nature, I pestered her a bit. Someone called her, and I heard that she had something to do with the police. Before I could interrogate her, she dashed into one of the side alleys. That's where things turned uncertain."

His take on the story differed somewhat from what I have witnessed when I was there. He omitted the presence of Judith as well the extent of his abuse of Historia. Regardless, I listened patiently.

"We run into the side allay, but it was a dead-end. The two doors that were there were locked completely from the inside. At the end of the side road ..." Leon paused. He didn't want to talk about the ending. He was playing a simulation of what the boss might say and then formulated a proper response. His hand wandered searching for a piece of gum in his trousers. Once found, he slipped a bit into his mouth. It was a stress coping mechanism which helped his body absorb the negative energy. "She wasn't there, she was gone."

"What do you mean?" I played the role of an amazed actor.

"She vanished. Not a trace left." He looked away.

"Jude and Dorian were there too?" the boss questioned, "I'd like to hear their interpretation of the story later." The boss gave of a sneaky gesture with his head. "Get the rest of the team. I'd like them to be here when we discuss the rest."

"Would you like Nathaniel to come too? He is just the driver?" Leon asked posing the name of another member. The boss waved in acceptance.

Although they were a family of some kind, the team looked as if it was in a state of war. Day by day they cooperated and worked together because it was the most beneficial thing to do, but underneath all that was masked a layer of suspicion—distrust of each other. They didn't know if they could trust each other, considering all the different points of view. The rebellious nature of the boss's subordinates spoke, but too softly. The boss was still the puppeteer holding all the wires and playing on the instruments that were his former colleagues.

Jude, Dorian, Leon and Nathaniel glided into the room. Their usual nature was clouded by a profound lack of sleep. Gone was the joking and idle chatter which was now replaced by the looks of men who might not think rationally anymore.

The boss showed a sketch of what looked like Magnus. It wasn't just similar. It was almost identical to the real person. Someone must have been a good artist to replicate a face he has seen only once and for such a brief time. Still, the most peculiar thing was the boss's self-confident attempt at changing the subject. "This man is presumable the one behind the killings of numerous of my teammates. Thanks to Dorian, who escaped him once, we have a sketch. Does he look familiar?"

The boss's keen eyes took aim at me. He analyzed my every emotion and reaction to questioning. I was adapt at concealing emotions and even lies, yet I wasn't so sure I could get him to believe an idea I just came up with a minute ago. Without a choice, I opted for the truth while withholding any unnecessary info. "He's responsible for some unfortunate event that happened to me. So, I do recognize him."

"Do tell us what you know?"

"Not much. One night he decided to play a game. Death is his weapon of choice. Every time he wants to meet, he chooses this place as the location." I jotted down the address of the phone booth.

"So you work for him? Was that the reason you were there when Kazuki needed help?" Leon roared.

"No, I detest him. If you could kill him, it would be a gift. Besides, the day we met when Kazuki was getting beat and my acquaintanceship with that man are just coincidence."

"Really? Do you truly want us to believe that?" Nathaniel slammed his fist against the wall and voiced his concern which clouded his judgment further.

"Jude, you're good at detecting a liar. Tell us." Dorian gave Jude a push. Jude held my wrist to check my pulse. He asked a series of questions that were exact copies of the previous ones. My answers didn't change, but my anxiety shook a bit more with each additional inquiry. He pressed on, trying to divulge if I'm connected with Magnus in any way. Fear rose to new levels as I wasn't sure if I could control my symptoms. My proficiency at concealing stress was nothing in the face of real danger. Upon his satisfaction, he ceased the interrogation. "He is telling the truth that his visit here was not ordered by that man, but the history why he met him needs a bit more clarification."

"It seems like the one in the picture loves games." I turned to the boss. "There was a classmate he killed and locked me up in his home. I was forced to find the exit. Solve the puzzle." I explained, letting my fear run loose as a method of persuasion.

"That's probably the case Judith told us about." Dorian yawned.

"You know Judith?" I asked. "A diverse crew you've got. A detective as determined as her working with people such as yourself."

It seems they sensed a hint of irony in my comment as most of the crew expressed a mix frustration and amusement.

The boss remained quiet for a bit longer. "I think it's time for you to leave."

"Do you know anything about the recent suicides?" I threw an idea out, pretending to be ignorant.

"No." Everybody sang at the same time as if the response was predetermined.

"Just what kind of a despicable human would do something so horrible?" I tried loosening their tongues and sparking a final bit of conversation. I realized that my time will be up. I only had 13 minutes left.

The boss loosened his tie. He rose from his chair and stepped closer. His posture contradicted his grand persona. "You want to know what I think? To do something like this, the mastermind would need to be part of something bigger. A lone wolf isn't capable of doing something on this grand of a scale because you need resources." The boss shed some light on his own point of view.

"Could he be one of your subordinates?" Fear was stuck into the hearts of the entire crew.

"I would have never suspected any of them. I use to trust my team, but I think it's safe to do some asking. We have arrived here on the fourth day. Three suicides took place before we arrived. Where were you four when this happened?" The boss demanded.

"Boss, are you seriously going to let this dimwit break our reliance on each other?" Leon jumped the wagon, and so did Nathaniel asking a repeat of the question.

Oblivious to their objections, the boss persisted with the request. Nathaniel scratched his nose, opened a can of beer, and told his concrete alibi that he was always with the boss—a full-time driver.

When Dorian's turn came up, he seemed ashamed and didn't want to disclose anything. He looked down on the ground as if the light coming from the lamp was blinding him. With no eye contact, he spoke. "I arrived on the plane just before our meeting took place, prior to our arrival here." The boss insisted on the whole truth, leaving Dorian no choice. "I spend the week enjoying beer with a girl I met." His voice was a blend of angry and shameful.

"I was home in Florida. Nothing to it." Leon spoke.

Jude sneaked down the stairs and out of the motel. Filled with surprise, the discussion was over, and I was pretty sure that none of them were the culprit. Of course, they could be lying, but I believed that the one behind this had beliefs like no other. He lived a life unknown to most human beings. He hated being under the wing of someone else. He was an independent thinker. None of the men in this room had an aura like that. My intuition was telling me this.

I was showed downstairs. The boss remained on the second floor, overlooking my leave. I was to be escorted by Leon and Dorian. The boss murmured something to them. It was 10:50. I was just about to leave when a loud knock on the door condensed into the room. Dorian looked astounded through the TV screen as he saw Officer Dyer. The boss instructed everyone to hide. Dorian opened the door and attempted a friendly act.

"I'm sorry to disturb you." Dyer started.

"Is there anything I can help you with, officer?"

"A call came in that someone was in danger. That's why I'm here."

"What's that?" Dorian faked a surprised look. "Not sure why. Everybody is asleep here. Peace and quiet all around."

"I'm sorry. It must have been a mistake." The door closed as Dyer turned his back to the building. The primary thought in his mind seemed to be to follow procedures. The thought of leaving the place at this instant pulsed strongly within his mind, but I think he was reminded of his conviction—he won't ever fear and be a coward. He reluctantly turned to knock again as if he overcame his fear. He would not belittle a call for help. He would always persist until he shed the blinds of lies and uncovered the truth. This time, he grabbed the grip of his gun, putting it at eye level, pressed the handle and walked right in to see the entire crew with me in the middle.

"All of you, hands high in the air." He spoke assertively.

Hidden behind the door, Nathaniel handled a crowbar over his head and slammed Officer Dyes on the elbow. As Dyer fell to the floor, he twisted backwards and shot Nathaniel countless times in the chest. Blood covered Nathaniel's white shirt as he fell with his eyes wide open onto the floor. He was soon drowning in a pool of blood. Quickly rising up, Dyer turned to face Dorian and Leon who raised their hands, unwilling to fight. The boss in his blind spot fired two shots one in the heart and another in the head. He was a true marksman, a professional killer. Dyer almost inertly backed up and banged against the wall. Falling into a sitting position, he could barely keep his head up. Dying, his hand opened up to reveal the note form Heather. Specks of blood showed on his blue uniform as the space was overtake by evil. He smiled honestly with triumph over fear before his head fell down—dead. The boss eyed the scene coldly, holding the gun in his left hand. Knowing well that the crew was shaken, I dashed forward seizing the note. Jumping out of the front door, bullets destroyed the entrance.

The orders behind me boiled up.

"Dorian, chase after him! Kill him! As for you, find Jude. We can clean this up later. I'll call Kazuki right away." The boss yelled with all his might.

It began raining. I felt irritation around my neck. Touching the spot, I saw my bloodied hand, thinking that a bullet must have scraped me. The clear water from the sky bounced off of my face and soaked my clothes and hair. The slippery surface of the pavement was a metaphor for my current situation. Today died a great man who was willing to risk everything for this town. He was the brake that slowed this town from rolling down the edge and into madness and despair. The last safeguard from anarchy was broken today. Those who are in power will watch this city from their safe heave as the mindless people do their bidding. This town will surely fall.

Obliging Heart

DORIAN CHASED AFTER me. I was almost out of breath, but he had a lot of stamina to spare. My goal was the meeting place right next to the phone booth. I could already see it in the distance, illuminated by the rays coming from the streetlight nearby. Magnus was nowhere to be seen until I got closer. He was sitting on the hedge. His mellow appearance was most likely caused by the recent events with Bridget, but I was questioning that theory since he was never sentimental. Could my comment have injured him this much? Reaching my destination, I struggled to catch a breath. My speaking must have been difficult to comprehend. "Would you take care of him?"

Magnus had a revolver in hand, the same one he has carried all those recent days. To my bewilderment, he said, seeing Dorian, "Not my problem. Besides he's too weak. I was anticipating you could find someone strong maybe that would've helped with my mood."

"This is no time to be foolish." I persevered.

"I met him once already. If it wasn't for that detective, he would've been dead. I would try again today, but I'm not in the right frame of mind."

"I remember you. Wow," Dorian slowly closed in, "my drawing was seriously accurate." He added, watching Magnus who was preparing to leave. Dorian gestured triumphantly. He remained cool and reloaded his gun. "Just watch for a second. I think your friend might get what he wishes for."

Kazuki dashed from the shadows, his shoes splattering water all around because of his velocity and strength. His trench coat unbuttoned, followed him like a cape, resonating with the wind. He had a knife in each hand as he prepared to strike the ignorant Magnus. At the last second, Magnus tried pointing his gun at the newly found target, but all was hopeless. Kazuki too close and aimed for his gun-equipped arm. The knife tore through the flesh of Magnus's wrist as he fired the gun once before dropping it on the ground. One arm immobilized, Magnus found his knife with the other hand. Kazuki rushed toward him, evaded a strike to the side, and followed by tripping Magnus. As Magnus fell, he remembered his former fighting spirit, however it was already too late for victory. Magnus screamed when his other arm was impaled by Kazuki's knife. The deep emptiness of the night clouded the scene as if it was getting further and further away until it was imperceptible.

"I think it's about time to conclude our meeting as well." Dorian directed the gun at me.

At the very moment, I realized that I lacked fear of Dorian. No matter the weapon, I knew that he's the powerless one. I had the "power" in mind all this time, yet fighting multiple people at once was overwhelming for fear that they might restrain and capture me. However, here things felt different.

His honest intention of killing me was of no meaning what-so-ever. He lacked understanding of my abilities—this was my advantage. His gun was loaded in his right hand. I charged forward in a replicated blind rage, aiming to punch him with my right fist. A bullet escaped the chamber of his gun, tearing through my clenched fist in an awe of pain. I landed my knees in the stream. I was unable to move my hand. The bones were completely shattered. Seconds later, the pain ceased gradually which was my signal to attack. By now his grip on the gun was getting looser. The pain still hasn't kicked in within Dorian's hand. His smile spelled out just how ignorant he was of his situation—a fiendish type of magic was in the works. I dashed forward, gripping his gun. Just as I tried to wrestle it out of his grip, the pain finally reached his mind, and blood begun dripping out of his hand. He screamed, letting go of the gun. Standing up, I assaulted him in the face with the butt of the gun, forcing him to fall right into the watery streets.

His wide open eyes stared at me. He coughed out some of the water that he swallowed falling. "What are you?"

I emptied all the bullets into the sewage before firing the last one in the chamber as a warning. The bullet was carried by the stream into the sewers, never to be uncovered.

"Which is the boss's dominant hand?" I inquired.

"Shit!" Dorian shrieked, holding his immobile hand. "What did you do to me?"

I flicked my fingers and reiterated the question.

"I think it's his right." Dorian lied, protecting his boss. I was sure to observe when I was there that his left hand is the dominant one.

"You know, out of all his subordinates you're the most dedicated one, yet he doesn't even realize it. He treats you like a nobody, and here you are risking your life for him." I brushed my wet hair back in an attempt at keeping them away from my eyes. "You see, you could be someone else. You could truly grow if you were to think for yourself and make your own decisions. On the other hand, if you continue to aid your boss, you'll be a servant and not a human being for the rest of your life." I stabbed his deepest desire.

"What could you know about dedication, dimwit?"

"I know that it can be self-thought." I threw the gun somewhere out on the streets away from Dorian. "Well, you get another chance and do consider what I told you. And the idea if I'm really the one you're hunting for? If I was that person, would I really let you live?"

I followed in the direction where Magnus was last seen, anticipating the outcome of the battle. The street was completely empty, but there was a trail a blood leading down into a garbage disposal area. Before I could continue my pursuit, my phone chimed. It was a call from my apartment.

"Are you alright?" Shannon had a vexed tone, contrary to her usually harsh attitude.

"Yea, I'm fine, but you called ten minutes earlier than I was expecting"

"It was just that ..."

Tired from the night, my voice escalated into a full verbal assault as I criticize her incompetence. "A person just died, and all you have for an excuse is silence! Can't you see that it's because of your mistake?"

"When you told me about making that call, I realize that you gave me an opportunity at freedom. I didn't want to lose what was just given to me if you had died!" She sank into anger.

I didn't know what to think, but I noted that if I continued the attack, she might become a problem so I backed off. It was my fault as well.

"Calm down. I apologize, I shouldn't have said that. The one responsible for the death was the killer and not you."

"What's with the sudden change of heart?"

"You know what? Remember that you are the lord of your life and never let anyone tell you otherwise. Always decide for yourself what you want to do."

"Don't get ahead of yourself with all the preaching." She replied calmly as she figured out my stance. After hanging up, I walked ahead. Magnus was resting among garbage cans, surrounded by a pond of blood. His leather jacket was ripped in three places. As steams of blood dripped down, he was still half awake and looked at me as if he recognized me. His eyes were red from blood. His limbs were resting motionlessly.

"If you think I'll be begging for help, you don't know me." he uttered his last words.

"You don't even know how much it would make my

life easier if I could just leave you here. Unfortunately, I made a promise to someone. Although, some promises are meant to be ignored at times. This is such time." I returned to the street and took a big breath before realizing that he had not kept his end of the bargain; I never got the goods. I returned to the alley to find him almost sleeping. I grabbed his garments, coiled his arm around my neck, and dragged him with me while keeping him awake.

The road to the clinic was harsh as the raindrops increased in numbers and persisted for what seemed like forever. My choice to keep him alive was mostly due to Christopher's life. After all, their one and the same, but Chris didn't deserve to end up like this—I tried to think that way. The wind was blowing vigorously which made every step feel punishing. There was no one present to help me, but I was not going to give up.

"Hey, Magnus, would you tell me why you had that awful mood."

"I … I realized that I might not have a soul … I realized that once this town dies, I'll die with it. My existence is coming to an end." He spoke on the verge of mumbling through the pain of his wounds.

The lights of the clinic shined dazzlingly. With ever step, I felt like I was at the end of a successful trip through the abyss. The main doors had a movement sensor, so they slid open as I got near. Walking in, I screamed. "Someone help!"

The nurses and the only doctor rushed to help and took him away, screaming that the pulse is faint and that there is an enormous loss of blood. I took a seat in the waiting room, and I noticed that my clothes were completely soiled. The nurses spoke in the reception.

"Another one called. He need some antidepressants." One said in an indifferent voice.

"I know, the cases of depression are only increasing." The other replied in a sleazy tone.

On the other side of the room, I observed Fredric seated, waiting for something. He was reading the newspaper, but because of all the noise he must have noticed me. I was about to walk outside when the nurse announced that I'll need to wait for the police. Behind me, I heard Fredric intervene. Outside, my vision was blinded by another hallucination. The blue image was much more vivid than before. An old man, severely injuries, was on the ground of what seemed like an old motel.

"Don't worry about it. I'll take care of everything. They're both precious members of the Unity." Fredric followed me, waking me from my dream. "I have a change of clothes inside my car. They might be a little big, but that shouldn't be a problem, right?"

With a change of clothes, I disposed of my former style. The new suit was in fact one size too large, but it was comfortable nonetheless.

"Why help me and Chris?"

"Everybody has secrets. This is one of yours. I'm hoping that once my secrets and sins are discovered, someone will be just as kind."

◆

I struggled to walk home. I was not only depressed, but overwhelmed by the new events. The nature of my actions, as well as my new view seemed to oppose the problems at hand. Even so, I tried my best to live in my own way. I even forgot my meeting with the believed perpetrator until the phone clanged in an almost mono-tone sound I wasn't familiar with. I grabbed the ruined phone I acquired today.

"Took you long enough." The emotionless voice sounded thought the speaker.

"I had some unforeseen matters."

Without another sound, the phone was mute. Half-way home, I paced down the streets, looking around. The sole notion that the perpetrator was watching me reso-nated thought my head. I was so preoccupied by the recent matters I didn't even notice that I was strolling thought the exact street I was instructed to. Suddenly from one of the roof tops, a body fell down banging intensely on the pavement right in front of me, sending a vivid wakeup call though my whole body. The earthquake of death that was created by the suicide clouded my worries and emancipated my presence. Before I could check the pulse, another corpse viciously hit the ground behind me—two suicides impeding my progress home. As I looked at the second body, considering a double suicide, the first one stood up as if the person was all well. The shades hid his identity, but he looked at me with a sense of pleasure as if he was enjoying the occasional spectator. That was when our meeting took place.

Confession

————————

I COULDN'T SEE his eyes, but I was sure that they were staring into mine, evaluating my character. This profound moment lasted for mere seconds, but it felt like an eternity. The emptiness that enveloped the culprit gave me a peculiar feeling—a feeling of helplessness. At that fated moment, I wasn't quite sure if this was just a coincidence, or if he was patiently waiting for my arrival. We faced each other as equals before the culprit would commence his escape. His abrupt choice made me feel as if he knew that I would stand against him. I determined that this was my chance at finding answers, and I would never let this pass. Before I could utter a single word, the individual race down the street, and I followed.

By now the rain has cease, and even though it was nighttime, the sky lingered visible in a gloomy way. The water had nowhere to go, and so it formed deep puddle on the uneven pavement. The avenues were mostly quiet and drained of any populous who mostly hid in their homes or in the Unity's headquarter. The pools splashed each time one of us landed in them running down the street.

The lights of some of the households were lit which acted as lighthouses, guiding us during our isolated voyage. At moments, I would have to take a leap of faith as light was absent and I was required to depend on instinct to survive—to continue onwards. A dead-end sign ahead told the perpetrator that he had to change strategy. He vigorously added velocity to his already fast pace while turning right. Losing my stamina I fell back. Around the corner, somebody was packing to leave town. As the culprit passed, he tripped a kid who fell on the asphalt away from the sidewalk. Hearing the cries and becoming aware of the oncoming traffic, he exchanged priorities. He returned to help the kid, apologizing hastily. As he saw me make my way around the corner, he attempted at crossing the street, startled by my presence as if he was losing footing. When he was almost across, a car rapidly zoomed in and hit him with strength that pulled him across the hood and into the windshield. The glass shattered partially. Yells from the startled driver woke up the entire neighborhood. "Are you alright?"

The culprit ignored the howls, ran down the street, and turned the next corner. He was barely limping ahead.

I saw Detective Dench, with the corner of my eye, arrive at the scene, but I wasn't sure if he saw me. This mattered not as the culprit hurried underground down the manhole and into the sewers. Without a second thought, I pursued him through the opening.

The spiral set of vertical steps led me downwards deeper into the lair of the fiend. The corridors were very narrow, so much so that at points it felt as if they were getting more contracted with each step. Coming to an end, there was a balcony overlooking a replica of a waterfall of second-hand water. Right at the edge was the culprit leaning on the barrier, his back to me. His accident seemed to be giving him a terribly painful lesson as any action took a big toll on his already throbbing leg. Before he could turn around, I gripped my knife and run to him puncturing his back. As he tried wresting against my attack, I lost the knife in exchange for grabbing the gun behind his belt as he shoved me back. With all the extraneous motion, his notebook fell on the floor. I held the gun loaded, but before I could utter a word, my mind felt blurry. I lost my footing, hearing the man scream. "Let me explain!" I felt a sudden worry that he might escape, so before completely losing consciousness, I fired four shots only to see the man tripping over and falling into the water below. I threw the gun in that direction as well before turning my attention to the book. I pulled out my cell and called home while I hid the diary under a sewage pipe in the corner.

"Listen closely. There is a manhole on Cove St. Go there. You'll find a book under a pipe in a room overlooking the water below. Get it, but be careful of the police. Make two copies."

I hit the floor. My vision was getting hazier. "You might not hear from me for some time, but don't trust the rumors." I couldn't even hear a word from Shannon, but I was hoping that it was her that answered and that she understood everything. My eyes closed as my body gave into to the melody of sleep. Falling forward, I lost consciousness.

◆

The next thing I knew I was seated in a rotating chair in the dream world. This time there was something very different residing in the dream world. There was another man seated with his back turned to me. The desk separated me from the teacher who was quietly resting behind it.

"Looks like all three of us finally meet." History's Most Preserving Teacher announced, enjoying the occasion while sipping on some tea in a tiny cup.

"Too bad it's not with cooperation in mind." A characterless tone came from the man sitting only a couple feet away from me. His idle stance seemed to represent the notion of not letting any of his habits show. The idea was only strengthened as I considered his voice. "You must have a hundred questions."

"That would be most correct."

"Since we're here, you must be the one responsible for the death of Michael Bailey, right?" I gestured in approval, listening to what else he had to say. "Well, looks like my hunt is over, at least in part, but you can probably say the same. I was foreseeing collaboration, but it seems your believes contradict mine in some way."

"Maybe I could reconsider if you shed light on the secrets of this ability. You see, he's not much of a teacher at all. Besides cooperation would be most beneficial as I have your book." I tried sparking a conversation while being as neutral as I could, but I had a feeling the man could see through me act.

"First things first, about the sudden sleepiness, since we both have that ability we are considered brothers by the universe. We shouldn't fight, so as soon as conflict arises and one person bleeds, we are both sent to this dimension to resolve any difference." He stared at the blank wall.

"What happens after we wake up? I mean, you're wounded."

"After we finish this little discussion, I'll be waiting until a person finds me, so that I could reclaim life. At that moment, you'll wake up as well, but before that happens, you'll be in a state of coma, and so will I." As he gave me a plausible explanation, I asked about his upcoming death. "You see, while we're here my body is preserved in a way, so death won't come as fast."

"Care to explain the general picture about the power and about him." I pointed at the teacher.

"Enough!" The teacher broke in an attempt at preventing the killer form spilling any more secrets.

Without paying attention, the killer asked, "You know who this is?" He pointed at the teacher with a resentful face. "He's the one that overlooks our activity, so he's somewhat of a mediator. He's been here ever since the first creature faced death. He's only capable of being in the human world for a short time, and he has to dress in a facade of an already-deceased person. Actually, this is his dimension after he committed a major sin—the sin of not doing his job. Still thinking of yourself as a teacher or a historian, huh?" The bland voice turned to face the teacher.

"What job?" Asking the next inquiry, I contemplated in my mind about Historia.

"What else? He's supposed to eliminate the people abusing the power." The sound of truth shook the room. The teacher fell quiet and vanished, dissolving into the imperceptible whiteness.

That's why he hid his purpose. If this despicable person would do what was assigned to him, no one would die. Bastard.

The killer returned to the most essential question. "And about the power? Anyway, I'm probably not the most knowledgeable, but I'll try to explain, or maybe not. We'd be wasting time, because after you wake up, you'll get your hands on my journal." He acted as if his keepsake had all the truths.

"I think you were ready for this question, so I'll ask. Why are you doing this?"

"That question screams 'I don't agree with you.' But that's not a problem. Let me explain. Human can be divided into noble and ignoble. During everyday life, you can't really tell the difference as everybody melts into a single heap of goo, but if there is a challenge, all those with a noble soul stand up."

"That's it!? You're telling me you created this massacre just so you could identify those who stand out in a way that allures you." I lost my temper for a second after hearing his irrational response.

"That's not all. While that is one of my pleasures, it isn't the entire reason why I would orchestrate something like this."

"What are your other reasons?"

"You should ask that question yourself as I have in the past."

I frowned at his nature. I reevaluated his every explanation, and while they did sound credible, I just couldn't accept his words as true. My last resort would be to read his notebook. Based on his reaction when he dropped it, it must be something he relished—something of utmost importance.

"Did you know a girl named Heather?" I asked devoid of any sense of emotion or feeling. Asking the question awoke a memory hidden deep within me that made me realize I've seen this man before. We met in front of Heather's apartment.

"Yes, I did. I was the one who helped her on her way. Her soul needed that after all." He gave of a chuckle as he talked to himself. "You don't even know how similar we are. I think everybody tries to do good when they gain this power. They follow their code and such, but at one point, everyone realizes that no matter how good they are, the pyramid of good deeds will collapse as soon as a dirty block is used. The good and the bad are not valued the same. What complicates matters more is that good and bad are one and the same at times. It's all just a matter of perspective. At some point you'll realize it, and you'll understand much more than you do now."

"I wish that day will never come true."

"You can't even envision how welcoming it was when I heard about Michael Bailey. As soon as I heard about it and read the police report, I knew that there is someone just like me."

I listened as the barrage of depressing words landed all over my mind. In the face of the recent events, I was much more determined than I ever was. No matter what he said, he didn't shake me of balance. I would only thrash about in my psyche for a bit before recuperating my equilibrium.

"You probably wander why you're like that, right? Why you've gained this power. Why you can watch everything unfold and never blink an eye? Why you can stand what could break other people? The answer is simple. All of it is interconnected. If your mind is clouded by unnecessary feeling, the chances that you'll make the most rational decision radically drop. That's why you've been bestowed with this power. Lack of emotions is the first prerequisite for gaining this power."

"And the others are?"

He raised his hand over his face as if bowing in defeat disappointed about the state of affairs. It was the first and only time when he dropped his bland act and begun acting human. "I don't know. I'm too low of rank."

"Rank?" I looked dazed about what he was talking about, but he seemed to disregard any additional inquiry, so I had to change the subject. "You said that we are here to settle our differences? What if we can't?"

"We'll be here forever." He let out a hearty giggle. "Of course not! We can leave this place any time, but we'll be in a coma until I find someone to inherit my wounds.

"Or die."

The man dismissed my remark. "That's when we'll wake up, but that should be the least of your worries. I was dragged by the current while you were left in the sewers. Don't you think that someone will find you? I bet it'll be that foolhardy detective. What's his name? Greg Dench. That's right."

"You saw him in the area too, right?" I asked thinking that the killer was right. He has probably found me by now, or will find me in the near future. In both cases, the result is unfavorable as I will be the primary and only suspect in the case. If I'm lucky, no one will find out about my power. Consequently, I doubt that the killer will try to escape. He'll continue his mission so I'll be soon dismissed, but what if there is more too it? I saw how Dench treats others. He'll be stubborn to the end, thinking that he has caught the one. If he announces that and discloses my info, the people will go crazy hunting for me. They won't accept any excuses. They'll hunt for me even if Dench were to publicly proclaim he was wrong. Oh, what am I talking about? Even if I'm free, he'll tail me. His diary is my best bet. It must have something nifty to eliminate him from the game.

"I know what you're thinking. You debated whether I'll continue killing. Rest assured this isn't over. After all, I bet you had a plan regarding my diary. I doubt you would have left it there. That would have been most foolish."

"One thing's for sure. If I'm dead, you won't find it."

"That would have been problematic as it contains a gargantuan load of info about my world. Oh, well, looks like we'll meet as soon as you're out of custody."

Once I'm free, I'll have to settle everything as soon as possible and leave this town or else I'll be a victim too.

"I think this resolve everything. I'll see you at the end of the line." I said.

"Good luck. It was a pleasure to meet you." The monotone voice tittered.

"Likewise. Thank you for the opportunity to learn." I remained indifferent. At the last moment, I was reminded of a question that was lost in the spring of ever-occurring events. "Can you get rid of this power?"

Our meeting ended in a vortex of kind words similar to a conversation between close friends. The man's attitude and behavior was unlike what I imagined. He lacked any serious nature, and despite his simulation of bland behavior, he's natural talent for dialogue and his charm seemed to surface and become vivid. The blackness enveloped the world of the dreams as the two of us went our separate ways. I seemed to be elevated somewhere without a floor, without a ceiling, lacking in everything material. Before I lost it to the hunger for sleep, I thought about the upcoming nightmare.

Chains

_____

TIME FLOW WAS very different when I slept. Hours passed like minutes, and days like hours. When you're conscious and you're sitting there waiting for something to happen, every second leaves marks on your body and your psyche, but when you're asleep things are very different. It's like you're flowing in a tunnel separate from the idea of time. It's almost like time passes you by the side. You feel as if you could see time flow right in front of you if only you could open your eyes. Things happen, but they're of no meaning to you. If you have problems, sleep is the best escape plan. It's where you should head when you have nowhere to run. You leave the vehicle that is your body only to teleport into a realm where you're the king. You feel that way, but it's all a lie. You don't escape. You're not the king. You're affected by all the things on the planet, you just don't realize it.

Opening my eyes for the first time in what felt like an eternity, I saw the ceiling blocking my view of the heavens. It had lights for eyes and a large leak that formed a smile. Any of my movement was restrained by handcuffs on each hand as well as around my ankles— all hooked up to the railings of the bed. My body resting still, my soul screamed in anger as it craved for freedom. It appeared to be day time as the rays sneaked between the window blinds. I recognized the view of the back of the police station right away. The rotten back was unappealing as always. I observed that my belongings were confiscated, and I was dressed in a plain white shirt and pants.

"You're finally awake." Judith walked in to the room.

"How long have I been asleep?" I said as I felt uncomfortable speaking. It felt as if I was doing it for the first time in a really long while.

"Eight days. The doctors didn't know what happened. You had no wounds, and you were practically fine, yet we couldn't reach you." She looked through her paperwork. She lacked any sympathy, which I expected, but it also seemed as if she didn't know what to say at all. The awkward silence filled the room as the detective persisted to avoid eye contact. She attempted to write something, but gave up and turned to nervously tapping her pen against the wooden board that held the papers together.

"What now?"

"Detective Dench is convinced that you are the one behind the suicide. He saw you running in the direction away from the scene. He wanted to announce his success, but I delayed it a bit."

"I told you that his nature would be problematic. So you didn't find any other blood around the area?" I asked thinking that there would still be blood from the culprit lingering around.

"No, you were the only one there. No other evidence, but I arrived at the scene late."

"Are you implying something?"

Judith disregarded my comment. "Last time when we spoke, you gave me a date. I think I understand your history now—" A slam on the widow of the doors suspended her confession. It was Dench who was calling for Judith to meet him.

"You have three more days before he announces that it is you."

"Thank you." I said welcoming her attitude toward me. As she exited, time embark on a lingering trip which seemed to last for all eternity. Hour begun moving slower and slower. I dreaded the idea that I'm here wasting time. If only I could get my hands on a copy of the killer's diary, I could study it and prepare for what's to come. I bet that I will get out, but will it be in a timely manner. Or maybe the killer will try to mock me by waiting until Dench broadcasts my guilt before he will commence with his usual work. That wasn't the only problem. As soon as I'm out, I'll be forced to deal with not only the culprit, but also Detective Dench as well as the mob. I'll have to hurry in order to leave this town as soon as I can. That's why I have to get in touch with Shannon. I have to make preparations. That's the only way I can make it out of here alive and in one piece. If only I could make a single call. All that I had now was time that would be devoted to waiting.

◆

The next day, Detective Dench came to hear my confession. I was unshackled so that I could sit up only to be cuffed again. His incompetence was buzzing more than usually as he was in a flowery mood, thinking of the success to come.

"Are you ready to confess?"

"I'll confess as soon as you'll do the same."

"This is for all those people you've murdered. Show some respect and explain your reasoning."

"I'm happy to know that you've found the blood of the other person that was at the scene." My mockery earned me a punch as Dench lost his temper and landed his fist in my face. I ceased at once with all my trickery and remained silent until he disappeared behind the door. I claimed that irritating him any more would serve no purpose but could disclose my power. All this time, Judith was in the corner with her head down. I could not decipher her behavior.

"You have a guest coming tonight form the Unity." She walked away.

I remained seated, forgotten with almost no freedom. The idea of a guest coming to see me was foreign. I knew nobody who would be even neutral in taking part in such endeavor which made me relatively anxious to meet the unforeseen visitor. Imagination evolved into my pastime until the time came to meet him. It turned out to be Fredric. He strolled in with a bag by his side. His act seemed suspicious, and I couldn't shake of the feeling that he fits the personality of the killer perfectly. Whenever I tried to recall the voices and the screams to compare with Fredric's response, it turned out they were not as vivid as I had anticipated.

"Life is quite problematic, wouldn't you say?" Fredric inquired.

"You're absolutely right, but I would be much more interested to hear why you're here?"

"The village is very much different now. Well, people are still depressed and such, but some of the effects seemed to be reverted at least to a certain extent. Waye and the Unity know that the culprit has been caught, and although there was no announcement of the closure of the case, I think the idea that the suicides have stopped has had a positive result on the people." Fredric was changing from a sensation of peace to one of dread.

"That still doesn't explain why you're here."

Fredric took a seat and rolled up his sleeve a little in order to see his old-school watch. Apparently our time here was limited to mere minutes. "Seven minutes left. Anyway, I went to check on you after the events with Chris, but the only one at home was Shannon. She begged me to find out what happened to you. Considering that I'm a representative of the Unity, after some fighting, Dench gave me ten minutes to speak with you. He never told me they consider you the culprit, but the immerse chains and their grave attitude sure gave it away." He felt somewhat triumphant as he stretched out his legs, giving him the feel of placid soreness as well as exhaustion. "This is for you. I bet they'll take it away but for now."

He threw a notebook in my direction. It was a worn-out softcover with pages dirtied, ripped and even soaked in coffee—an obnoxious gift until I saw Shannon's signature on the front. I blazed through the pages, aiming to find something of use. The book was very much filled with personal anecdotes like a diary. However, most were heavily based on slice of life scenarios which instantly made me feel that this is not the killer's notebook. Upon closer observation, three pages marked by columns of text and underlines words stood out. Fighting against the shackles, I ripped them out and threw the book back at Fredric.

"This'll be easier to hide and get rid of. Aren't you troubled about helping a suspect?"

"Helping? No, you misunderstood my intention. I just thought that the girl should have her wish granted." He walked closer, reached inside his black jacket and pulled out a cell phone. After dialing, he pressed it against my ear as if telling me to listen. Fredric stood close enough to hear everything. I expected Shannon to greet me from the other end. The idea made me uneasy as I didn't want Shannon to make a foolish mistake and ruin everything by disclosing unnecessary info. The future will greatly depend on if she'll be watchful and cautious.

"Hello." Shannon was her usual self at least in voice only.

"Hey, Shannon." I tired sparking a simple friendly conversation that wouldn't be suspicious.

"Are you alright? I asked Mr. Quinn to go look for you. Your abrupt departure made me troubled." Shannon had utmost respect for Fredric.

"I'm fine. I'll probably be back in a couple of days. We can leave this town then. I also want to thank you for the book."

"I bet you'll like it. It's about positive thinking. My mom always read it to me when I was a child. Oh, I wanted to tell you about your CV. I made two additional copies."

"Well done. That'll help us settle in a new home. You know, I realize that you might need something so look under the TV. Check number 4." I directed Shannon to get the note which contained all the necessary info to contact Aidan. He should be able to complete the task. Number four specifically talked about Dench's digital recorder—his diary. While it would never secure my escape, it'll be handy to shake him off when I leave this place. Displeased about the idea that Fredric listened to the conversation, I accepted his help as that was exactly what I needed to get out.

"I'll do so. I'll be waiting."

"Take care."

He turned off his cell and walked back to the door, ready to leave. "Not sure what it is, but you've got something very special going on with that girl, don't you? I wish you luck, you'll need it. Considering that tomorrow they'll announce you as the culprit, even if the suicides commence again, the people won't forget. They'll search for you. They'll desire punishment."

"Such unnerving words, but thanks for coming here."

Fredrick gazed the chains and then back at me. "I know how you feel. I feel just like you all my life—caged. The only time I'm free is when I fly a plane." He smiled.

The meeting came to an end, but I still had some time before the lights went out to finish a solitary page. I began reading in my mind as the notes seemed to be narrated by the mastermind.

They tell me that I'm on a mission. They lecture me that my existence has a profound meaning to it. They educate me that the world needs me to do something important. All the reason they've listed had only one goal in mind—to make me accept the ability with which I was gifted or cursed. It's the power to make pain befall somebody else instead of me. It's the power of a fiend. Every step that I take, it seems that I can smell the stench of death. It's like he follows my every move. Each occasion where the power trigger I feel as if I'm shaking hands with Death and begging him "Spare me! You can take the life of that other person." Despite the notion that this power is divine—a means to a greater good—I can't acknowledge it as a part of myself. Every time I try to consider other options, I get reminded about the hellish visions that I get after each use. All the wicked aspects contradict their claims that the power is given to humans to better the world.

When I concluded the evaluation of the text, I started thinking of a way to get rid of the pages. I decided that I'll be forced to consume them. The notion was extreme and quite disheartening, but it was a means to an end—an end where I triumph. I hid the other two pages under my back as someone walked in to turn off the lights and tomorrow's judgment levitated above me.

The Killer's Identity

LIGHT PIERCED THE glass of the window, and I woke up. Today was judgment day, and I had to finish reading those pages before anything happens. I had decided that if they announce my name, all I'll be forced to do is be more careful. My goal was to leave town in 48 hour, finishing every single task at hand and concluding my stay in this hellish place. I grabbed page number two.

I decided that if this power would come to use, it would be on the battlefield. I became a reporter with the sole idea of writing accounts about the most dangerous of places. In one such place, I stumbled upon an enemy soldier. He introduced himself as Sovereign, but I doubt that was his real name. Unlike me, he was a real sol-

dier, yet his goals were most bizarre. He ran tests regarding this power. Our first meeting didn't go as planned; he knocked me out before I could act. That's when I found out that this power doesn't work when my consciousness isn't right. When I woke up, I found myself bandaged up, burned. He gave me a choice of joining him or dying. I was behind enemy lines, so I had no real alternatives. Throughout my time with him, I came to understand many things about this ability.

I learned for a fact that it works for only 4 seconds, and after that it needs time to reset. So for example; if someone pours acid on your hand, it'll burn and soon gets transported to the attacker, but after 4 seconds, you'll be like a normal human. Prolonged pain leads to death. The duration of recharge is unknown.

I also discovered that it only triggers when there is blood. Pain is fair game in hurting someone with this power as long as it doesn't result in drawing blood.

My knowledge didn't measure up to his influence on me as I seemed to degrade mentally with each day. Whatever sympathy I had, seemed to be gone now, and my mission evolved into a meaningless idea. No matter how hard I tried to care about things that were dear to me a long time ago, I just couldn't—I didn't know how. It's like this man transformed me in some way. Disgusted by the thought, I had a fight with him. He fell into a pool of acid. For the first time, I was transported to the dream world where I met with him. His last words will corrode my mind until death. "Unshackle all chains, free your heart and stand above those puny humans because it's our destiny." Whatever he

had done to me, I felt sickened by it, but by now, I ac-
cepted this power as something of a gift.

The confession of how the killer lost his sanity made me think about how he wasn't so different from your everyday human being. One step and he flew of the staircase into the abyss, losing his mind. The anecdote made me think that the fiend that was haunting the other soldier found its way into the mind of the current culprit. It corrupted every last bit of compassion. The thing that once set them apart seemed to be disappearing with each morbid act. The idea of wearing the garments of the one you hate was in the works here as a man as changed irrevocably.

I swallowed the second page. A knock on the door signaled Judith's arrival. It was her second visit here since I woke up. Whatever was irking her seemed to give way to her visits.

"Dench is preparing all the formalities with closing the case. He's oblivious to anything, but his success." She said not looking me straight in the eyes. "You know that they'll broadcast your name on TV tonight."

"I was truly hoping that the suicides would resume sooner."

I should have expected it. The mastermind wants me to feel despair and helplessness. He wants to wear me out until I fall just like him.

"Aren't you disappointed or worried?" She gave me a defeated look. Despite what the scene might have looked like at first, the whole reason she acted this way was because she knew deep down that the case will go unsolved if Dench continues with his ignorance. She'll be out of this town in no time, and who knows what'll happen next. She became doubtful of Dench until she lost all the trust in his judgment.

"I was expecting that. He just made my life ten times harder. If anything, I'm frustrated."

"When they'll report the news, there'll also be a debate between Dench and the head spokesman of the Unity about how they should judge you." She spoke in a harsh voice as if her throat was aching.

"So in other words, Dench wants to get me out of town while the Unity wants to take justice in their own hands."

"Precisely." She picked up the bottle she sometimes carried and took a drink; "Remember the date you gave me last time? It really helped me understand how a person who just wants to be left alone gets entangled in the case."

"Care to share you hypothesis? Anything to kill a bit of time."

"I think that this power you have awakened on that day. Insensible that you had that ability, you realized that you could fake a suicide with it. Consequently, you had begun wondering that you could be taken for a culprit, so you investigated to find answers. The only thing I'm not too sure about is the death of Kasper. Could it be that someone saw the incident with Michael Bailey?"

"Everything's correct. A person indeed saw the incident, and once he fled, he told someone he shouldn't. He paid with his life for that. Alex dying was part of a plan to meet with me. Would you allow me to ask a personal question?"

"Go ahead. After all, we've gotten this far."

"The story that you told me days ago was incomplete,

was it? I mean sure the event could occur with minor variation, but what I'm curious about is your newly-acquired acquaintanceship right after the incident. I wondered why a woman with such strong beliefs would ally with a group of thugs." I forcibly pressed on, connecting the dots in hopes of being correct.

"So you knew." She smiled as if she was expecting that I might have known a couple of her secrets.

"Could it be that you former teammates in the task-force didn't trust you? As a result you were limited to insignificant cases because no one had enough bravery to be you partner. After all, who would want a person who might break down covering them? Somehow, you come to know the boss. This allowed you to solve cases even if you were on your own, and in case something went wrong, you had a backup in place in the form of assistance from the boss."

"They did limit me to trivial investigations. No one wanted to work with me. I inquired about this to my superior who gave me a chance. He gave me a worthy case, but one that was destined for a collapse. I searched meaninglessly until I was ready to give up. That's when I met the boss, or maybe I should say that he found me. He liked it that I was independent and that I had my own views. He offered info about the case in exchange for minor favors. That's how it all started."

"The only thing that stands to be asked is why didn't you tell them about my ability?"

"For the same reason that you told no one about my own secret." She crossed her arms across her chest as she leaned back in the seat. "Do remember that they'll be hunting for you once you're outside."

"I know."

With a touch of seriousness, she walked out closing the door. I turned my attention to the last page of the report send by Shannon. In my mind, the words emerged on my mental monitor as I read them silently.

The power sure is great and all. I'm undefeated, and the more I use it, I feel as if I should be revered as a godly creature. Today, I was in a fight against six and the panic-filled look they gave me was forever engraved in my mind. It felt as if the power was enticing me to take risks and fight like I never fought before. Massacring those pricks felt refreshing. People should just realize that the only thing they can do is bow and beg for mercy. I am gifted with the power of being a God.

The only things that lingers a question mark are the horrid visions. They seemed to be emerging in my mind within minutes of triggering the power.

What's more is that they seem to be getting longer each time, yet I haven't figured out why. My best bets are that the length is proportional to the injury, or that the more I use the power the more horrors I'll be forced to see. Recently, there was a hallucination which lasted four minutes, but that wasn't the only problem. It doesn't matter if my eyes are open or not, I'm forced to view the whole thing in one go. I have also been unable to decipher the meaning behind the vision. They're mostly random: the place and time. They seem to have nothing in common, but the vile nature. The idea makes me uneasy. Is this the price I must pay for using this gift?

Reading the passage made me recollect the images

that I saw. Fortunately, my visions were fairly limited since I only used the power about three or four times. I trust that I should keep it in mind in the near future and abstain for using this power as I want to get out of this in one piece. Then again, the killer has committed countless sins using this power, and he seemed to have suffered no consequences. Could it be that he found how to deal with the hallucination, or maybe he kills without using the power? The passages only invoked more questions, but the benefit of reading was some glimpse into the power, as well as some ideas on how to deal with the killer in the very near future.

◆

Outside, I heard a commotion. Det. Judith screamed in anger at someone before two shots were fired. Unable to reach the window, I could only fantasies about what was going on.

◆

As the night came closer, it was now about time for the announcement. My fall from grace communed. Judith turned on the TV in the room before leaving me alone to my forlorn self, listening. It was a simple studio recording with a circular table in the middle. The reporter sat in the center, while Dench was on his right, and Maximilian Waye on his left.

"First of all, I wanted to proclaim that we have finally closed the suicide case." Dench said with his arms crossed, siting proudly as if he had achieved the impossible.

"That is what we are here to broadcast. Based on the

detective's findings, the one responsible is Sebastian Snow, a citizen of the town for the past two years. Det. Dench, what could you say about the methods used to commit the crime?" The announcer shouted in an energetic voice as his goal was to get the viewer's attention.

"He used his charisma to instigate people to commit suicides."

"It's truly frightening that, with the right skills, someone could accomplish something so horrid. How do you feel about this, Professor Waye?" The reporter looked to his left.

"You know how it is; people make the wrong choice. A single bed deed leads to more horrid acts. Some are insignificant while this one had ghastly consequences. He turned a peaceful town into the den of despair. Thus, I believe the people should have the right to hear his explanation and judge him." The spokesman verbalized confidently while changing the subject a little to fit his agenda. Although he seemed calm, he had a touch of discontent and incongruity around him.

"The law is the same for everyone. There is no room for a vendetta here. He'll be judged in the court." Dench countered.

"You see, I'm not talking about burning him at the stake. I just believe that he should confess and voice himself right in front of the people."

"Don't you think that as soon as we put him out there, the people will tear him apart? There is no way two detectives can moderate a meeting between a hundreds of people yearning for blood. Besides, don't you think you're taking this too personally?" Dench riposted.

"That's right, spokesman, weren't you the leading

man in finding the culprit? Could it be that you are displeased that you couldn't achieve your goal? I also remember that you were promoting searching everyone's home. Is this some kind of retaliation for not succeeding in the first place?"

"No, this problem isn't about winning or losing, but about preserving the mentality of citizens. Sebastian Snow has taken away everything from them. How can they go back to normal life if the problem isn't confronted?"

The quarrel continued for some time until the debate ended. I looked at the clock on the wall, thinking that night is coming and the culprit is definitely satisfied by now. He made my life much more difficult—I had no way of knowing what will happen next. The TV was still screaming lively as the announcer spoke.

"Well, it looks like the nightmare is coming to an end. I wish everyone the best of luck in the upcoming season." The announcer had an apprehensive look as if he wanted to tell the citizens that revenge isn't the option—that they shouldn't harvest grudges—but understood that no matter what he would say, the outcome would be the same. He knew that if the people will get a chance, they'll deal the verdict themselves.

The Headless Society

———

THE CLOUDY DAY reflected my mood as I was still locked up in chains, waiting for my future to unfold. It was early in the morning, but I had no chance of falling asleep. Yesterday's message, even though expected, left a very negative image of the populace in my mind. Giving up every time the recollection of yesterday zoomed in my mind, I was fully awakened by a fight outside.

"I told you this changes nothing! He's still a suspect! All this proves is that he might've had a collaborator!" Dench screamed his heart out in the nearby hallway. He voice was mad in part, and at the same time chimed with authority.

"How can you be so blind to what's going on? This changes everything. The killer is still out there, and you're here acting self-indulgent because you don't care about finding the truth!" Judith announce, spilling all the anger and dissatisfaction that was crammed inside her. It was something that she shouldn't do as it angered Dench more and more, putting him on the edge.

"I don't care about finding the truth? You really think so? Finding the truth isn't always about uncovering every fact. It's, at least in part, about preserving people's morale and the police force's reputation."

"Reputation? Is that so? Who's reputation? Yours? For all I know, the rumors might be true! Tell me, did you frame innocent people for crimes they didn't commit?" As soon as Dench heard the vicious accusation, he slammed Judith's cheek with an open palm. Judith was nothing but angered that she was working under someone like Dench. She yearned to return a punch, but she knew that their disagreements shouldn't interfere with the case. Going against that belief because of her inability to fight her anger, she made a rush choice. "Do whatever you want! I quit." She announced and threw her gun and budge on the floor. As she was leaving, she clenched her fist and returned a punch at Dench. He was too preoccupied about being alone in this town that he couldn't fight back.

I called to mind the memory of the culprit yelling. It was still blurry. By now, I wasn't so sure of the belief that I would be able to identify the killer if I heard his voice. No, I couldn't think that way. While this idea might be erroneous, it's my best bet. At first, I wondered if Fredric is the killer, but I'm not too convinced anymore. I mean, he was in many places that I have visited almost like he trailed me, and he came to meet with me right before they announced my downfall. I also realize that he had a copy of the poem. I can confront him and see his reaction when I visit the Unity, but for now, I'll assume that he's innocent.

From the onset of the case the police believed that the culprit is an instigator. Why would that be? I mean they had no witnesses—no evidence—just a bunch of suicide cases. The only reason they would think so is because it was the only rational explanation for the ever increasing string of death. It was a universal explanation that someone could talk someone weak into quitting life. Based on that assumption, the killer would have to be someone who enjoys watching others fall into the reaper's hands. If so, could it be that in the past he might have been accused of a crime where he didn't help someone in need. That could narrow down the search, but I can't shake of the feeling that it'll be someone form the Unity.

In the evening, I heard a broadcast from the Unity. It was regarding future plans. "Based on the newly discovered facts, I have to say that I'm quite disappointed with the detectives. Let's face it, they've been running in circles. More so, they've postponed our initiative that could've put an end to the case. Another death happened today, even though the so-called suspect is in custody. Can we really trust people like that?" Waye spoke as he gained more live of this town's population with every word. "So far, I realize that many have left, and I respect them. You know why? Because they realized that they're not strong enough to bear the problems of this town. But for some, like me, this town is everything. It's my home, my family, my future, and I can't let that future die."

"Out of the 2500 residents, 417 migrated and 1724 are member of the Unity. What are your plans?" The reporter asked.

"I am not one to decide, yet at the same time, I strongly believe that we should search every home. Each member of the Unity was checked by one of our ten guardians. These people are free of any suspicions. That's why I trust in them. They are the ones who should make the choice."

The crowd of hundreds cheered in favor of the Spokesman's reasoning. It was an unquestionable sign that they were ready to take action. Today, they'll purge the city.

Someone came into my room, it was Dench. He looked like he had no life left inside him. He was utterly defeated. All the angry determination that was with him has evaporated as if he had lost everything. All his mistakes have taken a toll on him, and today there was one too many for him to carry. He came with the key in hand and released me from my chains. After telling me that my belongings are under the front counter, he left downcast to watch the rest of the broadcast, a bottle of whisky in one hand. Judith's leave and Dyer's unexpected disappearance have left him defenseless and shook his long lost guilt.

Once dressed and ready to go, I walked outside where I was greeted by a message on my phone telling me that I have a single new voicemail. "The murders commenced again so you should be free tonight. I acquired everything. I'll be waiting at the gates leading to the Unity for your arrival" The message form Shannon was quick and to the point.

I dialed Fredric's number.

"Hello?" He acted carefree under such terrible circumstances.

"Hey, it's me, Sebastian."

"So, they let you go?"

"Something like that. Anyway, I don't have a lot of time. I would like you to get me inside the Unity."

"Can this thing wait? Now is not a good time."

"This is urgent, but I can bet that Waye will be quite satisfied with the news."

Reluctant, Fredric said, "Fine, I'll get you in, but meet me at the side entrance. Just follow the left wall from the gate, and you'll find it."

The dusk sky took in all the negative emotion of the people of the town and dressed an appropriate color for what's to come. The stars residing on the pure black sky reflected the idea that in this sea of grief and anger there are still specs of goodness that shine brightly. The moon hid behind the copious clouds as if avoiding the sight of humanity. The way to the Unity was an easy walk since the member were still preparing for their upcoming raid. The gates shut tight with big lanterns illuminating the road. By a tree was Shannon sitting on the grass, her back leaning firmly against the trunk of the tree. She buried her face in her hands. At first glance, she looked ready to cry, but that wasn't the case; she was reflecting on what to say to the person who was responsible for her broken psyche —the spokesman.

As she saw me, she stood up. Her face showed a tinge of confusion as she was at a loss of words. I waited until she gathered her ideas and spoke. I walked by the 15 feet wall of the Unity.

"Aidan and I stole that diary recording. Unfortunately, your friend was injured."

"Marvelous. That's why we are here after all." She handed me the tiny digital recorder that was worn-out after countless uses and drops. She directed me to the most memorable confessions. "What about the notebook from the sewers?" I said in a voice quite satisfied, dismissing Aidan's fate.

"I have the original, as well as two copies. You'll get them once we're done here. Although I must say they're weird."

"Has anyone else come in contact with the notebook?"

"Once I got a hold of it, no one has seen it."

"I should praise you on your work during my absence." I patted her on the back as I was one step closer toward triumph. My mind was empty of all those unnecessary things and dilemmas. All that mattered was the problem at hand. We dashed into the woods. Shannon was preoccupied by her uncertain future. The giant wall that separated the Unity from everything else showed us around a corner and deeper into the emerald oblivion. On the other side of the wall, noises of all kinds could be heard which fused into a gargantuan howl of anger—a training for something demoralizing. As we finished our walk, we reached a small metal back entrance which looked tightly sealed. Before we could get closer, the door was opened by Fredric.

"I hope this is something important. If it's not, I'm not sure if coming here is worth the risk." Fredric said, loosening his tie.

"As long as I get to see the spokesman, I'm sure it will be."

"Put these on." He shoved two robes in my hands. It was an apparel of frequent use within the sect. When members did group discussions, and there is a very delicate topic at hand, they used it to conceal their identities. After putting on the awkward outfits, the hood covered my eyes completely so that no one could recognize me. Shannon did likewise. Fredric stayed in his regular day-to-day fashion. If it wasn't for Fredric, walking in this outfit in a crown of similarly dressed individuals could get problematic as I wouldn't be able to identify which one is Shannon. We marched through the convoluted grounds until we reached the very back building.

Finally at the top floor, stationed right in front of the Unity's head office, Fredric knocked to hear a cold welcome.

"Come in!"

"Look, I'm busy. I don't have time to lecture you." Waye said. He didn't recognize either of us because of the robes. "You should all concentrate on preparing for tonight."

"This might be important." Fredric said.

I took of the hood to reveal my face while Shannon remained in the shadows.

"Oh, it you—our presumed killer. Welcome." He spoke in an enthusiastic, yet gracious voice with absolutely no hostility. "We're preparing to go, so my time is limited." His attitude spoke louder than words to illustrate that he indeed wasn't suspecting me.

"I won't take long." I said and passed the recorder in his direction while playing.

Dench's confession was loud. "I don't know what I should do. I made many mistakes, but it's not like it was my choice. All this pressure just overwhelms me." Dench took a break from speaking in the recording as he sipped on some liquid which was probably his favorite alcoholic beverage—whiskey. "The cases have to be solved. Sometimes people have to sacrifice themselves. So far 27 sacrificed themselves for the greater good." He then began listing names.

"What is that? Wasn't that Dench's voice?" Waye turned it off.

"Didn't you hear of the internal investigation? He is suspected of this." I glanced at the recording.

"I don't know how you got a hold of this, but the recording is beyond compelling. So why show it to us? It's not like we can give you something in exchange." Waye responded.

"Yes, you can. All I need is some freedom, and that's precisely what you're capable of arranging."

"In other words, we'll arrest him and put him in a cage. That should also clear all charges against the grandson of the elderly lady." Fredric broke in.

The spokesman contemplated. "I heard that he let you go, but you still don't trust him? You're very much right about that. Before you came here, I spoke with Dench who was at the edge of despair, but someone visited him. He told me to wait, and after a brief conversation, he was a completely new person. It was almost like he regained a purpose—like new life was breathed into his soul."

"Do you know who might have visited him?" I asked.

"No, I didn't hear a single word from the dialogue, but your request is done. Are you satisfied?"

"I am, but I'm not so sure about the lady behind me." I introduced Shannon who stepped out of the murky shadows to face the Spokesman, revealing her identity.

"I don't understand. Who is this girl?"

"Do you remember Eleanor, Mr. Waye?" Shannon asked

"Yes, she was my ..." Waye stood there as he recalled all the necessary information to counterattack, although I wasn't so sure if he was able to do that at the time.

"That's right, and you abandoned her. Do you know how much I had to suffer seeing you every time and hearing your detestable voice on TV? Do you even think about someone else other than yourself?"

"Look, I don't think you understand."

"I don't understand? Do you even know what you've done? My stepfather was a wicked person, but he turned into something worse once my mother died."

"I'm not the one you're searching for. Your mother was my sister ..."

"Enough of this! All you do is lie! You've lied all your life! My mother told me very few things about you, but I heard your voice when I was a child. That voice is the voice of the only man in my mother's life, my father." Shannon continued her senseless assault, not letting Waye a chance to recuperate.

"Would you listen to me dammit? She was my sister, so as you can see there is no way I can be your ... since I would have had to commit an unforgivable sin!" He leaned in his chair triumphant over the girl. His evil smile was patronizing.

"You're lying! Mother told me that my father was fly-ing a plane in the army. You have pictures of planes"

"So what? I desired to fly planes, but I wasn't cut out for it. The one who allowed me to take pictures was ..." Max gazed at Fredric, realizing something. Before he could utter the truth, he poured a glass of whisky and gulped it down. He could bear problems of unidentifiable nature, but matters that related directly to him were too much to take—way too much.

"Shannon, he might actually be telling the truth." I said, looking at one of the photos. "You see, his outfit is from the navy."

"That's not true! It can't be! I was so sure. Hatred was all that I had left." She fell to the floor, tears dripping on the carpet. Her fists slammed against the floor in a flurry of anger.

The spokesman was still smiling as if he had won until something had gotten into him. He scratched his neck and tried to grasp something with his hands that wasn't there. It was almost like something has gotten into him, and he wanted it out, like a loop tied around his neck that impaired his normal self. He's voice became harsher almost to the point of screeching until he tried standing up only to fall head first into the ground beside his desk. His hand was still reaching for something, searching erratically on the desk before it fell dead. All this happened in an instance, so any reaction from anybody in the room was absent until Fredric's shock-postponed scream echoed. "Max!" He came closer to check his pulse. Sadness ripped through his face. "He's on the other side now."

At that moment, I think Fredric irrationally accused me for murder. Yet, he didn't voice any of his claims as his more rational side acted to stop his rage. I looked at Fredric and then at Shannon.

"Serves him right." She mumbled, wiping her tears in exchange for a serious face. Her sorrow and sense of defeat were completely gone. Hearing her finale, Fredric stopped breathing as if an awful thought crossed his mind.

As I saw Fredric emancipated in grief after a loss of someone he knew, I was sure of two things; either he was a magnum opus at acting, or his emotions were honest. Trying to find an escape route, I was at a loss. He was the only one who could get us out.

"As long as no one finds out about his death, you should be having an easy way out." Fredric stated still on his knees next to Waye, his life-long friend.

"Let's leave." I said to Shannon as a strident banging came from the other side of the door.

It rumbled across the room.

"Max, everyone is ready to proceed with the operation! May I come in?" Veronica Williams, the secretary, announced in an innocent voice.

Fredric rushed to the entry and looked though the knothole as sweat dripped down his chin. He fastened his blue tie before uncomfortably uttering "We're a bit busy, but we'll be right outside soon." It was an attempt at postponing her entry, with the aim of making her go away. Unfortunately, the words could not change the upcoming events. She insisted on coming in and haphazardly opened the door. Fredric hid in the corner as a scream filled the entire building.

She alarmed all members.

The Pawn

VERONICA WILLIAMS STOOD in the room gazing at the corpse. Fredric jumped out with a bat in hand. Before he could land a direct hit, she twisted around and backed up.

"What are you doing?" She gasped. Knowing that the strike is coming, she let out a frail shriek—a call for help.

Ignoring her cries, Fredric raised his bat over the shoulder and clouted her. A single blow left her unconscious, yet alive. Her screech ceased when he hit her on the head, but it sent an impulse that told everyone to head this way. Earsplitting footstep scuttled in our direction from down below. The whole building shook.

"You two should leave! Now!" Fredric stated in a firm voice. He was completely convinced that this is the best action to take. On the contrary, I thought he was at his mind's pinnacle, unable to form a plan.

"No, you take Shannon and get her out. I'll go my own way." I protested.

"Why question me now?" Fredric's eyes were filled with panic like a child's that lost his way.

"I can't have complete faith in you yet."

"Fine. We'll do it your way. I'll be sure to hold on to the testimony, and I'll make sure to take care of Dench."

"We'll meet at your place." Shannon said.

As they exited the room turning left, I overheard Shannon asking. "Aren't you frightened that she might have seen your face?" No answer came from Fredric. Any conversation was overtaken in noise level by the escalating footsteps.

I exited outside and went straight into the direction of the noise. At one point, the footsteps seemed to die down as I planned my next strategy. This was a crucial moment, so I had to muster my courage and use my panic. I'll use what has gotten me though most of my predicament before. I'll play with their minds.

The hooded figures mounted the steps as quickly as they could. Before they saw me, I hid my face under the hood and started backing up to the staircase, tripping and falling right at the edge of the summit. I grabbed my hand as if hurting and screamed. "Someone killed the spokesman! Help! Help! The killer is still here!" My emotions were true to the core. I wasn't acting, but playing with the meaning of my emotions. The act worked as most cultists ran down the hall. A single ignorantly kind cultist guided me outside. Right around the gate, I separated from him in order to find my way out of the complex.

♦

Walking home, I was truly hoping that Fredric would take care of Dench. For my plan to work, I had to get that obstacle out of the way, and no one else but the Unity could do that. The air outside had an unexpectedly cold touch which reminded me of death. The village has stood still waiting for the right time to strike. The streets—houses too—were mostly vacant. A few lamps within homes gave of light in the distance. Walking along, I called Aidan. No answer. In front of my apartment, I dug into my pocket and upon finding the keys, I made my way in. Before I could close the door, someone pointed a gun at me. His steady aim directed me inside as he slammed the door shut.

Shannon had her arms cuffed, sitting on the sofa. "I'm sorry. He was here when I arrived."

The lights shined unsteadily until they dug enough courage to keep completely on. The light revealed the face of Jude who sustained some major injuries to his appearance; there was inflammation around the eye and many bruises. He was sitting on one of those wooden chairs I had in my kitchen. His head dripped down which looked as if he had no strength to keep it up. Rain drops of blood accumulated in front of the seat. "I finally found you."

"Sorry to make you wait, but I was confined to a bed for over ten days." I thought about grabbing my knife. Seeing him like that made me think that the injuries were punishment for running off without giving an alibi for where he was during the initial suicides.

He reached for his phone in an attempt to call.

"What's with the big change? I mean, if you wanted to get me, you could have told the truth during the interrogation."

He put down his cell. "You see, I just thought that if you're telling the truth, you're innocent, so there is no need for you to die, but on the other hand, if you intend to kill the boss and you succeed, I'll be able to go home." He wiped his face with his sleeve.

"So much for loyalty."

"Unfortunately, Winters was the one who betrayed us first. He led us into this hell where we have no way of winning."

"So why not take him out yourself?"

"Leon and Dorian still firmly believe in him. They wouldn't dare betray him." Jude sighed. "That's why I'm here. I'll do everything for my family."

"Family is a lie." Shannon retorted cruelly.

"Shut up!" Jude redirected his aim to intimidate Shannon. "You two think alike? Looks like I'm the most normal one here." he added.

"Once you bring me in, they'll kill us both."

"We'll see about that."

"Can't you just leave?" My question was not credited with an answer as the doorbell rang. Jude walked, but someone kicked the door open, pushing him back in the process. Jude hit the wall. Ten muscle heads busted in like it was their own place. They were armed in various melee weapons ranging from baseball bats to pipes. They surrounded Jude who was just about ready to fight. Out of nowhere, the owner of the tattoo shop appeared.

"Look who we have here?" He walked around. For

whatever reason his name escaped my mind. It was a meaningless title. He had a senseless smile with a tinge of sanity that was long lost. He gave me a stare before licking his chapped lips. His body coated in markings. "They closed my shop, I lost everything." He bit his lip, and blood came out. "You see, I had no memory of who used me to write that poem, but when I saw that you were arrested, I contemplated that you were the one."

"News flash. I'm completely clean of any former accusations, so you should go look somewhere else."

"You think I care? You just fit my mental portrait of the one I'm hunting for. Even if it's not you, at least I'll be a bit more satisfied when I cause madness." He directed one of his thugs to grab Shannon before I could react. The thug put a knife close to her neck and held her tightly.

The tattooist took out a rope with the aim of restraining me. While I had enough strength to fight or even flee, I couldn't leave Shannon like that. Complying with his request, my hands were tied behind my back.

"What are you planning?" I asked.

"You, bastard, ruined my life, and you don't even know my name. Jason Fisher!" The tattooist stared at me. Hearing his drivel made me reconsider my questioning. "Why ain't you saying anything?"

"I hate to waste my breath."

The tattooist rose up, pushed me to the ground, and landed a couple of kicks to vent his frustration. The strikes made me straggle with breathing. "You should remember the name of the one who'll kill you. Jason Fisher." He whispered.

Lying on the floor, I continuously tried to free my

hands. All my attempts were futile until I found my knife in my pocket. The tattooist took a seat and watched as a couple of the thugs started a fight with Jude.

A sole thug rushed Jude with a bat, swinging it. The strike came overhead, but Jude ducked and uppercutted the muscle head. The thug lost balance. Jude ceased the change, grabbed him by the bat-equipped hand, and pushed him into the wall, planting his knee into his stomach. The thug bowed to the floor as Jude picked up the bat and slammed him with all his might in the back. Another one jumped forward and aimed his pipe at Jude. His hit was countered, missing. Jude bought his bat overhead and slammed at the thug's hand with the pipe. The thug cried like a child without a will to fight. The others stopped attacking.

"I guess, in a physical fight, you're the guru here, but what about dodging bullets?" The tattooist took out a handgun. "So drop the bat and the gun tacked behind your belt, bastard, or you're dead!"

Jude dropped his gun and kicked it in my direction.

"You know, people think that death is the worst? Let me tell you, they're wrong. Humiliation is worst, what else?" He strolled with his gun swinging by his side as if walking stimulated his thinking. "Whatever, let's work on humiliation a bit, alright?"

"Boss, but that's so overused." A thug wracked his train of thought.

In the magic of anger, the tattooist fired a few bullets in succession, erasing the thug from existence while yelling, "Shut up, shut up, shut the!" His clam attitude evaporated when someone disobeyed him.

The corpse collapsed to the floor. Its blood steadily spread in my direction.

The tattooist came nearer, his back to me, eyeing Shannon. Just as they were face to face Shannon hit him with her forehead. Stunned from the attack, the tattooist backed up. He coughed plenty and bowed his head forward. Blood splattered from his broken nose. He became utterly quiet until he was ready to retaliate. He stretched out his hand saying. "Give me that knife!"

I finally cut the rope. The tattooist raised the knife close to Shannon's cheek. Fear kicked in, and Shannon couldn't keep her stoic face. I picked up Jude's gun, took a breath, and fired three shots.

The tattooist fell to his knees. All the strength seemed to evaporate from his body. Before he plummeted into the floor with his face, he used up all his will to keep himself up for just a bit longer. He wanted to take a final deep breath of the splendid atmosphere around him. Lifelessly, he crumbled down with no chance of survival. The thug holding Shannon was stunned, but loosened his grip allowing her to run toward me. He gave chase, but a bullet pierced his shoulder.

"Whoever wants to live should run now!" I roared. All the thugs run like little mice, escaping from danger. All their hostility was substituted with apprehension. They just lacked any sense of courage. Only high numbers allowed them to do what they just did.

After the commotion, the only ones left were Shannon, Jude and I. Jude was perplexed about what to do. For a second, he still wanted to pursue the boss's orders, but all that vanished the moment he became aware that he could've died here—that I could still kill him here and now. He dropped the act with the goal of leaving my place.

"You should try to leave this town as soon as you can." I stated.

"That option seems like the best, yet it only reminds me that I couldn't save my two best pals."

"You can't make a choice for somebody else. They made their choices."

"Maybe you're right. Good luck."

"Hey, is it true that the boss will never give up with chasing me?"

"Year ago when I was just starting, he was formulating a new team since the other one malfunctioned." Jude took a seat and found his smokes. "One day, each of us got a name and a photo of our predecessor. He said 'kill them and you get in.' Out of the ten of us, only 4 succeeded. I have no idea what happened to the other six of the predecessors, but I heard stories that he searched all over the planet until he could kill all of them. I think he succeeded. I didn't know it back then, but now, I realize that his code is based on the notion of winning and losing." Jude rose and left without another word. Watching him go, I still held his gun.

The apartment was trashed and I couldn't stay there any longer. The living room floor was occupied by a corpse in a pool of blood, and all the furniture has been turned upside down. Whatever peace that was left here was consumed when tattooist made his final attempt at breathing.

"Take whatever you need, we're leaving." I told Shannon. She went inside to gather her things. "I'd like you to show me the place where you hid the diary."

"Alright, give me two minutes." She said from the inside, her voice somewhat distorted by the enclosure.

Waiting, I was again reminded about the circumstance surrounding Aidan. I wanted to make sure what he was planning, as well as the gist of the situation. I made one last endeavor to reach him with my cell.

"How does it feel to be uncertain, huh?" Aidan spoke in monotone on the other end.

"I heard about what happened."

"Shit happens, you know? But in case you're wondering, I'm having a nice chat with Judith here, who forgot her weapon. After all, she was the one who shot me."

"Where are you now?" His attack caught me off guard.

"I also called Magnus. It should be a splendid meeting."

"Where are you?"

"A long time ago, there was a factory on the western edge of town. I'll be waiting there." The call ended..

Making sure Shannon didn't hear anything, I got in touch with Magnus and described what to do if I were to get seriously injured while confronting Aidan.

Shannon was all set with packing. She carried a bag over her shoulder. As she got out, I locked the door with my key before tossing it in the grass never to be found again. I had no idea what to do with the corpses inside. It would be beneficial to burn this place, but this was not my style. Fortunately, if the Unity's plan works out, there'll be too much chaos, so I maybe nobody will link me with this incident. Maybe no one will care about the death of those two. The remoteness of the place played in my favor too. I had no intention of staying here anymore, and all I needed to settle this is a 48 hour period and a golden opportunity. Shannon seemed to understand what was happening. She didn't ask any questions.

"I forgot to tell you. Someone brought this when you were gone." She held a paper bag not unlike those the restaurants use for take-outs. Opening the bag, I saw that it contained a simple white plastic box. I opened it, and saw a note from Magnus with two syringes and a bottle of poison. Reading the note, I tacked the syringes into my pocket and turned to Shannon.

"You should take this in case you get into some kind of trouble." I handed her the bottle of poison, but soon regretted it. "Never mind, you don't need to do this. This is not your fight."

"Don't worry. I know that someone will die if I forced them to drink it. I'm not stupid"

"Well, promise me that you'll only use it in an extreme situation. I don't want you to have to bear something like that for the rest of your life."

"Thank you for earlier." She replied.

"For what?" I responded lost in thought about the confrontation orchestrated by Aidan. I had a feeling someone was directing him; kidnapping Judith wasn't his idea. If he really wanted just revenge, he could've killed Judith and me. Another person was playing the game.

"You see, people judge. They try not to understand, but only to judge. Humans have many emotions, but only a fraction is permitted to surface. Thanks for not condemning my behavior when Waye died."

"How many times do I have to tell you to be a bit more selfish?" I shrugged. "Allow yourself to do things and never ask for permission. You should make up for all

the selfishness that was absent from your life until now."
I gave her a smile as best as I could, but I wasn't use to
cheering anyone up, so I could never judge my perfor-
mance.

"I think you might have to keep reminding me. So
how did you meet Fredric?"

"When I first arrived, he was the one to show me
around. I think he was the first person I spoke to here.
He got me that job in the library too."

"Do you know who killed Waye?"

"Only speculation, no concrete evidence. If I were to
bet my life on it, I would bet it was the secretary. He
treated her worthlessly, and her abrupt entrance was just
too much of a coincidence."

"I know for sure that it wasn't Fredric. He seems too
kind to do something like that. I think he is trying to
make up for something that he has done a long time ago.
I think that's why he helped us."

Our conversation ceased from existence as if any fire
left was extinguished.

◆

I was a little wary of walking around for fear of stumbling
upon the cultists, but I think that Waye's death postponed
their plan as the streets were barren. An hour after we
have left home, we made it to the factory. It wasn't used
for what seemed like forever, so most of the place was
corroded and destroyed. The metal doors echoed through
the completely lifeless place as I opened them to go in.
The hallways had leaks and water was dripping down
onto the floor—maybe it wasn't even water. The greasy
and watery floor led me down a long hallway, and yet

another door greeted me before I faced Aidan. I insisted that Shannon stayed behind. Inside the huge room Judith was tied to a chair, facing in my direction. Aidan sat behind her. Her eyes were covered by a white cloth. There was another door opposite where I came from and another to my right. Aidan was resting on a chair. He was speaking with someone over the phone. Without even blinking an eye, he tossed the phone to me.

I answered to hear the computer generated voice of the killer again.

"I hope you're not too mad about my use of one of your pawns."

We're the Same

THE VOICE CARRIED a hint of triumph despite its emotionless nature. The killer was joyful that the game was continuing. His disregard for human life was the only thing that I considered honest.

"I was mostly done with that one, so you're free to take him if you so wish." I replied.

"I already did. I made him realize a thing or two. Say, how many people are you willing to sacrifice to face me?"

"Everyone, except maybe a single person."

"Such a conviction, but I'm certainly pleased. A couple weeks ago, you wouldn't care about anything and look at you now—fully motivated to get through this thing."

"That's all thanks to you." No, it isn't. I thought.

Opposite from me, Magnus entered thought the other

door. His pace much slower than usually. His wound were not healed.

"I'm glad you realized it. At first, I didn't know why you asked about Heather until I recognized that we met before."

"Do tell me the reason for doing something so horrible?"

"Guess you've earned it. What if I told you that every single person that committed suicide was actually willing to do so? You see, all of them ... they never had any support around them. They were on their last stroll. I helped them, and every single person agreed to do it. I never once forced anyone to do anything." He declared with a veneer of honesty. "I helped them end their suffering."

"Messing with their mind sure is easy if someone is weak."

"Oh, don't give me that. I know that you understand, and you know I'm right."

"You're kidding. Tell me, why someone on their last stroll would try to leave the city and sell their restaurant?"

"Outside behaviors don't mean anything in the face of inside thoughts. She certainly tied doing what you said, but she was too worn out. She couldn't care less what happens next. That's why she asked me to help her. Besides, a death when a human has reached their highest point is a beautiful death."

"You were the one sitting in that house when I helped Shannon, right?" I pointed in another direction seeing his indifference toward grave notions.

"Helped? You're overestimating yourself. Hearing you ask means that she hasn't disclosed any info. This makes me happy. One thing I don't understand is why you can't appreciate her more. You snatched her right for me, and you don't even understand what makes her unique."

"She's dedicated."

"Such a narrow view, my friend. I'll be off to show the world another spectacle of beauty today. I will be waiting for you once you decide to return my diary. For now, enjoy the play." The call ended with those simple, and yet extraordinary words.

This resulted in no rest as I still had Aidan to deal with.

"So now you had a chance to speak with my new mentor." Aidan rose from the chair. His mindset differed greatly from his usual one—his insides were boiling with a sentiment of hatred. He had a loaded gun in his hand, which he pointed at Judith in case something went wrong —in case I would try to make a move.

"Look, I don't know what you're getting at, but there is no need for this commotion. If you truly wish to get revenge, why not solely aim at me?" I asked.

"What do you take me for a fool? I can't kill you, at least not with physical violence. That's why she's here." He pointed the barrel at Judith, who remained extremely calm. Aidan limped off the chair and stood up. His free hand grasped one of the crutches. He was hobbling. "Of course, I wouldn't be able to get her in my current state, but she lacked a gun and I had the element of surprise."

"What do you intend to do?"

"It's not about what I want to do, but about what you want to do. Here, I'll help you." He threw a small bag to me. Inside, I found a pair of razor blades. "Do us all a favor and slit your wrists." Aidan was more and more soaked in pure enmity.

Was he serious? It would certainly be a way to kill as the power only activated when there is a third party involved. Yet, it was a vile and humiliating death after all that I've been through. I gazed at the blades, contemplating what to do next.

"You've always lectured me while keeping all the secrets to yourself. I trusted that stealing Dench's recorder was the last job, or so I hoped, until I got shot. She was the one to do it."

"If this is an act of freedom than you're gravely mistaken as you've just swapped masters. The one who allegedly opened your eyes is the mastermind behind the suicides."

"What did I just say? Take the razors, or I'll shoot her! This is no act of freedom, but an act of unshackling myself from the likes of you. I'll be finally free of this shit." He grimaced, looking straight up, searching for the heaven which was obstructed by the ceiling.

Aidan gave me no choice. There was no way to talk him out of this. It wasn't strictly the work of the killer. Something was nurtured within Aidan's psyche and he merely lit it up.

I unzipped the bag, my fingers pressed against the chilly steel. I could feel my hand turn freezing cold in an instant. Feeling the stress poured onto my, I pressed a blade against my arteries. Slowly the razor sharp edge pierced my skin in an almost painless way, slicing through my wrist. I sensed as if the pain was too rapid in onset to be registered by the nerve endings. The blood sped down my fingers and onto the ground.

"You think so?" I asked. "Do you truly think that an act of vengeance leads to liberty? If you think you're unique in your entrapment by others then you're fatally mistaken. What do you think, I'm the boss or something? If I'm truly free what am I doing here in this town struggling to find answers?" I screamed in anger. Once the pain kicked in, it felt derailing, but after a second or two, it twisted into a sensation similar to itching. Many found blood disgusting, but I came to understand it as the metaphor of life that flows through us.

Aidan's resolve was shaken a bit. He was searching for a good response, but in the end, was unable to find one.

"A person is only free once they overcome the idea of blaming others and analyze their own actions. Only then you can truly accept what happened!"

"So what you're suggesting is instead of blaming you and her I should be blaming myself?" He pointed the gun in my direction before firing a bullet in an attempt to shut me up.

A near-missed shot forced me to duck. I felt my ear go deaf before a headache was induced into my head. "You think I have everything under control? No, I'm mired down in this swamp up to my waist, and with each step I'm only going deeper!" I leaned against the wall a little tired form the constant standing. My vision became a bit distorted. "It's not like I'm blaming you for what happened! Who knows if Michael Bailey hadn't massacred me back then, maybe I would've been safe in my own little world. Did you think about that?" I ripped of a piece of my sleeve aiming to tie it around my wrists as to prevent to blood from escaping.

"Don't even think about it." His hands were shaking. "I got to say that your little speech has surely wrestled with my determination."

"Remember what I said about you being a hypocrite? Prove me wrong!" Magnus standing behind him spoke as if he was tired from all the waiting. His intentions were truly good this time as he aimed to prevent Aidan from killing any one.

Aidan was on his home stretch toward sanity. The words made him reconsider. He gave up on his revenge and it seemed as if he observed that he's not so different from Magnus and me. He was awakened to the lie that we're in control. Conversely, we're just hiding our true sentiments toward the world. "You're right. I don't need this shit. I'm better than the killer." Aidan confessed. He was set to leave. Magnus begun slowly strolling in his direction.

Ready to hand his gun over, Aidan stretched out his hand to Magnus. Before the exchange could take place, Judith freed herself from the chair and dropped on the floor. Startled by the sudden noise, Aidan twisted back and fired in awe. Within seconds, Magnus hurried and pushed him down. The bullet missed as Aidan fell to the ground. He stared at the gun before throwing it to the side in disgust. The gun banged on the floor, declaring his defeat. Aidan escaped through the closest exit. Judith took of the cloth and stared at Magnus.

Astonished, she spoke the words.

"It's you."

Survival

———————

MAGNUS RUSHED BACK toward the exit without looking back. He charged through the door and jammed it behind. Judith tried followed, but she got nowhere close before the passage sealed.

I tied the cloth around my bloodied hands.

"Explain yourself."

"We have no time for that. All you need to know is that the one you saw is not responsible for the kidnapping." I walked to the door behind me and called for Shannon.

As she saw my wounds, she panicked. "What happened? You need to get to a hospital."

"It can wait. This whole thing was arranged by the suicide mastermind, and Aidan might be in trouble. I've got to follow him." I turned to Judith. "Are you coming as well?"

With a simple nod, the three of us followed through the door that Aidan used. The place waiting for us on the other side was a squalid labyrinth of corridors. The water could still be heard in the background, but it was much more subtle. Any light that was there seemed like its only purpose was getting a person though the corridor and not good illumination. As we made it to the first intersection, I was hesitant about where to proceed until Shannon pointed at the left hallway. There was a sign.

I realized my mistake. I overcame my anger. I was a thief and a criminal; what kind of fate was I asking for? Of course, sooner or later I would get hurt. Realizing this, I escaped committing murderer and proved that I have some goodness left.

Words that seemed to be spoken by Aidan led us down the left corridor. Up the next narrow hallway and to the right, the next sign pointed the way.

Unfortunately, very few humans change. The feelings we try to hold only last seconds—in the best scenario days. In the end, any progress is reverted with time.

Following the hall, we were lead into a mostly empty cafeteria. The lights were much brighter, yet that didn't change the obscurity of the place. The floor felt dirty from the greasy food and the impoliteness of the workers that once been here. Seated on one of the empty stool and leaning again the counter was Aidan. The stool's black finish was now vibrantly red, and the black gave in to the vivacious crimson. Aidan had his hands on the counter, forming a pillow where his head lie. His eyes closed, sleeping. Behind him was more writing.

The most proper death is at the point when a human reached enlightenment and perfection. Only then one can hold the idea for longer than a second.

Shannon gasped and put her hand to her face in terror. It must have been her first time seeing the gruesome face of death. As for me and Judith, we showed no emotion what-so-ever. I didn't know if the town changed Judith, or if she was always immune to the gruesome, but she wasn't shaken even a bit by the scene.

"I'll call this in to Dench and the medics, but I doubt the killer left any evidence except the quotes written in blood." Judith said and turned her attention to her cell.

"We should go." I glanced at Shannon.

Judith finished her brief conversation, and turned to me. "Considering how unnerved the people are, I'll go into hiding. My companions might come after you, so find a good hiding spot as well." she recommended.

"Hiding is the last thing I'll ever consider." My last statement evaporated in the acidic air of sadness and grief at the time of Aidan's death. We went our separate ways. The blood that I've lost was truly getting me to familiarize with the feeling of sleepiness and despair as my strength was slowly escaping. I was only able to pass a couple of blocks, and soon I needed Shannon's support to walk upright. I knew that I won't make it in time in this state— not home, and certainly not to the clinic. The screams of the mad cultists could be heard form buildings ahead.

"Let's stop for a second." I attempted at standing straight but gave up after the first try. The dizziness was way too strong. I clang to Shannon for support.

"You really need to get to a doctor." Shannon looked

at me with those eyes that care. It wasn't the look of someone who says something because it's proper, but the look of someone who had strong feelings. These feeling backed up her advice.

I took out my phone and made a call. "Magnus, I think it's about time."

"Are you sure about this?" He asked curious about what I was planning.

"That's the only way. Plus if everything works, one problem will be no more."

"She'll hate you for the rest of her life if she finds out." Magnus exclaimed in a voice as if he begun studying to understand other humans.

"Since when do you care about other people's feeling?" I asked Magnus trying to joke around, but he could sense that I'm on my last lap. "Make it convincing." I said. After hearing Magnus agree to follow my plan right through, I hung up.

I put my shoulder over Shannon as she dragged me ahead toward home. She looked at me as a tear gathered in her eye. Her sad look only reflected the despair that dwells in this city and its current form—rage. We haven't even walked for mere minutes as someone stood behind me.

He lunched himself with his back foot, a knife in hand. Any attempts at taking Shannon to safety were in vain because of my physical condition. The hooded assassin pushed me back and upon seeing Shannon's fighting spirit planted the knife in her thigh. The smile from underneath the hood made me speculate if I had gone too far.

"No! Let her go! Don't hurt her!" I screamed with all my heart as I knew Shannon was at his mercy.

He pushed her to the ground and said. "I'd like my notebook back."

"You'll get it! I'll bring it to you! I swear."

"We both know that's not going to happen." He patted me on the back. He called a number, and I heard an emergency operator rumble on. "I saw some suspicious activity going on the intersection of Locust Dr. and Green Meadow Boulevard. You'll send someone? Great. Thank you so much." He turned to give me a one final look. "You should probably leave the girl if you want to live, although with your health, I doubt you'll get anywhere." He disappeared as the noise from the surrounding buildings redoubled. I stumbled closer to Shannon who fainted, her body motionlessly resting on the pavement. Seeing her bleed, I panicked.

In horror, I took out my phone and called Judith. My voice was hectic and gasping for air. "I need your help, or she'll die! We've been attacked, and the cultists might find us! I beg for your help!"

She spoke not a word. It sounded like she was talking to someone. The debate on the other side boiled with enthusiasm until she posed the final question.

"In exchange for saving her life, will you turn yourself in?"

The Paradox

_____

WITHOUT A CHOICE in the matter, I had to agree if Shannon was to be saved. While her wound wasn't as lethal as I initially thought, after the panic has worn off, I came to realize that her current state was the least of my worries. The screams of flustered denizens of the town and their victims echoed everywhere. The notion that any second someone with an intention to kill might arrive worked in my body in an uncomfortable way that only increased my willingness to agree to Judith's proposal.

Time flew slowly until two vehicles had arrived: a silver four-door sedan driven by Judith, and an SUV. Out of the SUV jumped out Leon, Dorian, and Kazuki.

Judith soon dragged away Shannon to her vehicle after whispering. "I'm sorry that it had to end like this, but I promise you that she'll live."

"Alright, enough talk! Put this on." Leon said in determination to get this done.

He threw a white strait jacket toward me which signaled just how petrified they really were. This power poured fear into their hearts of men. After putting it on, Kazuki tied the loose sleeves behind me which restrained my movements completely, and any willingness in a standard human being would evaporate instantly, but I still had a fraction of the usual motivation left.

Judith drove off into the distance with Shannon on board, but before we could leave, over a dozen cultists arrived with various weapons. One towered over the rest. His tall posture instantly made his out to be the boss of the pack. "What's going on here, lads?" Although friendly in sound and meaning, the question grew into something else in this context, something composed solely of mockery. "Unfortunately we're going to have to take you in for questioning. The Unity demands so."

Dorian turned around, holding a gun in each hand; he seemed to be a bit more irritated than ever before. With the loaded guns, he used the power of persuasion; "Do you think I care? Get out of my sight at once before I change my mind, and a massacre will commence!"

At the sound of the response most of the cultists dispersed in the opposite direction like ants running to their nest, leaving only a few stranded on the side walk in awe. The boss roared in authority at the retreating members, forcing some to reluctantly comeback.

Annoyed by the growing commotion, Kazuki took out his firearm and fire with the intent to kill. After a single brainwashed thug descended to the floor, the rest of them withdrew in glorified terror.

"Let's get going before anything unforeseen happens." Leon said to Kazuki who took a hold of my vest and dragged me into the car, throwing me on the leather backseat. He then took a seat right beside me. He was the only one that retained his composure even in the face of danger that I supposedly posed. His bravery lingered somewhere on the edge of wanting to die and rationally risking life.

"Don't act like you're the boss!" Dorian uttered and their usual friendliness was gone. Something was eating at both of them this very minute, something that won't ever let go.

"Look, I know Jude is gone, but the only way we can make it through this is if we cooperate."

"Cooperate? Where was the cooperation when Jude objected to our stay here? You know very well that if all of us rebelled, the boss wouldn't have a chance."

"We all knew the risk!" Leon retorted.

Leon took out a cigarette out of an almost empty pack. His hands were quivering a bit, but I wasn't sure what it was form. He took a lighter and ignited a fire which lit his cigarette. The smoke escaped his longs as he took multiple unconscious deep breathes that proved he was a long-time smoker.

"Don't give me that bullshit. We were a family, and where are we now? The three of us gave up on life becoming nothing more than meat chunk, ready to be replaced by another." Dorian leaped into the seat alongside the driver, complaining about the situation. The venting backfired as with each complaint his anxiety only escalated.

"We've got no time for this! Let's go!" Kazuki spoke

in an almost mindless voice, one that has lost sanity and is indeed just a chunk of meat.

Finishing his smoke with a final deep lungful, Leon took the driver seat. The car was a luxurious SUV, taking into account the black leather of the seats. It was an automatic drive with cameras for backing us as well as a built-in GPS.

The town was most lively today. Countless buildings had lights on, and screams could be heard from every direction. Our destination was unknown, but I would guess it was that old motel, so my time here was very limited. Magnus had a microphone implanted on the crew, but I doubt there would be one in the car. He still has his injuries too. With their current unstable state, with mere words I could be about to put them against one another. It's my only chance.

"Hey, your name is Dorian, right?" With a simple nod I could continue. "I don't get you. I told you last time that you could achieve greatness if you made decisions for yourself, and yet you're still going with the flow."

Leon sped up past some helpless youth on the street, trying to escape from his oppressors. From the window, I saw him plummet into the pavement with no strength to stand up.

Dorian gave me the stare, "I'm not in a mood for this so shut up."

"That's quite sad because the reason why you're angry is because you're afraid you could be next."

"Shut up!" Kazuki exclaimed, hitting me with the butt of his gun.

Tremendous headache ensued and my mind was dazed by the assault, but I chose to push on. "If you do something for someone once maybe twice, sooner or later they won't even think twice about taking it for granted. They'll use you. One day you'll wake up as a pet dog." I paused for a second. "I once heard someone say that."

"Look, shut up! You're thinking that we're all going to listen to this bullshit because we're scared? What do you think about the idea; I'll put the gun to your head and ram a bullet into your head. That should work."

"You think so? Are you ready to try? That'll be your first and last conscious decision." I laughed at Dorian. Flustered and helpless with nothing to grasp to reclaim his stability, Dorian raised the pistol and cuddled the trigger. His muscles tightened a little all around his hand. On the verge of killing, Dorian gave me a closing stare of resentment. Before he could proceed, Kazuki fired a shot into his face. Dorian's head fell back partially shattering the side window. Blood coated the front windshield as well as the majority of the side.

"What the heck are you doin? Shit!" Leon hit the brakes. He freaked out, blindly searching for the handle to open the door. He fell onto the pavement onto his back. His pupil widened as he saw his friend dead. Tears dripped from his face, a feeling which he never felt. He took both of his hands and dug his face into them. He begun weeping on his knees, realizing that he is the only one left.

Kazuki got out of the car and heaved me onto the floor with full force. He towered over me, and I couldn't predict what will be his reaction. He's cold stature knew nothing about feelings. He stared at Leon as if this was the first time he saw someone crying, or maybe this event reminded him of the time he lost this ability. He gave of a shrug before saying. "I don't know what the big problem is? He was ready to fire and it's safe to assume that he would be killed anyway. The orders were clear, bring him alive."

"It's your fault! What is wrong with you? You messed-up freak, don't you have any reverence toward the value of human life!" Leon was on his knees sobbing, his whole face covered in tears as he lamented at the loss of a friend. He was looking at Kazuki through his covered face. The only thing that showed was his eyes which had a tinge a fury to them.

Both of the man reached out for the gun and fired. Leon was much faster and managed to hit Kazuki in the jaw. The bullet tore through his face, ripping out multiple teeth in the process. Kazuki bowed, profusely spitting blood and facial tissue. He miss and Leon exited unharmed.

"I'm done." Leon said, giving up on his assignment and slowly retreating. He was still prepared to counterattack in case Kazuki reloaded his weapon. Aiming to disappear, he was interrupted by the voice of a man, who exited form the depths of the shadows.

"So they were right. You're a very quick draw and a fine shooter as well." Magnus spoke, sauntering. His face was pale from the loss of blood, and he stood there with major insecurity. Lacking in strength and endurance, he still had that same lunatic smile, but his eyes were weak and tired—dying.

"Who are you?" Leon asked.

"The one who eliminated your comrades."

At the sound of those words, Leon raised his gun in an attempt to shot Magnus, who was already way to close. Magnus bent down, and the bullet flew right over his head. He zoomed close to Leon, grabbing the hand with the loaded gun and turning his back to Leon. When he had Leon's hand over his shoulder, he grabbed it with both hand and pulled down with all his might. Leon's pathetic struggling had no meaning, and the hand just snapped. Hearing Leon feeble scream, Magnus swiveled landing an elbow into his face. Leon flew back onto the floor, howling in pain. Magnus took a hold of his gun and fired a few rounds ending his life.

"Looks like you're the only one left excluding the boss." Magnus said. His movements still lacking as his contusions haven't fully healed. He had his regular attire which most likely covered the bandage that he had on himself.

Kazuki tried to fire, but all he heard was a silent click.

"I had a bug planted in your car, I was quite positive that my bullet count was correct." Magnus marched.

When Kazuki haphazardly tried to reload his gun, Magnus threw himself forward as he grappled a knife and flanged it at Kazuki puncturing his shoulder. Kazuki ripped out the blade and took a fighting stance. Magnus was already close, and he picked up another dagger from his pocket. He raised his hands overhead, preparing to jam the tip into Kazuki. Kazuki blocked, crossing his arms in front of his face. They went into a stalemate as Magnus was on the offensive, yet their strength was evenly matched.

"Stop this! We might need him." I said.

Blood spilled from the corners of Kazuki's dry lips. Magnus backed up as he was just about to overpower Kazuki, who was now constantly spitting blood. The blood was not only from the wound on his face, but from an internal problem.

"I'm dissatisfied. Where is that attacker who almost slaughtered me that night?" Magnus signed as he lost his blood-thirsty self.

My plan fell apart as Kazuki was just about ready to die. He must've been sick for a very long time. His face showed no surprise; he was expecting this to happen. "I always believed that, no matter where you are, if you and the person you're searching for want to meet each other, sooner or later you will. The only condition is that both of you have to desire so. I have always dreamed of seeing my wife and child, but I never could see them since I lost them. Does it mean that they didn't want to see me?"

I stooped down unable to move my upper body. "Worry not, your family is safe living a normal life. The boss told me that they think you're dead, but they're safe."

Only half of the words seemed to reach Kazuki. He died in the middle of my story telling.

"A kind gesture. You've granted his last wish. He was yearning all his life to make sure that his family is safe. Now he knows that they indeed are." Magnus leaned against the SUV.

"If only he heard me before he died."

"'If not, sooner or later, he'll meet them.'"

"Say, why did you stop?"

"He was too weak to pose any kind of a challenge." Magnus took a step back as he saw his jacket colored red. "My injury must have reopened." He took a seat on the hood of the SUV. "So what now? There is one more enemy we have to deal with tonight."

While the circumstances of the last hour have kept my mind off my unfavorable state, I was now on the verge of falling sleep. I persisted to keep myself awake, knowing that once I lose consciousness I'll be done for. "Untie me and give me your gun."

"What?"

"You heard me right."

Magnus helped me get the vest off. Not sure of my intentions, he passed me the gun he had in hand. I took a deep breath and pointed it at me leg. I fired a shot which drove a piercing sensation running through me body. I screamed as the pain was one that I never felt before. My limbs usefulness shattered in immense pain, making me cry and scream.

"What are you doing? Have you lost it?" Magnus screamed.

I fired another shot into my left hand—the Earl's dominant hand.

I glanced at Magnus through my watery eyes. "The boss is left handed, and my injury will prevent him from retaliation. The other wound will prevent his escape. Once he has all those injuries, he'll be an easy target. As long as I confront him, I win. Oh, yea, and don't do anything. Just watch the ending."

Magnus disposed of the bodies in an alley. He helped me into the car. He started the engine, let off the hand brake, and the car rolled down the incline. It was already the middle of the night, and soon, it'll be daybreak. I only had minutes left before my possible departure, so I had to hurry.

◆

Every second, I was reminded of how my consciousness was tearing away—how empty my body felt. The roaring of the engine sounded in my barely awake ears like a lullaby, pushing me into sleep, yet keeping me lightly awake.

As we got to our destination, the boss was stationed overlooking the place from his second floor apartment. Magnus gave me a knife which I hid in my sleeve. He opened the door and helped me inside before he let go, and I crumbled to the ground. He soon vanished. The boss was, by now, walking down the steps.

"You have no idea how long I've been waiting for this." He went closer as he gave me an evil smile. "You created quite a lot of trouble for me. You destroyed my team's respect toward me, as well as my position as their leader." He bent over. I kept resting on my side, ready to fall asleep. "Hey, I'm talking to you!" He gave me a kick in the shoulder which propelled me to fall on my back. The knife slipped out of my sleeve and onto the bloodied ground. The kick, which should have hurt me, kept me alert just a little. "What do we have here?" He bent down and took a hold of the blade. "Were you hoping to win? You've lost it all. The only thing you can do to keep your name alive is disclose the name of the one who killed my teammates, your reason for helping him, and everything you know about the fiendish power that Dorian told me about." His voice slowly drifted away as if it moving away from me, but it was my consciousness which was moving away. The roof spoke to me with its lights. It gave off a signal, flashing occasionally. I felt as if I was drifting on a boat away from the shore with no destination.

The elderly man stumped on my injured hand, sending pain thought my body. "I'll ask again. I want the name and address of the person who eliminated my team." He stated, this time in a much more vigorous tone, trying to stir me up again. I tried speaking, but had no strength what-so-ever. The voice that I tried to transmit got lost, unable to overcome the barrier of distance. He came closer and kneeled, putting his ear above my face. The knife that was in his left hand levitated above the ground close to my right hand.

"Chr ... Christopher ..." I began speaking while I tried to reach for the knife. As I felt the blade, I prepared to grapple it while I said. "Look like I win. "Before I drifted off, I used up all my might to wring my hand around the blade. As more and more blood poured out of my hand, I wondered how much of it was left in my body.

"Pathetic." Earl Winters took a confident stand. "Look how low y-you've f-fallen." His determined strong voice was suddenly twisted into mere mumbling. The boss didn't realize that his time has come. He wandered backwards as he groaned when the pain entered his body. He lost his balance and bent holding his hand over the counter in order to regain his composure.

The dizziness evaporated as my vision became clearer until it was ideal. The blood that was on my hands seconds ago began to drip to the floor from the boss's right hand.

"I, Earl Winters, demand an explanation! What did you do to me, you monster?"

My strength was coming back. I lifted myself up to a sitting position on the ground. Behind me, the boss searched for a gun, and once he had on in hand, he aimed, but couldn't. He's hand was twitching unsettled by the pain until it was too late. It broke completely. He fired a round at the ground as the hand dropped down, pulled by the weight of the pain. With his last final attempt at a shot, he aimed with his other hand, but before he could fire his leg ruptured until he was forced to a crawling position on the ground. His shrieks redoubled into the room as he yelled. "What did you do?"

By the time the ghoulish procedure was over, I was the one standing up and he was the one in the arms of death. Whatever imperfections I might have had were completely gone. All wounds and harms disappeared in an instant. I stood with full strength as I felt that my body had every ounce of everything it needed to exist in perfect harmony. I strolled to the counter and called Judith form the receptionist's phone. I took a refreshing breath. "I have the boss's life in my hands. In exchange, I would like to see the files of every person in the village that was indirectly involved in a murderer and didn't help the one in need. I'm sure there will be notes about the most suspicious of cases. I'll be waiting where I should've died."

Judith was stunned. I bet that, for a second, she didn't know what to say. I'm guessing that she had a mixture of happy and sad feelings. For once, I would like to believe that she didn't want me to die. However, I was uncertain how she'll feel about seeing the detestable man on the floor. He was about to depart this life, yet he meant something to her. Still on the phone, I was yearning for a response until Judith said.

"I'm not cop anymore. Only Dench has the necessary authorization."

Believing that Fredric succeeded, I stated the tentative. "Dench has been discarded from this game. You're free to do as you please at the station. Besides if there is someone who is lawful, it's you." I hung up the phone.

I turned to the old man. "I'm not sure how this power works, so I can't tell you how much time you have left. On another note, you're a fool, you know that?" I said as I walked to the dark backroom and turned on the TV. I wanted to hear the news about Dench. The reporter spoke about a lot of unnecessary information. Clamor came from the back of the room. As I killed the darkness with light, I saw Jude on the floor. He had numerous severe wounds. There was red all over his clothes. It was certain that he was tortured, and all the wounds that he had avoided any major arteries. Struggling to voice any comments, he was about to die.

"P-Pocket … letter … family …" He spoke in a broken up language as if his muscles didn't want to cooperate in speaking the words. In his right pocket of his coat, there was a letter addressed to Francesca Lane. The correspondence was bent right down the middle of the envelope. It had bend corners as well as a mild red stein on the front, which avoided the mailing info.

"I'll be sure to mail it." I said as I was unsure about what to say. I saw his eyes, and I knew what they were telling me. I was not an executioner and didn't want to attack a defenseless person, but the notion that he won't live much longer and all that's left is suffering was eating at me. Taking his life would leave a bad taste in my mouth, or so I thought, until I realized it that he was waiting here for me. I felt anger bottle up in the pit of my stomach. The sensation of no escape was ever-present.

"Don't ask this of me."

"P-please."

Hearing his pleas irked me and shook my conviction. Going against the idea that I'll do everything for peace, I went to the hall and picked up the boss's gun. Upon my return, I fired multiple shots into his chest, ending his life, and wishing that he'll find peace. I took a hold of the gun as if expecting that I might need it for something. Before departing the room, I found more bullets that fit the standard police firearm.

"You know, I would like to hear your take on the story of why an extraordinary woman such as Judith would hang out with someone life you." I said, walking next to the boss, who was bleeding but still had some strength left.

"She was unable to come back to work because of the events with the murderer." The boss coughed. "I had power in the city. I spoke on her behalf with the higher-ups and because of that she could return to work." His words were fighting his cadaverous body.

"That's why she's here in this village, right? I mean, it's no coincidence that she was chosen as Dench's support?"

"That's right. I trusted her like no one else, and she felt the same. Our cooperation here was arranged as you've figured." He coughed abundantly.

A bell sounded from the door, and on the monitor in the backroom Judith showed up. Apparently, she had the papers as she was carrying a stack of them.

"Promise me that she'll get out of here alive." The boss exhaled without any power left.

"That's a weird request, considering that you thought I wanted all of you dead." I stared at him. With the silence growing, I said. "She's likely to survive if she doesn't lose her spirit." I walked to the door and unlocked them.

She seemed composed, but as her eyes met with the boss, she lost her cool and shoved the paperwork into my hands. Passing me by, I sneaked the extra bullets into her pocket. She rushed for the boss and called for the ambulance. "Help will be here soon." She said at the verge of crying.

I opened up the folder and begun flipping through the profiles of various suspects from this town. The search was simple as I instantly dismissed most of them. I was halfway through in a minute, but she interrupted my work.

"What did you do to him?"

"I merely reversed our positions. Minutes ago, I was the one on the floor." I declared my point of view without looking her way. I was consumed by the search. At last, I found the one, and I threw the rest of the paperwork on the floor. "That's the one. I would also like the keys to your car." I said.

"Here." Judith through them unwillingly. The boss caught all of her attention.

"Don't forget to check your pockets." I interrupted her.

She bent down further in order to hear the boss's now tiny voice that was requesting water. She reached for the bottle as I walked outside.

"Shannon, I wonder if you've completed your mission." I said to myself in my mind. The horrors of the night followed me even thought I was back in full health. No matter how hard I struggled, I felt a foreign sensation that I would became a tastier meal for the shadows that were born from the night. I made it across the street and jumped into the sedan. Shannon was seated on the back seat. Her pulse was a little weaker, but she was on her way to health.

"I did what you told me." She uttered half-asleep. Her eyes were almost fully closed. The words were spoken though a fog as if she was dreaming about something.

"Good job. We're halfway there to escaping this town." I turned the key, and the engine growl softly. The tank was full of gas. A flash of two humans burning under azure flames recoiled in my mind for a prolonged period before disappearing. As I drove, I saw Judith run out in full rage screaming in the distance. She emptied her gun into thin air. Only one bullet reached my car and blew out the back windshield. Once her gun was empty, she took an angry stance in the middle of the road. The noise create a center of attention for all the residents as numerous became present at the scene.

Her last words echoed in my head as I drove down the street. "You're just like all the others! You're like them!"

The words developed into a weaker tone as the villagers encircled her. Her anger at my betrayal engraved her demise into stone.

Restrained Hatred

HER WORDS PIERCED my heart. "You're just like all the others! You're like them!"

I knew sure well that I didn't want to be grouped with the animals like those people that she considered, yet I had no choice.

I drove down the road, aiming to get out of town. A certain serene spot was what I was looking for. Every intersection gave me an uncomfortable sensation like someone was tailing me—staring me down. Meticulously, I surveyed my surroundings, making sure no one was hunting for me as I headed into the forest. The moon barely shone like it turned away from humanity disgusted from the barbaric view.

Shannon showed me to the place where she buried the diary. We found a concealed spot on the outskirts of town where bushes would mask the car. I turned off the head lights and contemplated about tomorrow. Instinctively, I spend the majority of the night reading the mastermind's diary. Knowing his identity didn't help as I was still at a loss as to how I could triumph over him. I fell into the dream world where I was met with the teacher.

◆

"Looks like tomorrow you'll face destiny?" The teacher was reading his notes with his face hidden behind the book. The look of the world was identical to every time that I visited, yet there was a thin breeze or movement in the air.

"I hope so. As long as a confrontation takes place, I'll end this nightmare somehow."

"When I still served the world with all my heart, it was forbidden for brothers to kill each other. When a killer surfaced, I took his life." He closed the book and smashed it on to the top of the desk. He stood up, stepped around the desk, and took a seat on the chair.

"Why stop?"

"Let's just say that I too have lost something dear. Afterward, I couldn't kill the one responsible because the Will of the Universe saw him as righteous. Everybody gets burned out sooner or later. That event burned me out. " His signature smile was much brighter than typically, concealing his true emotions.

"Is that why you want to find a successor? You lost the meaning of your existence."

"You see, humans look for eternity. They lust for eternal lives. Yet, there are very few of them that would be able to bear the burden of eternal life. I'm tired of life really."

"You know, the killer and you, you're very similar—your look of life, your way of mind games."

"Well, his school is probably identical to mine."

"I'll be going. I have life to catch up to." I gave of a faint smile as our days of conversing were coming to an end.

"Don't worry. We'll meet at your road's end. I wish you luck. Thank you for curing me of boredom even for just a little."

"Despite your infuriating presence, I think my stay here was one that spiced up my life a little." As I said those words the world crumbles, twisted, and melted like a stone consumed by lava; and soon I was in the real world. My eyes were opened, but still vastly asleep yearning to drop into slumber. When I rose up the clock indicated 5:30.

◆

With whatever sleep I had and my resources of strength still depleted, I set out to complete my task. I stepped out of my car and stretched. Out of nowhere something hit me on the head. I felt dizzy as the entire environment shook up and down. I felt my memory go cloudy then come back to life again—reset. Before I could seize my return, another hit made me plummet into dirt. I turned around onto my back to see Judith pointing her gun at me.

"How could you do something like that?" Her voice was trembling for the adrenaline that came from the struggle she endured.

"I had no choice. You know very well that in the end, I would've died if I didn't act."

"I'm not only talking about his wounds, I'm talking about the poison that was in my water bottle. Were you expecting it to take me out as well?" Her mind was barely gripping her hatred. All she wanted to do was act on her emotions and shoot, but something was stopping her and it certainly wasn't the fear of my power. "I could have been the one to drink out of that bottle!"

"The situation required the risk."

"Shut up! I don't want to hear any more of this bull-shit! Tell me the name of the person you found in the files." Her finder caressed the trigger.

"Have you seen Jude Lane? If you did, you saw how the boss tortured him. Look in to my eyes and tell me that you have not a tinge of reservation about the boss."

"And you think that with this doubt I'll start to believe that he should've died?" She kneeled closer, constantly looking into my eyes as if searching deep within my soul for a reason that would allow her to restrain her urge to kill. Her pupils filled with insanity that was eagerly striving to overcome her consciousness and control her whole.

"No, with this doubt, you can understand that he had many chances to turn back and all I've done was retaliate with all the tools I had at my disposal. Look at me and tell me that you would've gone a different route in my situation, Judith." I demanded.

She hesitated for a second and glanced at me. She grappled her gun and said, "You're right. I would've done the same. The boss turned into a monster. He changed as he saw his team turn to dust. I respected Winters, and not the newly formed monster, but I can never forgive you for poisoning him. He had only a few minutes of life left, but you couldn't honor that." Judith stood up.

"I had to be sure. If he lived for a little longer, he could have a chance to contact someone he trusted. I could have been hunted for the rest of my life."

"I should've known. You planned this; Shannon poisoned my bottle. You had a plan. You turned a helpless situation into one of triumph. Or maybe you were the one who stabbed Shannon?" Judith chuckled a little from the disappointment. "Tell me, what would happen if I was to drink it."

"Your bottle was poisoned as you were driving Shannon back. There was a chance that you might've died, but it was very slim. On the other hand, if you would've tried to drink it in the boss's hideout. I would've stopped you." I inhaled as I tried to relieve the stress of tonight. "If it'll make you feel better, you can take that gun and shot me, but know that together we can stop the killer."

"If we argue, we fall right into his trap." Her eye looked up in the sky. "Dench was taken. I'm sure the Unity would've wanted me too, so that I won't get in the way. Why was I left alone? It was your doing, right?"

"I just told them you had nothing to do with his work."

"Yet, how can I trust someone who left me there surrounded by all those maniacs, huh?"

"The killer knows my identity. He knows I'm hunting for him. He could've been keeping an eye on me back there. If he was there, he should be convinced that we're enemies. That should give us an upper hand. Besides, who was the one who provided you with a means of repelling those cultists? Would I do that if I wanted you dead?"

She shook her head in disgust. "Fine, let's put our differences aside." She stood up, and we shook hands.

At that time, it seemed as if as long as we cooperated we'd be able to catch him.

The Gamble

IT'S ONLY BEEN meager hours since our pact, but this time, I told Judith everything—about Magnus, anything I knew about the killer, including his theoretical identity, and about the power. Although, I felt as if I was playing actor again just trying to reclaim something unattainable, it was the only thing I could do to mend our twisted partnership. Before the dawn come, we discussed what to do and formulated a plan, as well as tested out a couple of things about the power. In preparation, I really wanted to read the entire notebook of the killer since I believed it would train me for what's to come, but yesterday's night had me so tired that I managed to only read a tiny portion of it. Even though I spend much of the night reading it, it felt as if I just wasn't able to register all the knowledge—like insomnia took a huge toll on me, and I unquestionably needed sleep. No matter, I had an overall understanding of his methods as well as the ability and how to eliminate him.

"Do you remember what I told you about the plan?" I asked Judith.

"Yea, as long as he's there, it should work. I'll be setting out in a couple of minutes to get to the TV station." She said, closing the copied diary as if implying that she was done for now. She had a cup of coffee in her hand. "I was wandering how do you know he'll be there at the station?"

"Just my intuition. I spoke with him on occasions, and many times he seemed to enjoy how the town is going mad. Seeing people fall pleases him. He treats this as a play. If he's pushed to the limit by disclosing his personality, he'll play on anger. Plus, he can't leave since he wants the diary. Angered, he'll yearn to erase me in front of a bigger audience."

"I truly hope you're right." She said crossing her arms tightly around her chest. "I'll get to the station, but the only problem is what if the people don't listen? I mean, he could just kill them all if they stay there."

"Do what you can. You have your budge, so that should help, but we have no idea how much influence the Unity has over there. The people might ignore your argument."

"Which means I won't argue with the heads, I'll inform every single person there? If they want to stay, they can do it at their own risk." she said calmly and sipped her coffee.

"There is one thing that might be troublesome. The killer plays on emotions, so I need to be certain that if he uses Dench in some way, you're not going to do something reckless."

"If that happens, as long as we persuade him who the real killer is, he shouldn't get in our way. At least I hope he doesn't. But if he does, you can play your cards."

"That settles it. I'll be on my way as soon as Shannon gets better."

"Yesterday, we haven't come up with a decision on what we'll do with the killer after we catch him."

I took a plane white napkin and carved out an answer before leaving it on the front seat. "We could just find a peaceful place in the forest, dig a ditch, and throw him in. The ability only works for three seconds. We tested that out last night, didn't we?" Judith eyed her bandaged hand. "He should have enough oxygen for those three sec." I remembered last night when Judith took a knife and made multiple cuts on my hand in succession. After three second, the transfer stopped.

"You know, call me crazy, but the people are searching for a monster, right? If we leave this town as it is, the Unity will take a hold of it and never let go, stripping those people of freewill. If he was to be taken by the Unity and executed, the people might get scared off and break away from the Unity and flee after seeing his power...or they might praise it for succeeding."

"I think you're right, so does that mean I'm crazy too? I think that if people saw his ability, they would panic and most would leave this cursed land. I think that would be one of the best scenarios, but it's too hazardous."

"And it would mean that he would face ..." She took a hold of the napkin read "Execution in front of a huge crowd." With an ironic chuckle, she rose up, ready to go. "Are you sure we should be taking Shannon with us? I'm against that decision."

"I think so too, but it's even more dangerous leaving her here alone. She might do something stupid."

Judith finished her drink, and gathered her belonging in a flash, ready to depart. She had a pile of pictures of the culprit—the result of her trip to the police station after our agreement.

"Take care of yourself."

She hesitated. The sentence must've been something she was unaccustomed at dealing with. She was at a loss of words. She never learned how to respond to these types of sentimental situations. Her beliefs contradicted my actions which were kind to her. "Good luck." She uttered before leaving behind the closed door. Judith's aim was to make it to the station, but before that, she was to hand out the pictures to kids, so that they could go around and stick them to walls around the town. She left in Dench's car while she left her own vehicle with me.

The rest of the morning passed with a blazing sun of summer. During the time off, I considered the use of Magnus, but I went against it as he was unpredictable and much too close to *him*. Looking at Shannon sleeping ignited a yearning to tell her something. The wound she sustained was indeed my fault. I prepare a note that I would like her to have when it's all over. She was slowly regaining her strength around mid-morning, but remained mostly absent until late noon. Once she woke up, we turned to some small talk for a bit before addressing to the case. Her half-awake eyes looked at me patiently.

"Was this the man that visited you on the day when I

took you away?" I asked, holding up a photo of the killer in one hand.

She averted eye contact as she lightly said, "No."

"So it is him. The only question is why you're defending him." My questioning seemed to have no effect on Shannon as she locked herself up mentally, determined to never say anything more. "What are you hiding?" I spoke in a resolute tone, trying to influence her to disclose her hidden agenda if there ever was one. Continuing with the silence, she turned away from me and attempted at falling asleep. "You don't have to say anything as he'll tell me everything once he is about to die" The words irritated Shannon until she could not hold he composure stable any longer.

"That's why I never told you about him."

I turned to face her.

"You two are the first people who respected me. I have only met that man twice, but each time, he cared for me. I cherished every moment I spent with him just as I do with you. You two are very similar, yet I know that if you were to meet, you would've killed each other." A tear travelled down her cheek. "No matter how similar you are, you have different believes and different paths."

"You should rest up." I said, preparing to leave within mere hours.

Once we were ready to leave we packed up. Shannon was still too weak so she slept on the back seat. I gathered all my belongings in the trunk of the car as I prepared to leave. Before leaving the village, I stopped by my former residence. The notion that Dench might come back irked me to leave a note for him pertaining to my location. I placed a note on the door saying, "Shannon, meet me at the TV station."

◆

The distance took 8 hour to cover from the village to the TV station as it was deep within the woods. The station was a multi-floor building that aired both TV and radio broadcasts. During my days here, I have never once visited this place. I parked the car around the front parking lot as I noticed that the only floor lit was the first. Leaving Shannon behind, I headed inside. The doors sprung open automatically as I walked into the near vicinity. Inside the strong lights irritated my eyes as they aimed to blind any person walking by. Straight ahead the corridor stretched to the far back of the station. It was until I walked further that I observed, a person hanging by a rope in the middle of the hallway. Blood was slowly dripping to the floor around the levitating corpse which imitated the movements of a pendulum. Pressing my back again the wall, I sneaked past the dead body.

Moving into the open scene where the news reports typically recorded their stories, more hanging corpses in the center unnerved me. Realizing that Judith's persuasion failed, I stepped forward. Behind the counter, facing all the turned-off cameras, was the culprit. He had his boots high up over the table as he tired killing time.

"I knew you would get here. It was only a matter of time. Although, I'm disappointed that Dench didn't hinder your progress." He was chewing gum, pretending to be blithe, but in reality, he was oozing with anger that seemed to increase as he saw me. Playing with the reddish gum which he spit into his hand, it was obvious that he could barely keep still. One of his upper limbs was twitching lightly as if some harm was done to it.

"Looks like we finally meet face to face, Virgil." I spoke with a feeling of repugnance for the creature that stood before me—the creature that ruined my tranquility.

Shameful Defeat

———

VIRGIL CHUCKLED AND spat on the floor. "Splendid tactic, I must say. I would've never foreseen that you'll correctly identify me and spread my picture. You see, coming here I was attacked by nine cultists. Most are now dead from injuries they dealt to me, but they were determined enough that one broke my arm. They died before it could heal."

"Not as godly as one might've thought, are you?"

Virgil dismissed my comment. "I'm very much annoyed. If it wasn't for your determination, I wouldn't have all this trouble. Sure some would try to find me, but in essence, they would've been just running in circles."

"Don't you think that you lost because you were too careless?"

"Not really, in my life time I've met three others just

like myself. Every single on joined me. So it was only natural for me to put myself out there for a brother-in-arms, but you turned out to be a pathetic ideologist."

"I was just struggling to find out more about the ability. It wasn't until I got detained that I was determined to clear my name."

"You think you're better, don't you? You don't even know how much I've sacrificed. You don't even know how many people are willing to help others, but in reality they're giving useless advice. They pretend to help you, but in actuality, they are not even going slightly above the line of kindness. I went way over the line. I helped those who the society considered were fine. Do you think I do this because I want to? No! I watched them suffer, and after getting to know them, they agreed to this. Even your classmate, Heather. She didn't even cry when the end came. She was that determined to complete her life."

"Is that how you see it? What about instigating them to suicide?"

"There was never any instigating! I have never taken an innocent life without a reason."

"Is that so? What about Aidan? What is going on in this situation then?" I put my hands out, implying that he should look around.

"That's completely your fault. And so your life ends." He spoke as the light went out. I sneaked back into the hall and up around the corner. Behind me, I heard loud noises as if somebody was coming in. Dench ran into the room where the killer was stationed while I sneaked back, hiding behind a wall close enough to take notice of everything.

"It's you!" Dench uttered in a surprising tone as if he

knew the person. My guess that Dench would be a perfect victim to put up against me were confirmed as the two faced without any hostility.

"You failed, you know that? What kind of a detective are you anyway." Virgil spoke, losing his cool only to realize that Dench's arrival wasn't a coincidence "How did you get here?"

"I found a note in front of Snow's home. I followed the note. Show some respect would you!"

"You fool! Don't you think it's a bit suspicious that there was a note left for your convenience?"

Virgil's announcement was interrupted by a broadcast in the room they were in. The big scream flashed with a recording of my discussion with Virgil. Virgil was stunned as they both listened to the confession. "I helped those who the society considered were fine."

The passage awoke Dench into his justice-glorifying stance – something that was mostly absent from his life. He raised his gun and pointed it at Virgil.

"You think you can just arrest me?" Virgil gritted his teeth.

"Put your hand up!" Dench pointed the gun in Virgil's direction, holding it decisively with both hands.

"What's with you now? It never bothered you that the culprit is still on the loose, so what's the problem? Put down that gun and walk away."

"Maybe so. I have made many mistakes, but I have never let a killer free when he was standing right in front of me. Making all those mistakes, catching you will be like doing something good for a change."

"I once had you for a fool, I now have you for an even bigger one" Virgil grappled his knife as he rushed

Dench, who fired his gun. Vigil dodged to the side and back, making aiming difficult until he got close, at which point he dug the knife into Dench's torso a few times one after another. We his last strength, Dench fired the rest of the bullets into Virgil, who was a little more than annoyed as he started to climb the stairs after the whole endeavor.

◆

I was awaiting him on the rooftop, where the moon illuminated the whole place. As he reached the top, it was apparent that one of his wounds didn't heal.

"Now, you've pissed me off!"

"Could it be that the wound didn't heal because the person who caused it was already dead before the power kicked in?" I asked sitting at the periphery of the multi-story building rooftop, which was overlooking the forest and a fraction of town. The darkness made the forest liquefy into a blob of murky greenish colors. The moon's rays bent out of proportions as they intentionally avoided lighting up the town and the very nearby areas, giving of a feeling that the town was abandoned by the heavens.

Virgil tried to conceal his pulsing frustration and irritation. Something aided him in doing so as he erupted into a laugh. "You don't even understand how close this whole play with Greg has gotten us. The gap only decreased. I still can't believe we can't cooperate." He stalled forward a little, but concentrated more on conserving any and all strength until there is a definite end to this whole play. "You see, I hate stories with no end. I hate stories with feeble ends. Human sure can change, a lot actually; but there are very few who can preserve that change. Most revert to their old self within a day, sometimes a week. A death where a person achieves enlightenment on a moral scale, or in terms of personality, is something I'd like to call a noble death."

"Was Aidan's death an example of that?"

"Exactly. He knew that he'll die if he backs off. I told him that I'll purge him if he overcomes his rage in a way other than to kill. He died at the time when he defeated his anger and understood more of himself. He accepted his life as it is. He chose the goodness within. That's a splendid end to his tale."

"Splendid? You've left him there forgotten by everyone."

"A noble death isn't one remembered by the people or history; it's a death remembered by the Will of the Universe. That's exactly the end you've written for Dench, if I say so myself."

"Is that what drives you? The desire to see the end."

"At first I was mad, but right now, all I can do is praise you. Remember how you sacrificed your own pawn to win against the mob. That was something else." He reached into his pockets where the light of the phone tore through the cloth. After taking it out, he flipped it upright, and turned it on. The music coordinated with the light as the phone activated enthusiastically. He played with the touch screen and slid it in my direction. "You should watch the finally of our most valuable assets. I've already seen it."

The video played, showing Chris walking into his home where Bridget stood ready to confront him. As they begun the meal, a conversation broke out.

"I could never depend on you. From that day onward the only thing you've done is …" Bridget started.

"Remind you of the pain you've carried. I know and for that I'm sorry." Chris was too tired to flee.

"You think you're just going to walk away? It doesn't work that way."

"What else can I do?"

She passed the revolver that was a priceless item owned by Magnus. "That's what. You can die."

"If you think I'll take that gun, you're out of your mind!" Something triggered a defensive mechanism and Chris put on a much more comfortable smile. His tone changes as Magnus surfaced. Bridget started for the gun, but Magnus's fast reflexes gave in, and he was the one holding the revolver. He took out the bullets as he left, tacking the gun behind his belt. Without any intention of fighting, he said. "You're free now."

As he reached the summit of the steps, Bridget gave into her resentment as she rammed him off the stairs. Propelled by the push, he tripped and span around with his limbs out of control. Magnus tried to stop, but gravity was stronger, pulling his weightless body downward. With each hit, he could feel his bones slam against the rocky steps. With a final strike, he landed at the bottom. His vision wobbly, he could feel his head rumble in pain as he saw Bridget walking down. Quickly loading the gun, his finger froze in time the moment Magnus tried to press the trigger. Muscles didn't react to any impulses, but he made every attempt at firing. He lost complete control of his hand, and the gun fell. Thinking back, he became conscious that he could never fire at Bridget. Chris cherished ever memory of her even with the fresh taste of her disgust in mind.

As the video ended, the screen jumped back to the

pick-a-playlist window on the phone. I stretched out my hand, holding the cell phone loosely with two fingers as I dropped it from the roof. No objection came from Virgil as we were nearing the end of our discussion. The plastic shattered into pieces down below, emitting a pale sound as if screeching that we should prepare for battle.

"You know you seemed quite surprised at how I found out your identity." I said with my back turned to Virgil, who took a seat at the other end of the roof, listening patiently to what I had to say. He was looking over the horizon in the opposite direction, implying that we have opposite views of life.

"The key was when I found out that you can't use the power indefinitely. You told me that there was a price to pay, and that the currency is time spend viewing those awful visions. That's when I realized that someone had to be proficient in speaking and understanding others. A profession which is based on that idea is psychology." I took a deep breath of fresh air. My chest became a bit tense from the edgy situation. Taking a brief pause, I observed a car leaving the village driving in our direction. "Not only that, but one had to have charisma as well as a friendly outlook on life. When I checked the record of the police, I saw your profile. At that point, I knew you were the one."

"You have my admiration. You've changed. You've certainly changed."

"Tell me, why do this? Give me an honest answer without the usual half-truths."

"I was telling the truth when I said that I tried to help free those whose life was grim. However, I can't deny that I take enjoyment in doing so—that seeing a noble death brings me joy, and that observing this village degrade is a splendid phenomenon. It all started when someone asked me to help him die."

"Tell me, was it really the truth that you didn't have to use the power often."

"Partially, at least half the times I had to use the power. Some people felt better dying that way. You might think I'm a monster since forging on suicide only bred more, and I do know that. But after hearing Waye's vision, I couldn't stop. He wanted to unite the town. He wanted no one to be alone. He wanted to be a father figure for everyone. Within the Unity, he wasn't the bloodsucking ruler that some believe him to be. He wanted to help everyone. His beliefs about the village made him a caring figure. Anyway, enough of this. I would like my diary back now."

"I have it here" I grabbed it form within my jacket. "First of all, I wanted to thanks you for sharing all the knowledge about the power with me." I rose up and rid my pants of the dirt that lingered everywhere on the roof. "After deep consideration, after hearing your testimony, I wonder what I'm doing here, trying to understand a murderer."

"Why do you insist on being a protector of morality?"

"No, that's so not me." I chuckled at his feverous comment. "My moral dilemma is over." I poured some alcohol over the diary and lit the lighter.

"What are you doing?" A protest surfaces from within Virgil's facade of full control.

"You said it yourself, there is no instigator, and thus this diary shouldn't exist." The fire ate the diary whole.

Virgil grimaced as I could sense that he had an honest

intention of erasing me from existence. He drew closer and said. "That's a good one. Fortunately, I have a strong doubt you would've destroy something so precious." He smiled as if triumphant that he didn't fall for my mental trap. By now the edges had burned to a crisp and begun turned to ash. Still glowing, I kicked the notebook in his direction, so that he could make sure that it was indeed his treasure.

"Once I'm done with you. I'll walk downstairs and take Shannon with me. As a present for you perseverance, I'll find the most justice-filled person, Judith. She'll join you soon. You won't feel lonely on the other side that way."

Virgil walked forward full of confidence. As a head-strong combatant, he learned to keep a steady hold of his emotions. He blocked my punch unconsciously and retaliated with a jab in the face. The quick punch under-mined my poise as it was full of power, which made me conscious of my inability as a fighter. As I tried to land a single blow, he dodged to the side, came closer, grabbed me by the neck, and pulled my feet forward which propelled me to fall to the ground. Guarding against his onslaught of kicks, I was in no position to counterattack. His kicks seemed to avoid the face and felt quite dull as if he consciously avoided making me bleed.

"You're pathetic. You're a human without a meaning —a senseless existence. Wouldn't you say that a selfless act before death could give you a proper noble death?" He let off on the assault. "Would you die—sacrificing yourself—while chasing a supposed madman? Heather would be proud." Virgil wiggled his head to stimulate his sore neck.

"Heather wanted me to live—change!"

"What if I told you that the note was fake?"

"It wouldn't change a thing. Even if written by you, they were her words."

"Why not just give up?"

I screamed as he landed a stump to the stomach. He saw that I was sneakily hiding a syringe in one hand, so he kicked me in the shoulder. The syringe slipped out of my grip, and he stumped on it, breaking it into pieces. The shattered glass was dipped in liquid as his shoe left watery tracks.

"Did you really think you could've put me to sleep? That certainly was a good idea as that's exactly what I'll do." His words echoed through the air. Judith surfaced coming upstairs. Her movements as quite as a snake. She held a syringe in one of her hands.

I had no strength to speak.

"That's precisely the best way to take someone out as once there is no consciousness the power doesn't trigger."

"I pity you, for losing your way and succumbing to the teaching of a madman." I spoke as he was getting ready to knock me out.

"You know, what Heather told me when she died? She despised you. Dying here, you could redeem yourself."

"Do your worse."

Before he could succeed, a needle pierced his neck. I saw Judith standing behind him. She squeezed the tip, pouring the liquid into Virgil's veins.

Wrestling out of her grip, he screamed. "What the hell did you do?" He turned around as if he wanted to escape, becoming aware that he can't fight. He walked back unsteadily, dizzy bit by bit. His knees hit the floor as the medicine kicked in. For the first time, his eyes showed an enormous fear that went beyond human emotions.

Judith gave me a hand as I rose up, aching form the attacks.

"Are you alright?" She said as I could hear somebody pull into the parking lot.

"I've been better."

I let her use my help as we dressed Virgil in the strait jacket that I once had and dragged him downstairs.

Our intention was to bury him somewhere in the forest.

◆

Walking down the stairs, Judith said. "Here. I've made a copy of his confession just like you asked." She handed me a voice recorder.

Opening the door to go outside, we saw multiple cars awaiting us from the Unity. Over 30 cultists armed in weapons surrounded the new leader—the secretary. As she took off the black shades, she gave away a glorious smile, and our dreams of leaving this cursed land shattered in an instant.

The Noble Fiend

DESPITE BEING A new leader, Veronica William quickly found herself known for being a chief of the ever-growing sect. Her confidence was the exact opposite of when I last seen her. Her timid nature seemed to have left her body to make space for the power-hungry side that took over. She lacked the calmness and shyness of her former self as she turned into a self-confident fool.

Instinctively, I tacked the voice recorder with Virgil's confession into his pocket after considering that they're much more likely to favor him.

As soon as she saw us, she instantly gave the order, "Take Virgil into to my car." She then waved her hand, giving a stoic glance at the cultists behind her. The believers had no intention to question her, and so they hastily run forward. They ripped Virgil out of our grasps who remained unconscious.

I didn't know what'll happen next, but I was convinced of one thing—I had to complete this undertaking. For all I know, she might join forces with Virgil, and he might never see the judgment day until it is too late. I could never run away. I could never let this end like that but at the same time I realized that I crossed the line of no return.

"How did you know we'd be here?" I asked desiring an answer.

An extremely tall cultist, whose height could only be rivaled by Jude's, towered over the rest and stood in the front. As soon as he heard my inquiry, he rose his baseball bat. "You there, don't speak unless you're asked a question."

"That's fine. He has a right to know, but before that take the detective into the other vehicle." Veronica Williams commented. She was eager to tell me how she out found me, fueled by the notion of out smarting others and rising to the top, in the end putting the town in her own palm.

Judith had a look of a fighter ready for an assault, but she recognized that fighting here would lead nowhere but death. She backed down, dropped her gun, and got into the vehicle without a second thought.

"You see, a certain girl left a message for a devoted cult member, Fredric, who's currently hunted for the murderer of our beloved spokesman. Thus his office is vacant, so I was forced to listen to his messages. One of them stated that his help is needed at the station."

We heard something approach us.

I heard Shannon's voice. She was awake and was stumbling in our direction. Her frightened face looked at me as she broke through the swarm.

"Do you know that girl?" The secretary asked in a calm voice I knew that if I answered affirmatively, she would be forced to come along with us. I shook my head, aiming to convince her that she's not an accomplice. "Take her as well." The command awoke every single one of the cultists who were ready to fulfill her will.

Shannon panicked. She came closer, her hand tightened into a fist holding my jacket out of unrest before freaking out. "What's happening? This is not how it should've been."

Seeing her naive look ignited anger. Just thinking about her foolishness, which ruined my plan, sent me flying off the cliff of tranquility. Yet, it was indeed the foolishness—the same foolishness that had good intentions of helping me—that was to blame. Loosely holding onto my calmness, I reminded myself that I don't want Shannon to die. Within mere seconds, I rummaged around for an answer until I couldn't keep a hold of myself. My fury went into a stalemate with the thought of saving Shannon. The scorching anger soon overcame any rational idea. Rage was the perfect answer.

I pushed her back with all my strength, making her trip and fall into the soggy dirt. "Get off me, you filth! You must've mistaken me for someone else!" I kneeled as I grabbed her ready to shove her down.

Slipping a dirty note into her pocket, my final words freed her completely. "Leave this town, and do remember to be a bit more selfish, alright?" Giving up fighting, I rose up. With a closing act of antagonism, I threw a kick at Shannon that sprayed the mud all over her.

"Never mind. I don't want all that filth in my car. Leave that trash. But you're coming with us." Veronica jumped right into a navy blue sedan where Virgil was sleeping on the back seat. I was forced in beside him as well. The cultists scattered into their respective vehicles, and we were on our way back to the Unity.

Not looking back, I left Shannon to be reborn anew.

Hour have passes as the monotonous drive back continued. Light and darkness were fighting their last battalion as small freckles of light illuminated the sky form the horizon line. Yet, nighttime wasn't going to end without a big bang as the heavens were vastly populated by the absence of any sort of light. The vehicle run calmly. The only sounds I could hear were from the animals and insects residing in the greens. Driving into town, measly tourists wouldn't even recognize the horror that enveloped the land as the streets were now mostly barren—peaceful—and the only place brimming with life and clamor was the headquarters of the Unity. By now, Virgil has awakened and regained his consciousness fully.

The situation was dire, and he most likely hated being powerless, but at the same time, he didn't let up with his comments. He mocked. "Greeting Veronica Williams, the secretary, the murderer of the person who initially tried to unite this town"

The secretary ignored him for the time being, so he turned his attention to me.

"Ready to join forces and show them who's the divine being here?" He asked having a smirk similar to the one always sported by the historian who haunted my dreams. I looked out the window as we were nearing the headquarters. Countless people surrounded our vehicle and tapped on the roof and sides, cheering Victoria Williams for her success.

"It's our last chance." Virgil added.

"You're on your own, and so am I."

"Do you truly think that they'll let you walk away if you prove me guilty?" Virgil has lost his cool and was sick of being bound by the vest.

Before the secretary could get out, the tall man asked. "What was he talking about?"

However, the secretary quickly brushed off his comment but to no avail. "You told us that Fredric was the killer. Was that a lie?"

"He's a madman. What did you expect?" The secretary jumped outside where the populace welcomed her. She waved her hand. Her bodyguards opened both of the back doors and dragged Virgil and me outside. The swarm was ready to tear us apart, and the only thing protecting us for the time being were the bodyguards. They formed a circle around us as the head led us to a huge podium. The wooden stager towered over the horde of spectators ready for the show. On top of it was a pyramid of planks and other wooden objects with a huge wooden beam sticking out from the tip, prepared for the one who'll be executed. I took a stance on one side of the stage while they let Virgil out of the vest on the other side. They shackled our feet with chains, so that we wouldn't escape. Standing on my side, below in the crowd, was Judith who was cuffed surrounded by two bodyguards.

"Welcome to all who supported the salvation of this town!" The secretary spoke in a loud voice which emanated with confidence and reassurance. "One of our beloved members, who would like to stay anonymous, called us hours ago foretelling of an incident at the TV station. Following the lead, we are here with two final suspects in the suicide case. Today we will put an end to this madness as you will be the ones who'll point at the guilty." She gestured at someone hiding in the back of the stage, insisting on coming up. "But before that, we also have an eye witness who will point at the killer."

I was left puzzled and so was Virgil. While I was prepared for all kinds of lies, seeing the supposed eyewitness gave me a bitter feeling.

The girl who came up was the same one I met in the store weeks ago when this whole thing first started. The girl who had her purse stolen stood on the stage, giving me a malicious look. Her face showed a tinge of discomfort as if she wanted to get this over with as soon as possible.

"He is the one!" She pointed her finger in my direction, her voice trembling.

My heart began beating viciously. Fear was the name of the emotion I felt. The strongest sensation I could recall.

"So the debate begins! Would you to voice your argument?" The secretary passed the voice to me and led the girl down the steps into the mass of people.

Virgil gave of a smirk as I eyed the horde of cultists right in front of me. At the start, the people were hushed, but as soon as any evidence was poured onto the stage, they lost their way. Supposedly humans are thinking animals, but that wasn't what I saw. Their mechanical comments escaped their bodies, their voices merged into a pile of goo, and an inaudible racket redoubled that conveyed almost no information. The only thing that could be read from their lips was madness, which clouded their thought in anger. I doubted if they would even listen to what I have to say.

One thing was definite—my position was bleak. The notion that I made it this far only infuriated me more and more, but what kept me silent was the idea that this scenario had two ways in which I can win. Either, I walk away and Virgil burns, or we're both going to die here and now. I'm not ready to give up. I can't attack the Unity, Virgil, or the spokesman directly until the people listen and I loosen up their beliefs. Another thing that stands against me is their preconceived notion that I'm evil which I doubt I'll be able to wrestle against.

"Quite down everyone!" The driver spoke in the background.

"I think everybody knows me in this town. Everyone is suspicious of me. No one trusts me, yet I came to love this town for its peaceful nature. All I ever wanted was to be left alone."

"Burn him already!" A scream came from the back of the swarm—a mindless voice of hate.

"Thus, I detest the one who started this massacre. Despite what you might think, I care for this town as much as anyone here. I might not be a citizen in the eyes of the people, but I am in the eyes of nature." I walked forward, the chains mumbled behind.

Virgil jumped in before I could get my point across. "Everybody agrees with me that these detectives didn't come here to help but to show off. You believe that you're one of us, but you partner up with Detective Page?" Virgil said.

The crowd burned with a flare of anger. Their voices made it impossible to continue the debate until they settled down remained by one of the mediators. The people seemed to have great respect for him which took me back a few weeks when Waye told me about the guardians. The extremely tall individual was a guardian.

"That's true." I staggered, thinking that I can't mention anything about Dench as that would lead me into a blind alley with nothing to gain. "But no one can argue that the only detective who should be loathed is Dench. Who as you know make horrific mistakes. Page is nothing like that. You all remember how he arrested that young man for killing a student. Page fought against Dench. She fought against his incompetence and blindness!" Walking up to the front, I saw the lad who was arrested then. He confirmed my testimony, saying that she really wanted to help. "Now let's face it, why haven't the police been able to find anything?

"Get back on track!" Veronica Williams demanded, getting bored.

"Killing, no, excuse me, instigating this many deaths is no small feat, don't you think? To instigate, you need to be charismatic, and most of all, you need the other person's trust in most case. Who would trust me? No one! People hate me. Therefore, I wouldn't be able to persuade a single person!"

The horde seemed to get a bit reluctant. There was a lack of a collective response. The people murmured between themselves until someone yelled. "Why not burn them both! That would settle the problem!"

"If we do that, we're no different from the killer!" Another voice came from the side.

"Why should we trust him with his nonsense about instigating?"

I chose to continued, trying to fight the discouraging comment. "The only person capable of finding the killer was the spokesman. He was the wisest of them all, determined to find the one destroying the village. He united us all under a banner of determination. He cared for every one of us. What if the killer used the thing that made us love the spokesman in order to further his plan? For you see, someone once told me that to succeed in a grand wicked act, you need to have the correct position. You need to have the right background."

"That's ridicules! Are you implying that the spokesman helped the killer! That's absurd!" Virgil spoke instigating the crowd.

"No, quite the opposite! He believed in his guardians! He believed that the killer is outside of the Unity! He cared for the citizens of this town so much that sometimes he gave false info to clear his dear members of any suspicions." I stepped up pointing my finger at Virgil. "To commit a crime this grave, one would need freedom to roam the night, the trust of the populace, the charm of a kind spirit, and a psychology background. Now stand up everyone and tell me that the people that died were not all visited by this man!"

Virgil resisted the natural urge to back up. For a second, he has lost his footing as well. "That's no argument as I was seeing the majority of residents with problems." he said.

Nods came from the crowds as the people agreed.

"That doesn't prove anything! He was seeing most if not all citizens who had any kind of a problem just like he says!" A shared response was voiced after a prolonged pause.

"Well played, but you see, their trust is in me and I don't even need to say anything." Virgil whispered to me.

"We want Snow dead! He's the one!" The horde echoed.

I helplessly laughed. I rose my head up into the sky. My attempts were rendered futile by the ignorance and blind trust of the people in this fiend. Taking a breath of fresh air, I turned to face the tall guardian.

"Check Virgil's pockets!"

Virgil was restrained at which point a recorder was uncovered. Played, it stated. "No one ever paid any attention to their despair. All I ever did was free those souls filled with despair from this world. That's what they wanted after all." Virgil's voice resonated from the speaker. The final argument lit a different kind of fire within the resident's minds. Their convictions were turned into nothingness and reshaped into hatred for Virgil.

"This is some kind of a misunderstand." Virgil uttered before something smacked his head instantly. His body fell numb as blood gushed from his head. He eyes filled with surprise as a certain man sneaked up on Virgil after hearing the confession. The number of people on the stage drastically increased and many more rushed up. They restrained Virgil who was constantly looking at me, congratulating me for my victory. His final words were engraved into my memory. "Unshackle all chains, free your heart, and stand above those puny humans because it's our destiny." he whispered.

The driver came closer as he freed me. "Take this." He said, tagging a bunch of keys into my hands. "Or you'll be next soon."

"Thank you, but why do this?"

"Some people just can't live with injustice. Next thing they'll want is have you dead as well." He smiled as he pushed me and Judith into the crowd. The roaring voices cheered with an emotion I couldn't identify, but it wasn't happiness. Soon, I lost sight of the stage swallowed by the horde of onlookers. We made our way past the small garden and into the central deepest part of the Unity. The halls were quiet, and no one seemed to be here. I unshackled Judith from the handcuffs that had a hold of her wrists.

"Why are we here?"

"Since we're here, we might as well find Dench's diary. It might've been left in one of the offices. It could free a lot of innocent people after all."

Upon making it up to the second floor, we entered the spokesman's office in hopes of getting a hold of the diary. The room was turned upside-down: books spread on the floor, drawers left opened, and most of all, his hidden vault opened—all his secrets divulged. Gone was the formality of the place. Any attempt at finding our goal was futile as the secretary made sure there would be nothing of use left here.

"She's probably the one carrying it." Judith looked at me.

Outside the window they had already tied Virgil to the stake. Two masked executioners had fire in their hands which was about to lit to the wood encircling Virgil. As the fire overtook the pyramid and spread, Virgil had a solemn look. He never regretted any of his actions. As the fire finally caught onto his clothes, Virgil closed his eyes. Before he uttered a single scream, the two executioners were spellbound into panic. They started scratching themselves, running, turning, and screaming. The crowed stared in awe as seconds later the two men lit on fire. Soon the power expired, and Virgil's mad scream merged with his killers.

"Unfortunately. We should leave before they'll look for us." I said.

"I knew they wouldn't let us go free." She gave off a hopeless smile that seemed to make fun of the current, heinous situation.

Outside the office, shoes smacked against the floor of the building. In the background, loud taps could be heard coming upstairs. Someone was returning, and it was no one else but Veronica Williams. A different and heavier footstep caught up to her and asked.

"I've lost one son to the plague that attacked this city. Today, I have just heard my other son died fighting the man we are about to burn. You knew, didn't you? You knew that it was dangerous, that he had this wicked power?"

"That's absurd. How could I? I wasn't the one who posted those pictures. Shouldn't you have a grudge against that person?" She said, reaching for the knob to check the spokesman office.

"No, I asked the only one out of the group who stayed alive. He told me that you gave the order to find Virgil and bring him in."

"You can be happy that your sons didn't die in vain."

"No! No! No! It doesn't work that way. There is a

price for everything." The dialogue grew to a standstill. No words were ever spoken and silence ate up the atmosphere of the building again. A cacophonous blast sounded outside the office. Fast footsteps could be heard until they were gone in the distance.

Noble Death

———————

THE DYING BODY of the secretary rested in front of the office when we exited. Her success didn't last for long, and I wondered if she knew that she would die this young, would she still strive toward power within the Unity. She was still conscious of our presence and showed no surprise that we were here. Her panicking eyes were very much like the once in dreams. Those dreams where you feel like you're dying, but you can't call out for help. Her plane white shirt was oozing with a deep crimson color. On the verge of dying, she felt no pain and fear, but a touch of sorrow lingered on her face.

"Were you searching for this?" She could barely utter a comment. In her tightened hand, she was holding the diary.

"Exactly, you know that the dairy could do some good." I bowed next to her.

"Take it then." She knew her time on earth came to a close.

I took out the recorder out of her slightly-bloodied hands. Seeing traces of blood on mine, made me feel a foreign sensation of discomfort.

"You're making a good choice." I stood up.

"One of only a few."

She showed no sentiments as she peacefully closed her eyes and drifted off.

We grabbed a pair of robes. With our identity hidden and the denizen's bloodlust temporarily sated, escaping was easy, or so I thought. Right outside, we were stopped by the girl who accused me of being the killer. She halfheartedly grappled a gun with hands that shook chaotically. Her makeup was drained and ruined by the tears that never stopped.

"This ends here." She shrieked.

"Is death really the price you require for that incident at the store?" I joked, thinking.

"You have me for a fool? When I saw you in the store, something told me that I know that look. Do you remember the time when you were oblivious to a life and death fight nearby?" I shook my head in agreement. "That was my brother who was massacred!"

Judith tried to close in possibly to disarm her, but the girl quickly saw the hidden motive and pointed the gun in her direction. As she was ready to push the trigger, I shoved Judith toward the wall. The hail of bullets pierced my body. I felt pain oozing out of my chest. My torso filled with lead, bleeding. The pain was much more vivid than any time before. With the clip empty, the girl showed a tinge of satisfaction as I flew back lightly. I made one final eye contact with Judith who was bent over against the wall, looking distressed.

On the floor, I searched the night sky for stars that would give me an insight into what the divine were thinking orchestrating the events in this town. I saw Judith stooping next to me. My eyes heavy and ready to fall asleep, the pain felt as if it never had any intention of stopping. I soon felt a sensation similar to rain as warm droplets covered my face. The next thing I knew the pain stopped, but I didn't wake up—not in my world.

As I became conscious inside the dream world, the one and only person I saw was the Mankind's Most Persevering Teacher. The bland colors that coexisted with him in the dream world were nowhere to be found. Darkness was surrounding us, but it didn't just proclaim the absence of light. It felt as if the tangible side of this world was completely gone. My feet levitated above a ground that wasn't there. Nothingness was surrounding us, and we were just drifting slowly in eternity. The teacher seemed to be quite accustomed to the idea as he was as carefree as ever.

"So that's how it ends, huh?" He asked me.

"Aren't you the Lord of Death, you should know?"

"Sorry, I'm a little discouraged that I couldn't find a successor in the end. Asking you would be meaningless."

"I'm on the other hand delighted that I won't have to see you ever again."

"Let me show you something." He clicked his fingers at which point the darkness subsided. The forest surfaced from below me, and a building not unlike the radio station elevated from below. We were back at the scene of the final confrontation. Shannon was still there, but I could barely see her. My view was obstructed by the bushes—it was a view of a stalker.

Shannon was gazing at the road ahead. The weight of her life was pulling her mood down. The two people of opposite beliefs who she cherished were long gone. Neither could've been saved. Searching for something in the pocket, a tiny note dropped like a rock to the ground despite being extremely light. Upon reading my note, she uttered. "You were right about not giving me the note earlier."

A car pulled up into the parking lot, and Fredric jumped. He breathed heavily from the trauma of the current events. "A friend from the Unity told me about the message."

"Well, you're too late." She gave him a disappointed look, attempting to get into another car.

Fredric hesitated for a second before confessing what was bothering him to no end—a thought that was eating at his heart by infusing him with unimaginable pools of guilt. "Shannon, I … you blamed the … spokesman …" Fredric's words stuttered now and then as his thought run in loops.

"So what?"

"Well, you see, I'm the one … I'm the one you should hate."

"What are you talking about?"

"18 years ago, I left this town when everybody turned their backs on me. I made a wrong investment and lost all my wealth. Waye claimed it was my fault, and my pregnant soon-to-be wife sided with him. I fled. A year ago, I came back in search of the one whom I have betrayed. You'll be 18 soon, won't you?"

Shannon grimaced, realizing the bitter taste of Fredric's confession, and continued listened. "Ever since I came here and found you, I could never bring myself to confront you. I guess I'm just a big coward."

"I've spend my whole life under the wing of that fiend, and you're telling me you knew about it and didn't do a thing."

"I've only known for 8 months. I'm a fool. I know." He fell to his knees and made Shannon grab a gun that he took form the Unity. "That's why I'll give you a chance for revenge."

Shannon had a surprised look. She couldn't understand what this man was thinking. Surely she wanted revenge, but not against a man who wasn't fighting back. Tears dripped down when she spoke. "Yes, you're a fool, but that makes two of us." Her grip on the weapon became wobbly until it was lost completely. "Sure revenge might be sweet, but I much rather see you struggle by making up for all your past mistakes." She hugged him as he cried apologizing for every one of his actions.

Consumed in an emotional moment, the father and daughter were startled. My vision zoomed in. The greens that were obstructing the view were out of the way. I saw a bat to my right. "I finally found you." An unknown voice spoke. "Once I bring justice to the killer of our beloved spokesman, things will be on the right track."

"Look, you've got the wrong idea. I don't want any trouble." Fredric stretched his hand out with an open palm as if showing that he means no harm.

"I've got the wrong idea? No, I have the right idea!"

"It was Veronica Williams, the secretary, who murder Waye out of jealousy." Fredric made a concluding attempt at negotiations.

The camera zoomed closer, I saw Fredric take a hold of the gun and fire multiple rounds. As the assault was over the camera fell the side and back, pointing at the night sky. In the background, I heard Shannon and Fredric drive off. The room returned to the unfathomable darkness.

"I thought you should see what happened to Shannon and Fredric." The teacher said.

"So that's how you were able to show me the past. I was looking through the eye of an already dead person, right?"

"Precisely."

"Thank you for showing me that scene." I said happily with a smile. The motion was foreign to me, but only on the outside. Deep down, I was joyful that they made it out of that cursed town. "You know, you've never told me how I knew that story about the pit I told you a long time ago."

"You should know."

"In all honesty, I have never encountered anything pertaining to this ability until recently."

"The only thing worse than lying to others, is lying to yourself." He ran his hand through his hair and flicked his fingers. The room returned to a bland empty-of-life colors, and it reshaped into the white physical form that it had before. "Perhaps, you've met someone who told you a story that only he knew was true. Perhaps it's a child's memory."

"Fine"

"Your perseverance had made me reconsider. I think I'll struggle a bit more with my existence."

"Say, Virgil once mentioned having brothers."

"Speculating that they might search for revenge?" The teacher chuckled full heartedly. "The idea of brotherhood as a family never existed. Those gifted with the Exchange of Death lack strong bonds. Most are solitary being, living in solitude. Even when they meet, their beliefs and missions are so different that they frequently can't even communicate without a fight, let alone become companions. On another note, aren't you going to ask what's next?"

"No need. I'll find out soon enough."

"You can't get rid of this gift." He said honestly.

"I don' think I care anymore."

He looked out the window, opened it, and jumped out. Coming closer, I finally read the writing on the desk.

It said. "Reaper, Death, God of Death." My grip on consciousness loosened, and I fell to the floor in a matter of seconds, ready to fall asleep.

The last thing I recognized was the sound of bells.

EPilogue

───────────

THE TINY BELLS sang outside propelled by the faint wind. Water rushing down the stream startled me out of my slumber. The sun illuminated the room through the open window as the breeze caressed the curtain. I was sleeping in a mid-size bed. The wooden frame gave of a feeling of being in a village. I sat up, hunting for clues as to where I was. Hearing me make a ruckus, someone entered through the wooden door. It was Magnus.

"Took you a while to wake up." He said, grabbed a wood chair, flipped it around, and took a seat, placing his crossed arms on top of the backrest.

"How log was I out?" I looked at my clothes which were the same ones I wore on that night. Every ounce of dirt, every stain was still there.

"19 days. To be honest, I had my doubts if you're ever going to wake up." He gave of a different vibe from his usual nature.

"Care to fill me in." I said, stretching next to the bed, I took a look out the window. We were still somewhere deep within the woods. The greens coexisted perfectly with the wooden hut we were in.

'In the news, they told a story where Dench was killed by the mastermind behind the suicides and Judith was the one who ended the mastermind's life."

"What about the town?" I asked curious.

"They say that the town is no more. Right after the people saw the ones putting up the flames burn before their eye, the vast majority left everything and migrated as far away as they possibly could. The Unity crumbled. Only a hand full of members stayed with a mission of giving a proper burial to everyone who died that night." He bowed his head. "Supposedly they also cleaned every inch of town—even the TV station is crystal clear without a trace of murderer. After their work was done, they left as well, so it's pretty much a ghost town now. But that was the idea, right?"

"Those people will definitely have a better chance at leading a regular life away from that cursed place." I turned around. "What happened to Judith?"

"In the news, they said that Dench gave her the diary during his last moments. If everything goes right, they'll free 31 innocent people based on his recording."

Hearing his words, I was content that she made it out and that Dench's confession will see the light of day.

"But they said that some evildoers might go free as well." His word had a tone as if he wanted to ruin my day, but I paid no attention to his final remarks.

"How did you end up at the Unity during that night?"

"I had a fight with Bridget. Afterward, he was gone." Magnus pointed to his head, giving me an angry look. "So now, I'm cursed with living a normal life." He grimaced. "So how long have you known the identity of the murder?"

"Since we settled the score with the mob. As you might realize, I didn't tell you because he was too close to you. Something might've gone wrong."

"Just don't tell me that everything went as planned?" He had a bitter tone as if he sense that I might be looking down on him. I dismissed his comment without saying a word. "I was just a puppet in his game. I know that. He kept so close to me and Bridget, so that he could watch me." Magnus sigh heavily as his mood swung to the side of depression and soon frustration.

"Are you going to search for Bridget?"

He swiftly rose his head up with a smile and laughed at the irony of those words "Not a chance. There is no reason for doing so. That fight has freed her, and now she can have her life back." Magnus went to get some water. He was back with a glass full, small droplets were cumulating on the outer layer of the glass. Pulled by gravity, they flew down one by one. "It's really difficult to swallow, but in his own way, I think that Virgil helped Bridget overcome whatever was bothering her. I think he made her realize that staying with Chris will lead to nothing."

"Are you trying to tell me that there are very few people completely corrupted by darkness?"

"How about you? Are you going to find the detective and that other girl?"

"You must be joking." I gave a short answer. I had no idea what to say. The only way I could collaborate with Judith is during the worst of times. As for Shannon, hopefully she has found her place. "So what now?"

"I should be the one asking that question as I have nowhere to go."

"I'll travel for a bit before finding another place where I can find peace."

"Boring! Here, I was thinking that you'll tell me that you're going to go hunt for more adventures."

"Maybe Virgil was right. Maybe people don't change after all." I said in a form of a joke as I realized one truth. I have no idea what it was, but I was certain that something changed inside me during these past weeks. My perspective of taking action changed as I accepted the consequence of all my decisions and ended up with no fear of the unforeseen resolution. I even forgot my distaste for getting involved. The case has devoured me and escape was not an option. Even now, I am eager to look into the future and take it into my hands. No matter what's ahead, I strive to follow Heather's belief and prove Virgil wrong every single day.

"Why did you save me back there?" I asked.

"My choice wasn't influenced by a feeling of obligation for repaying a debt. With no point in life, I thought that maybe one day, I'll be able to face off against a fiendish opponent if I keep you around." Magnus gave an honest answer.

To this day, I have no idea who I was fighting. Was it a lost soul? A deranged maniac? Or someone sick of the world trying to do something that ultimately made him evil? However, the fact remains that Virgil has cast a spell on the village turning it into a feast for evil. The worst was brought out of the bodies of most while some retained their sanity and shone like passionate stars, enlightening the way for others. I will forever remember those people I have met during those times because some of them had the best of humanity in their souls. For whatever evil lurked in their hearts, in the worst of times they made the best of choices. Choices that eventually led to the end of a fiend's serenade which would otherwise continue to no end.

This wasn't a victory, but a struggle which allowed some people to leave their grief behind on a battlefield.

Overcoming a struggle is worth much more than a meager victory.

MESSAGE FROM THE AUTHOR

Thanks for reading. I hope you enjoyed Noble Death. If you did, please take a moment to leave a review on Amazon and/or Goodreads.

I would also like to tell you of a place, where stories are told and adventure awaits. The Unreal Castle is my website, where you can read short stories and poetry, as well as leave comments and offer suggestions. You can also become a knight of the Unreal Castle by signing up for my newsletter. With your adventurous nature, I think you'd fit right in. I hope to see you there.

www.unrealcastle.com

—Patrick Rain

ABOUT THE AUTHOR

PATRICK RAIN is a writer with an interest in fantasy, mystery, and supernatural fiction. When he's not working on a new story, he likes to read and play games. Fueled by his fascination with language, he is learning Japanese. He loves to swim while listening to his favorite music.

www.ingramcontent.com/pod-product-compliance
Lightning Source LLC
Chambersburg PA
CBHW051329250626
47155CB00007B/2516